Bello

hidden talent rediscovered

Bello is a digital-only imprint of Pan Macmillan,
established to breathe new life into previously published,
classic books.

At Bello we believe in the timeless power of the imagination,
of a good story, narrative and entertainment, and we want to
use digital technology to ensure that many more readers
can enjoy these books into the future.

We publish in ebook and print-on-demand formats
to bring these wonderful books to new audiences.

www.panmacmillan.com/imprint-publishers/bello

Richmal Crompton

Richmal Crompton (1890–1969) is best known for her thirty-eight books featuring William Brown, which were published between 1922 and 1970. Born in Lancashire, Crompton won a scholarship to Royal Holloway in London, where she trained as a schoolteacher, graduating in 1914, before turning to writing full-time. Alongside the William novels, Crompton wrote forty-one novels for adults, as well as nine collections of short stories.

Richmal Crompton

WEATHERLEY PARADE

BELL◎

First published in 1943 by Macmillan & Co.

This edition published 2017 by Bello
an imprint of Pan Macmillan
20 New Wharf Road, London N1 9RR
Associated companies throughout the world

www.panmacmillan.com/imprint-publishers/bello

ISBN 978-1-5098-5952-8 EPUB
ISBN 978-1-5098-5950-4 HB
ISBN 978-1-5098-5951-1 PB

A CIP catalogue record for this book is available from the British Library.

Typeset by Ellipsis Digital Limited, Glasgow

Visit **www.panmacmillan.com** to read more about all our books
and to buy them. You will also find features, author interviews and
news of any author events, and you can sign up for e-newsletters
so that you're always first to hear about our new releases.

Contents

PART I

1902

Chapter One

Arthur's Home-coming from the Boer War

Anthea added another series of whorls to the ornamental border of "WELCOME HOME", then leant back in her chair to consider the effect. Her tongue, stained deep purple, protruded slightly from her lips, as it always did in moments of tension. "WELCOME HOME" in large uneven purple letters, surrounded by a border of roses, violets and forget-me-nots, joined together by whorls of red ink. It was the sixth she had done that morning. The other five, in letters of red, blue, yellow, green and orange, lay scattered over the schoolroom table. Six were enough, she thought. In any case, she was tired of doing them, and the taste of the paint was beginning to make her feel sick. She had spread a piece of newspaper over the end of the table where she was painting, but a good deal of paint water and ink had found their way through it. Not that that mattered, because the schoolroom table was so ink-stained and scratched and scored already that a few more marks on it would never be noticed. Both Father and Grandfather had done their lessons at that table when they were little boys . . .

She tilted her chair back, put her hands behind her head, and gazed dreamily out of the window. A sweep of lawn and herbaceous border was framed by the neat arcs of Nottingham lace curtain and the lace edging of the holland blind. The window was open at the top, and the little wooden knob on the end of the blind cord tapped against the pane as it swung gently in the breeze. She was trying to remember what Father looked like . . .

There were photographs, of course, — he had had a photograph taken in uniform just before he left England — but they didn't seem quite real. And, in any case, he would have changed after three years. . . Probably he was trying to remember what they looked like. She had been ten years old when he went away, and Clive had been twelve, while Billy had not been born.

She looked at the big cuckoo clock that hung on the wall. They would have started from London by now. Mother had gone to Plymouth yesterday to meet him, and they were staying the night in London. The village had wanted to make a ceremony of his home-coming, but Mother had discouraged the idea. He had had enteric fever very badly (that was why he had not come home sooner) and had still not quite recovered from it. All the neighbours had been invited to a party tomorrow — in the garden if it were fine enough — but his actual home-coming was to be as quiet as possible. She saw the picture of it clearly in her mind. She stood at the open doorway, in her white muslin frock with the blue sash, her hair tied up with blue ribbons . . . The carriage drew up to the door, and a tall figure in khaki leapt out and took her in his arms . . . It was a satisfying picture, slightly marred by the fact that Clive and Billy would be there too. And Mother . . . But at least she was his only daughter. He had always called her "Baby" before he went away. Billy, of course, was the baby now. She felt a sudden stab of jealousy. Not only was Billy the baby, but he was Mother's real child, whereas she and Clive were only her stepchildren. She could not remember her real mother, though she had invented an imaginary figure — sympathetic, understanding, exquisitely beautiful — to comfort her when people were unkind. Mother was never unkind. Sometimes, without quite realising it, Anthea wished she would be. She liked to see herself as the central figure of a drama, and either a cruel stepmother or an adoring real one would have given her the desired role. Mother was quiet and aloof and—just. You couldn't rouse her, and you never knew what she was thinking of you. It made things dull . . .

She spread out the six "WELCOME HOME" notices on the table and looked at them with deepening pride. Perhaps she would be an artist when she grew up, and people would go to the Academy to see her pictures and point her out in the street: "That's Anthea Weatherley, the artist." She would be very rich and give a lot of money to the poor. Painting was interesting and she found most interesting things easy. She could learn by heart much more quickly than Clive, though he was the elder by two years, and she could read and recite with much more expression. Perhaps she would be a famous actress. "That's Anthea Weatherley, the actress, getting out of that carriage. Isn't she beautiful?" She could play the piano quite well, too, but she didn't think that she would like to be a musician, however famous, because of the practising . . . Perhaps she would just marry — a handsome man with a title, of course — and have a lot of beautiful children . . . She was glad that she had missed sums and geography today. Miss Berry, her governess, had given her a holiday because Father was coming home. Clive had a holiday for the occasion as well, and had arrived home yesterday. He was in his carpentering shed now, finishing a table that he had begun to make last holidays.

Just as she was thinking of Clive, the door opened and he came in. He was a tall boy, with dark hair and a regular-featured serious face. He looked neat and well-groomed in his Eton suit.

"Hello, Clive," said Anthea. "I've done six of them. Look!"

Clive came over to the table.

"You haven't kept to the lines of the letters," he said.

Anthea's face clouded.

"That doesn't matter," she said.

"Yes, it does, Carrots," he said kindly." It spoils the whole thing. It makes it look — slap-dash. And those red things round the edges——"

"They're roses," said Anthea stormily. "You *know* they're roses."

"They just look like red splodges. No one would know they were meant to be roses."

Anthea burst into tears.

"You're hateful," she sobbed. "I've been working and *working* at them all morning and I feel *sick* with paint, and all you can say is that they're slap-dash and don't look like what they are."

"Well, it's true, Anthea," said Clive patiently, "and it's silly to cry over it. If you'd taken the same time you've taken over all these to do *one* correctly, it would have been much better——"

5

There was the sound of wheels on the gravel outside, and Anthea, forgetting to cry, ran to the window. Looking down, she saw a large picture hat, a floating feather boa and a foam of silk flounces as the visitor descended from the cab.

"I believe it's Aunt Lilian," she said. "I didn't know she was coming."

"I don't suppose anyone did," said Clive. "She just comes."

"Well, Mother had a postcard from her from the South of France only the other day, and she didn't say anything about leaving it."

"Perhaps she's heard that Father's coming home."

"We don't want a crowd," said Anthea sulkily.

Her picture of herself leaping down the steps into her father's arms was being completely spoilt. The idea of dozens of people leaping into his arms was ridiculous . . .

"Thank goodness she's not brought her fiancé with her!" said Anthea. "I didn't like him."

"The man who came last holidays?" said Clive. "I didn't like him either, but he's not her fiancé now. She broke it off and got engaged to someone else in the South of France."

"Well, thank goodness she's not brought any of them! . . . Shall we finish decorating the hall?"

"I've practically finished it," said Clive. He looked at her with mingled concern and disapproval. There was a ring of purple paint round her mouth, and her pinafore was stained all the colours of the "notices" "I say, you've made a frightful mess of yourself. Look at your face and pinafore."

"My face doesn't matter," said Anthea. "I can wash it. But — goodness, I hope it hasn't gone through to my frock."

She stood up, slipped off the starched frilly pinafore and, planting her slender legs — in long black stockings and black button boots — wide apart, anxiously inspected the front of the white muslin dress.

"No, *that's* all right," she said, drawing a quick breath of relief. She looked again at her "notices" on the table. "Anyway, it's old-fashioned to keep to lines and things. It's called New Art not to." Her air of superior erudition faded into sententiousness as she added, "And Father will like them just because I did them."

"Perhaps," said Clive, "but that's not the point. You drew the lines to keep in them, didn't you? If you didn't mean to keep in the lines, you shouldn't have drawn them."

"You don't know anything about art," said Anthea indignantly. "You're just *stupid"*

But she knew by experience that it was impossible to make Clive lose his temper. His fault-finding, though persistent, was always kindly and patient, and he never grudged any trouble to help her.

"Oh heavens!" she said, as a sudden thought struck her. "I said I'd go into the village for the flags after breakfast, and I quite forgot."

"I got them," said Clive. "I thought you'd probably forget, so I went down on my bicycle. They're in my bedroom."

"Oh, good! Let's get them."

They went along the passage to Clive's bedroom — a small square room, austerely furnished and immaculately tidy. Ranged round the room on bare tables — made by Clive himself — were his various collections of stamps, butterflies, coins, fossils and birds' eggs. Each collection was methodically arranged and indexed.

"I don't see the flags," said Anthea.

"Well, naturally, I've put them away," said Clive.

He opened a drawer in his writing-table and brought out a bundle of flags.

"Oh, aren't they lovely!" said Anthea excitedly. "I didn't know you were going to get such nice ones as this."

"They had them left over from the Peace Celebrations," said Clive.

He wondered whether to remind her that they had agreed to share the expenses of the decorations. He knew that she would never remember of her own accord, and, in any case, she probably had no money. "Frittering away her money" was one of her gravest faults in Clive's eyes. Clive himself apportioned his pocket-money carefully and exactly to various funds — church collections, "grub", hobbies, incidental expenses — and always had a considerable sum put aside as savings. He could easily have afforded to pay for the flags and was inclined to say nothing about it, but he took his responsibilities as the eldest of the family seriously and felt that it was not good for Anthea to be allowed to shirk her obligations.

"They were a shilling each," he said. "You said you'd pay half, didn't you?"

Anthea pouted.

"Yes . . . You've *paid* for them, haven't you?"

"Yes."

"Well, I'll owe it you."

"I'll ask Mother to let me have it out of your pocket-money."

"Oh, all right." No need to make a scene yet. She could always do that — if she felt like it — when the sum was actually deducted from her pocket-money. She had no time to waste this morning. "Come on. We must get the decorating done before lunch."

They went downstairs to the big lounge hall, from which doors led to dining-room, drawing-room and library. The front doors stood open, showing the gravelled drive that curved between trees to the tall iron gates, flanked by stone piers. A smaller door opened from the opposite side of the hall onto a terrace with a stone balustrade from which a double flight of steps led down to the lawn. The hall itself was festooned with red, white and blue bunting, and old Quimp, the gardener, who lived at the lodge by the side of the iron gates, had brought flowering plants — lilies, petunias, begonias, early chrysanthemums — from the conservatory and massed them at the foot of the staircase.

Clive's table stood against the wall. In the centre he had put the large silver-framed photograph of Major Weatherley that usually stood on the drawing-room chimney-piece, and had ranged round it the smaller photographs of Baden-Powell, White, "Bobs", Buller and Kitchener that had been on sale at stationers' shops during the greater part of the war.

A step-ladder on the hearth showed that the decorations were still incomplete.

"We'll put the flags up now," said Clive. "I've got some little ones to put round the photographs on the table. How do you like it now it's finished?"

Anthea inspected it critically. It was a solid table, plainly made, except for the elaborate interstices of fretwork between legs and top. Clive's criticism of her "WELCOME HOME" notices still rankled.

"I can see that you've put a lot of work into it and done it very well," she said judicially, "but I think it's ugly."

Even that failed to ruffle Clive.

"Yes, I see what you mean," he said, standing back to look at it. "There's too much ornamentation, but fretwork *is* like that. It was the most difficult pattern in the book, and I wanted to see if I could manage it."

There was no triumph or even complacency in his tone. It was a simple statement of fact.

He set to work, draping the smaller flags over the photographs, fixing Anthea's notices prominently about the room, while Anthea pirouetted around, her muslin skirt swirling about her knees, her red-gold curls flying.

"Oh, I wish old Oom Paul could see it," she said, stopping at last, out of breath.

"Poor old chap," said Clive. "After all, he was fighting for his country and probably thought he was in the right."

"Don't be a beastly pro-Boer," flamed Anthea.

Clive mounted the step-ladder and fixed the largest flag over the chimney-piece, concealing the portrait of his grandmother that hung there. Anthea went to the table and thoughtfully inspected the silver-framed photograph.

"What a lot of changes there've been since he went away!" she said.

"I know," agreed Clive, coming down from the step-ladder. " The Queen's death and the Coronation and——"

"Oh, I don't mean those," said Anthea impatiently.

"I mean *real* things — Billy being born and the elm avenue cut down and the Harmers getting a motor-car and——"

There was a rustle of silk on the staircase, and they turned to see Lilian Weatherley coming slowly downstairs. She wore a wine-coloured silk dress, with leg-of-mutton sleeves and a yoke and high collar of white lace. Her chestnut hair was brushed up from the back and coiled on the top of her head. She held up the front of her dress, with one hand, while the flounced train fell softly from step to step behind her. In her other hand she held a lighted cigarette. Her lovely mouth curved into a quizzical smile as her eyes fell on the scene in the hall.

"Ah, decorating the home for the return of the warrior," she said. "We did it for my father's return from the Zulu War, I remember . . . Yes, Union Jacks and bunting. Just the same." Her eyes moved to Anthea. "I was much younger than you, but, I believe, very like you."

With grave courtesy Clive drew forward one of the straight-backed Jacobean armchairs, and she sank into it, inhaling a mouthful of cigarette smoke then leaning back her head to send out a succession of smoke rings.

"My latest accomplishment," she said. "Childish, but gratifying."

Clive watched her with ill-concealed disapproval.

"We didn't know you were coming, Aunt Lilian," he said, "and I expect the servants are busy. I hope you have everything you need. If there's anything Anthea or I can do . . ."

Her eyes met his in smiling mockery.

"Nothing, thank you, dear boy. In such a perfectly-run house as this the unexpected guest is always expected. My room is ready for me, and hot water, in the usual spotless brass can, arrives almost as soon as I do myself."

Major Weatherley's young sister was one of his most serious responsibilities. She was ten years his junior, and their parents had died while she was still a child, leaving her in his guardianship. The loveliest debutante of her year, everyone had prophesied a good match for her. She had been engaged in her first season, and again in her second and again in her third. The ominous word "jilt" became attached to her. Thereafter she flouted the accepted standards of her day by travelling alone and unchaperoned on the Continent, smoking cigarettes in public and consorting with Bohemian sets of dubious morals. It was rumoured that she gambled at foreign casinos and that she had been seen "not exactly tipsy, but — near enough, my dear". She was now twenty-six years old — lovely, well-off and well-connected — but rumours followed her wherever she went, and discreet matrons warned their sons against her. That fragile and precious Victorian possession, her "reputation", was considered to have lost the untouched bloom that an Englishman has the right to demand in his bride. Despite all this, she still became engaged with almost monotonous regularity.

Clive and Anthea knew little of her history. To them she was just Aunt Lilian, who would arrive for occasional visits — unlike other visitors in that one never knew when she was coming or when she was going. Anthea found her strangely disturbing. Clive felt an instinctive hostility to her that he did his best to overcome. Their father had always seemed worried and out-of-temper when she was in the house.

She was looking round the hall again.

"And I suppose that Clive's children will one day be decorating it for Clive's return from some future war."

Clive spoke with an effort, as if steeling himself to the task.

"Aunt Lilian, Father doesn't like ladies to smoke here."

"I know," said Aunt Lilian, unperturbed, even faintly amused, "but he's not here to disapprove, so why worry?"

"I don't think we ought" began Clive slowly, but Aunt Lilian was looking at Anthea with narrowed eyes through a haze of cigarette smoke.

"Yes, my dear," she said, "you're quite pretty. You're going to be *very* pretty."

A feeling of exaltation seized Anthea. She was going to be pretty — like Aunt Lilian. She would wear a wine-coloured silk dress, with a white lace yoke and collar. Its train would sweep the ground, and it would rustle as she walked. Men would fall in love with her, as they fell in love with Aunt Lilian . . .

The luncheon bell sounded, and Aunt Lilian rose, throwing her cigarette carelessly towards the fireplace. It fell on the rug, and Clive stooped to pick it up, his face set in lines of disapproval.

"Come along," said Aunt Lilian, holding out a hand to Anthea. "I'm ravenous. I don't think I've had anything to eat since yesterday."

Anthea slipped an arm through hers. The feeling of exaltation still upheld her, as if she had entered into an alliance with Aunt Lilian — against Clive and all he stood for. She longed to toss a half-smoked cigarette towards the fireplace and watch someone pick it up with that faint mocking smile.

"Aunt Lilian," she whispered as they went towards the dining-room, "will you teach me to do smoke rings?"

Chapter Two

Clive went out onto the terrace and down the flight of steps to the lawn. There he turned to look back at the house — a well-proportioned two-storied stone building, with a pillared portico at the front entrance. He approved of the house, but he disapproved of the Virginia creeper that covered most of it and of the verandah that ran along the back. The verandah, of course, was convenient (his stepmother liked to sit there with her sewing, and Billy could play there on wet days), but it kept light and air from the downstairs rooms, while the Virginia creeper actually destroyed the stonework beneath it. He had remonstrated with his stepmother on both these points, and she had replied, rather shortly, that his father loved the house as it was, and would not, she was sure, wish to make any alteration. He wondered whether it were unfilial to decide to make several alterations when he was the owner of the property, and decided that it was not . . . He would have the trees round the lawn cut down. The ground under the big cedar was almost bare . . .

As he walked across the lawn, his thoughts turned anxiously to Anthea. After lunch, Aunt Lilian had taken her to her bedroom to show her the new dresses she had bought in Paris. Aunt Lilian, Clive knew, was not a Good Influence, and he felt responsible for Anthea in their parents' absence. Suppose that even now she were teaching Anthea to smoke . . .

Beyond the lawn the ground sloped sharply up to a hillock on which was a little summer-house. A small boy in a sailor suit was trying to push a large wooden horse on wheels up the steep path to the summer-house. Whenever he had managed to push it up a few inches, the weight would force him down to the bottom again. His face was set and pink with effort, his golden curls plastered on his forehead. Inside the summer-house, a nursery maid, in print dress and apron, sat with her sewing. A sunk lane ran beneath the summer-house, and Clive knew that the nurses liked to sit there, so as to converse with any of their friends from the village who happened to pass along the lane.

He watched the scene in silence for a few moments, then said: "Hello, Billy."

Billy, intent on his Sisyphean task, did not answer.

Clive glanced disapprovingly towards the summerhouse. Surely it was the duty of the nursery maid to assist her charge. It was obviously impossible for the poor little chap to push the horse up by himself.

"I'll do it for you, Billy," he said in a voice loud enough for her to hear and in a tone that would, he hoped, recall her to her duty.

He took up the horse and carried it to the top of the incline.

"There! Now you can push it yourself, can't you?"

A miniature fury flung itself on Clive's legs, beating at them ferociously.

"Wanted to do it mineself," screamed Billy, his voice choked by rage. "Wanted to do it mineself."

The nursery maid came out of the summer-house and gathered the small kicking fury consolingly into her arms.

"Never mind, pet," she said, "we'll put it down at the bottom again."

Clive looked at them in bewilderment.

"But he couldn't possibly have pushed it up," he said.

"No, sir," agreed the nursery maid, "but he likes trying. He doesn't like being helped. He'll go on trying all afternoon sometimes. He enjoys it, bless him!"

"Surely he's too old to cry like that," said Clive.

"Well, he's a bit over-excited," said the nursery maid indulgently. "What with his Pa coming home this afternoon an' all."

"Yes, of course," said Clive.

The nursery maid had carried Billy and the wooden horse down

14

to the bottom of the slope, and Billy was once again intent on his impossible task.

Clive watched him, smiling.

"Sorry I interfered, old chap," he said. "Look! Here's a penny. Would you like it?"

Billy shook his head and went on pushing his horse.

"He doesn't really understand about pennies yet," said the nursery maid. "They just go into his moneybox."

Clive wandered along the path that ran at the top of the moss-covered wall bordering the lane. He had not seen much of his stepbrother, who had lived the usual secluded nursery life of the period, but he hoped that he was not being spoilt . . . Still — Clive's face softened — he was a dear little chap. When he was older and more sensible, it would be a pleasure to help and guide him. Clive saw himself — a man of twenty or so — taking an eight-year-old Billy to the Zoo, to the pantomime . . .

"I say, Clive!"

He looked down the moss-grown wall into the lane below and saw a small stocky boy with untidy hair looking up at him.

"Hello, Ronnie!"

"I heard you were coming over, so I thought I'd slip round and see you. Give me a hand up, will you?"

Clive leant down, and the boy scrambled up the slippery wall, grasping Clive's hand for the last lap and landing on his knees on the soft earth at the top. He got up, laughing, and brushed the earth from his suit and stockings.

"Thanks awfully . . . I say, when do you expect your father?"

"I think about three. Aunt Lilian's here."

"Is she?" said the boy without interest. His snub nose and wide mouth gave him an appearance of irrepressible good-humour. "Why didn't you tell me you were coming home?"

"I didn't know in time to let you know, and we've been busy all day. We're having a party tomorrow. I expect your family's coming to that."

"Yes, but nothing's any fun with the family. It's you I want — without crowds of people messing round. Let's go to our place.

It's not nearly three yet. There's heaps of time to have a talk. They'll call you if they want you for anything."

"All right."

Their "place" was a point in the spinney that ran along the top of the wall, where the low-growing branches of a beech tree made a sort of tent. Stooping under the leafy branches, they entered the shadowy hollow round the trunk. It had a dank earthy smell and was thickly carpeted with decayed leaves. Ronnie began to swing himself onto the lowest branch, where they usually sat. Clive looked up regretfully.

"Perhaps I'd better not," he said. "I've got my Eton suit on, and Father might be coming home any minute."

"All right." Ronnie dropped down again. "Let's just sit here." He took off the belted jacket of his Norfolk suit and laid it at the foot of the tree-trunk. "What price Sir Walter Raleigh? We can both sit on this."

"Won't you get into a row if it's messed with leaves and things?" said Clive.

"I shall get into a row anyway," grinned Ronnie, "so that won't matter."

"Don't they know you've come?"

"No. Father's gone into the village to do some parish visiting, and he said I was to read to Flora till he came back. I waited till he was out of the way and then just slipped off here."

"Oh, Ronnie!" said Clive reproachfully.

"Come on. We haven't much time. Tell me about the term. Did Walsh get his colours?"

Ronnie Hayes was the son of the Vicar of Cokers End. His mother had died at the birth of her second child, Flora, and Flora had been crippled by a fall from a swing when she was four years old. The Vicar — a reserved morose man with a genius for self-torment — considered himself responsible for the accident and had ever since devoted his life to the little invalid. That, of course, would not have mattered. What did matter was that he expected Ronnie, too, to devote his life to his sister. There was no question of Ronnie's going to school. Ronnie must join his sister in her lessons in order to provide company and competition. Flora was quick-witted and intelligent, Ronnie slow and backward, with an inbred aversion from study and a craving for out-of-door pursuits. In every subject Flora outstripped him, and he was constantly in trouble with his father. Not only had he to do his lessons with Flora as his classmate and his father as teacher, but he was expected to give up all his free time to her. He must take her out for "walks" in her spinal carriage, read aloud to her (she tired easily of holding up a book), wait on her, play games with her — and he was expected to be glad and proud to do these things. Any sign of reluctance was treated by the Vicar as a serious moral fault. The Vicar himself loved his daughter with an almost morbid absorption. She filled his entire life. Ronnie existed for him only as a means of helping him fulfil the task to which he had dedicated himself. Whenever he had to be absent on parochial duties, Ronnie must, as a matter of course, take his place.

The adjective most frequently applied to Flora was "saintlike" She gave voice to pious moral maxims that the Vicar recorded in a notebook kept for the purpose, she learnt pages of Mrs. Hemans' poetry by heart and she sang hymns in a small sweet voice that brought tears to the eyes of quite hardened people. And she saw to it that Ronnie did not too often shirk his subordinate but important role.

If Ronnie had not been a healthy little savage, accepting punishment philosophically, living wholly in the present, he might have become warped by this existence. As it was, when the need for exercise and adventure came upon him, he would play truant, roaming the countryside, fishing in streams, climbing trees, and would cheerfully regard the consequent thrashing as due payment for his pleasure. There were few boys of his own age in the neighbourhood, and Clive was his only contact with the normal world of boyhood. Clive's two years' seniority invested him with glamour, and, from early childhood, Ronnie had focussed on him all the affection and hero-worship that found no outlet in his own surroundings. The world of school and schoolboys in which Clive lived had an irresistible fascination for him. He was a practical boy, and the dream worlds of more imaginative children held no appeal for him, but he knew every corner of Clive's school as well as if he had been a pupil there himself and could have found his way blindfold through corridors and classrooms. He was familiar with the personal appearance, history, nicknames and idiosyncrasies of both pupils and masters.

Clive, on his side, felt an almost paternal affection for the younger boy. He wrote to him regularly from school and during the holidays did his best to mitigate the rigours of the Vicarage regime. The Vicar approved of the friendship, considering Clive a responsible serious-minded boy, and Ronnie looked forward eagerly throughout the term to Clive's return from school.

"Yes, Paul got his colours," said Clive. "He played a ripping game in the Upcombe match."

"That was Saturday, wasn't it?" said Ronnie. "I was thinking about it. You did win, didn't you? I was certain you would. Tell me about it. How many runs did Peters make?"

Clive described the game, while Ronnie sat, tailor fashion, his elbows on his knees, his chin in his hands, gazing dreamily in front of him . . .

"I wish I'd seen it," he said at the end, drawing a deep breath. "I say! Do tell me. Has old Stinker been less crabby this term? And does Piggy still cheat, and have Marks and Law made it up yet, and what about Sprigg's chameleon? Did anyone find it?"

"One at a time," smiled Clive.

He answered the questions slowly and carefully, and Ronnie stored every detail in his mind.

"You never tell me half enough in your letters, you know," he said at the end. "There are always hundreds of questions I want to ask you."

"Well, you do, don't you?" said Clive.

"I suppose I do," grinned Ronnie. "Is Walsh coming to stay with you next hols?"

"I think so," said Clive.

Clive and Walsh had gone to the school at the same time and had been friends ever since. Despite his prowess at games, Walsh

18

was a quiet studious boy and shared most of Clive's interests. Ronnie regarded Walsh's visits to Hallowes with mixed feelings. When Walsh was there he did not like to obtrude his presence on the two of them. He watched them from a distance — even followed them, without their knowing it, on their walks over the countryside. On the rare occasions when he made a third, he listened to their conversation about school and schoolfellows in spellbound silence. He did not know which was better — to have Clive to himself or to have the world of school brought before him in miniature by Clive and Walsh together.

Conscientiously Clive tried to hold his hero-worship within bounds.

"You know, I'm not good at games or anything like that, Ronnie," he would say. "I'm not what you'd call popular, either. I haven't any real friend but Walsh. I've never wanted any."

But this, of course, only added a hero-like modesty to the other heroic qualities with which Ronnie endowed him.

As he answered Ronnie's eager questions, Clive's eye wandered in kindly criticism over the small figure. There was a scruffy neglected look about it. The Vicarage housekeeper was old and cantankerous and short-sighted. She knew that it was as much as her place was worth to neglect Miss Flora, and she tended her carefully, compensating for the demands this made on her time and energy by ignoring Ronnie. The Vicar would have noticed at once had Flora not been kept as fresh and dainty as a flower — the long golden ringlets brushed to smooth silkiness, the small white hands well manicured — but Ronnie's air of neglect he took as a matter of course.

"Did you wash your neck this morning, Ronnie?" said Clive suddenly.

"Well . . . p'raps not this *morning*," admitted Ronnie, hunching up his shoulders to hide the offending member.

"You ought to, you know," said Clive. "Physical cleanliness is a sort of foundation for all the other sorts of cleanliness, if you know what I mean. You ought to have a cold tub every morning and wash properly as well."

"There's only the one hip bath," explained Ronnie, "and it's kept in Father's bedroom except on Saturday nights, when she brings it into my room and puts some hot water in it — and a jolly little bit of it and not very hot, I can tell you."

"I know it's difficult without a bathroom," said Clive, "but you could give yourself a cold sponge down every morning. Will you?"

"Yes, I will. I promise, Clive," said Ronnie.

"And brush your hair, too. You oughtn't to go about looking like that."

"No one cares two pins what I look like, anyway," said Ronnie.

"That's not the point. It's a question of forming good habits. The habits you form now go to make your character, and bad habits are difficult to break once you've formed them. Getting up early and cold tubs are very important."

"Yes, Clive," said Ronnie. "I will try . . ."

"That's right," said Clive, "and don't get depressed if you find it hard at first. Just go on trying."

The church clock struck three.

"By Jove!" said Ronnie, self-consciously using an expression that was forbidden at home under the general head of "swearing". "I'd better go, hadn't I? Your father will be here soon."

He stood up, brushed the leaves from his jacket and slipped it on.

"Will you really get into trouble?" said Clive.

Ronnie grinned.

"Yes. I'm supposed to be reading *Ministering Children* to Flora. It's a beastly book and she loves it. I pronounce the words wrong and she corrects me. I think that's partly why she likes me reading to her, so that she can correct me when I pronounce words wrong. Anyway, I hope I do get into trouble. If I don't it'll be because she's begged me off, and I'd rather get into trouble than have to be grateful to her."

"You are as decent to her as you can, aren't you, Ronnie?"

"I don't get much chance not to be."

"It's a rotten life for her, you know."

"She enjoys it . . ."

"Ronnie!" reproachfully.

"I'm sorry, Clive. Honestly, I do try to feel as I ought to about her. Perhaps if Father wasn't always dinning it into me how I ought to feel about her, I'd feel it. Sometimes I nearly do."

There was the distant sound of carriage wheels entering the drive.

"I say! I must go," said Clive.

Anthea's imaginary picture of her father's homecoming was realised, after all.

Clive was still in the spinney, Billy in the summerhouse, Aunt Lilian in her bedroom . . . and Anthea alone ran down the steps to be gathered into the arms of the tall thin man in khaki.

Chapter Three

Helena Weatherley stood at the bottom of the terrace steps, talking to a group of guests. The day had turned out fine and warm, so that it had been possible, after all, to hold the party out of doors. Despite the warmth of the sun, however, there was a faint tang of autumn in the air, and most of the women wore thin coats of silk or alpaca over their dresses. From beneath the coats, trains and flounces foamed and billowed round elegantly booted feet. Feather boas floated over arms and shoulders. Heavily trimmed "picture hats" dipped over foreheads to sweep up at the sides over waves of carefully dressed hair. Many of the women carried lace-trimmed parasols, for delicate complexions must be protected even from the September sun.

As she fulfilled mechanically her duties as hostess, Helena was aware in every nerve of her husband, who stood beneath the cedar tree at the further end of the lawn, surrounded by some of his old friends. Through the long years of their separation she had prayed desperately for this moment. She was a deeply reserved woman, giving few signs of her feelings, but there had hardly been a day, hardly an hour, in which she had not missed him poignantly. Yet, when she saw him coming down the gangway of the boat yesterday, her heart had contracted with fear. He looked so worn and tired, his eyes ringed and hollow, his brown hair flecked with grey. He held his tall soldierly figure upright, but his uniform hung on it loosely.

"Well, you know, I've had fever pretty badly," he had explained, smiling at her anxiety. "I shall be all right now I'm at home again."

And in his tone she glimpsed a home-sickness even deeper than had been her longing for him.

Watching him now across the lawn, immaculate in pale-grey frock-coat, with an orchid in his buttonhole, she thought that he looked better already after a good night's rest. If only Lilian had not been here to spoil his home-coming! Helena's heart hardened as she thought of Lilian. Determinedly she had forced herself to look on Arthur's children by his first wife (a pretty empty-headed little creature who had early worn out his devotion) as her own, but she could not conquer her resentment of the sister who had troubled his peace ever since she left the schoolroom. Always over-conscientious, he blamed himself for her vagaries, ascribing them to some failure of duty on his part. Yesterday, when alone with Helena, he had seemed happy and at rest, but Lilian had soon brought back the lines of anxiety to his thin face.

She had announced the breaking of her engagement immediately after dinner, speaking in a light mocking voice that, Helena could feel, jarred Arthur's overstrained nerves. He was standing in front of the fire, smoking a cigar, and Lilian was lying back with studied negligence in an easy-chair. She looked very lovely in the soft lamplight, her curly chestnut hair massed on her shapely head, her blue eyes narrowed, her lips curved into a faint smile of bravado. Her evening dress of white satin enhanced the transparency of her skin, but Helena suspected that her lips were artificially reddened. Well, as long as Arthur didn't notice . . . Going into Lilian's bedroom earlier in the evening to make sure that the maids had forgotten nothing, she had noticed the smell of tobacco and seen a box of cigarettes on the chest of drawers. But even Lilian would hardly dare to smoke in Arthur's presence, and that was all that mattered. Helena was secretly a little ashamed of her lack of concern for the girl herself. The effect of her conduct on Arthur was all she cared about . . .

As Arthur listened to her story, the furrows of his cheeks deepened. He had known and liked her latest fiancé and had been glad to hear of her engagement, taking for granted that his own responsibility was now at an end.

"But, my dear girl," he said, when Lilian had finished, "what on earth possessed you to break it off? St. Aubyn's a thoroughly good chap — well off, good family and as decent and clean-living a fellow as you're likely to find anywhere."

"Oh, I agree," drawled Lilian. "It was all eminently suitable."

"I suppose you were in love with him when you accepted him?"

"I suppose I was," said Lilian, as if considering the question for the first time.

"You can't go on breaking engagements all your life, you know. You're old enough now to know your own mind."

Lilian said nothing — only smiled that maddeningly secretive little smile.

"Why did you break the engagement?" persisted Arthur.

"I didn't break it, my dear Arthur. He did. He offered to do the gentlemanly thing and let me break it, but, if the decision was his, I didn't see why he shouldn't stand by it."

Arthur was silent for a few moments, then said quietly:

"Tell me what happened."

Lilian crossed one leg over the other with a rustle of silk and a swirl of lace petticoat flounces and moved the toe of a white satin slipper up and down, gazing at it absorbedly.

"He said I drank too much."

There was still that note of mockery in her voice.

Arthur stared at her in slow horror.

"Drank too much?" he repeated. "What on earth do you mean?"

"Just that," said Lilian. "I drank too much. I can carry my drink quite well as a rule, but I suppose he happened to see me on one or two occasions when I'd had more than I could carry. And he didn't like my gambling, either."

"Good *God!*" exploded Arthur.

Lilian continued calmly:

"On the whole, he didn't think I'd make a suitable mother for his children, and I agreed with him. It was quite an amicable arrangement. I gathered that I was the type of woman he'd like for a mistress, but not for a wife."

"*Lilian!*" said Arthur sternly, and Helena echoed "Lilian!" in a tone of helpless expostulation.

"I'm sorry, Arthur, but at least I'm being honest about it. Quite a lot of people cut me after it happened, but they were the duller sort of people. I had other, more amusing, friends, so I didn't miss them."

Arthur sat down on the big leather armchair by the fire. His face looked so drawn and sunken that even Lilian felt a sudden compunction.

"I'm sorry, Arthur," she said again. "I mean, I'm sorry to worry you like this when you're ill——"

"I'm not ill," interrupted Arthur shortly, and continued. "Now listen to me, Lilian. You're over twenty-one, and I haven't any legal authority over you now, but I do feel that perhaps I'm a little to blame. A brother can't be the same as a father, and Helena, of course, is not much older than you are yourself. Somehow we've not made a success of the business, but do believe me that if you don't take yourself in hand now, you're going to make a mess of your whole life. Can't you see that?"

"Most plainly, my dear Arthur."

"Won't you get in touch with St. Aubyn again — or let me get in touch with him? I've no doubt you were very provocative——"

"I was," agreed Lilian, smiling again to herself.

"——and that you both acted hastily and are too proud to acknowledge yourselves at fault. Couldn't you suggest making a fresh start? You were fond of him, weren't you?"

"Fond of him?" echoed Lilian. "No, I was bored with him. Bored, bored, *bored*!" The hardness and mockery had gone from her voice. It quivered hysterically. "I'm bored with you all . . . bored with everything . . ."

Her voice broke into a sob, and, springing tempestuously from her seat, she flung herself from the room. They heard the rustle of silk as she ran upstairs, then the distant slamming of her bedroom door.

Arthur gave a short sigh, expressive partly of exasperation, partly of weariness.

"Hadn't you better go after her?" he said to Helena.

Helena shook her head.

"No . . . I should say things that I'd be sorry for afterwards." She hesitated, then went on, "You see, I don't love her, Arthur. I resent her. I always have done. You can't — get through to a person if you don't love them, and I don't even like her. I'm ashamed of it, but — there it is!"

Arthur held out his hand, and she went to sit on the arm of his chair, slipping her hand in his. He held it closely.

"I suppose that's where I've gone wrong, too," he said slowly. "I've felt responsible for her and tried to do my duty by her, but I don't think I've ever really loved her, either. She used to irritate me, even when she was a child."

"You've done everything you could for her, Arthur."

"I've taken trouble . . . I've worried . . . but that's not enough."

"Nothing would have made any difference." She bent down and laid her cheek against his head. "Oh, my dear, don't let's think about it . . . not now . . . not tonight."

Arthur stayed in bed the next morning, and Helena came down first to breakfast. There was a letter on Lilian's plate, addressed in a sprawling masculine handwriting, with a London postmark . . . Helena looked at it with interest. Suppose it were from Reggie St. Aubyn . . . Suppose the lovers' quarrel were made up and she and Arthur freed from this dragging sense of responsibility. Lilian as Mrs. St. Aubyn, with a settled position, with Reggie and his relations to bear the brunt of her whims and caprices . . . Perhaps she wouldn't have any after marriage. Lots of women who had been "difficult" before marriage settled down into happy conventional wives.

Lilian came down a few minutes later. Though trim and elegant, as ever, in her long full braided skirt of navy-blue serge, her white blouse tucked neatly into her small belted waist, she looked pale and sulky, and responded shortly to Helena's greeting. As soon as her eyes fell upon the letter, however, the colour flooded her cheeks. She slipped it into her pocket, made a pretence of eating, and left the dining-room just as Clive and Anthea were entering it. Going upstairs after breakfast, Helena met her coming down. She had put on her outdoor things — a short tight-waisted jacket and a small hat secured by a veil. Beneath the veil Helena could see that her cheeks were still flushed, her eyes starry.

"I'm sorry to miss your party this afternoon, Helena," she said, "but I have to go to London. I shall probably go on to Baden afterwards. It will be a relief to you and Arthur, won't it? I'm sure that Arthur's worrying about my influence on the children."

"Was your letter from Reggie St. Aubyn, Lilian?"

"My God, no!"

"Lilian, *please*."

"Yes, Reggie objected to my language, too. It was one of the many things that would have made me an unsuitable mother to his children. Don't tell Arthur till I've gone, and don't let him worry about me. I can take care of myself."

"You'll just catch the ten-fifteen. I'll order the carriage."

"Thank you. My trunk's ready."

Arthur heard the news more calmly than Helena had feared he would. He was in his shirt-sleeves brushing his hair at his dressing-table when she went into the bedroom. He listened in silence, then shrugged his shoulders.

"Well, after all, she's twenty-six. Whatever mistakes we made were made long enough ago now, and it's too late to remedy them . . ."

His gaze went round the room with its air of solid comfort, then through the window to the garden, with the shady lawn, gay flower borders and the distant sweep of meadow and woodland, to return finally to Helena . . . Helena was not the fashionable "milk and roses" type. Her honey-coloured skin and velvety-brown eyes consorted oddly, some people thought, with her hair — "the colour of ripe corn" as Arthur loved to quote — hair that was straight and plainly dressed, not twisted into waves or curls. Her body was firm and compact and well proportioned and she moved with grace and dignity, making no effort to attain the "hour-glass" figure so popular with her contemporaries. He remembered how he had

27

clung to the pictured vision of her through the stress and horror of the war, remembered the despair of those moments when it had eluded him and he could not recall her features . . .

"Gad, Helena!" he said with a catch in his voice, "I'm terrified of waking up and finding it a dream. I've thought of it all these years and wondered if it would ever come, and now it's come I can't believe it."

She smiled at him without speaking, and in the silence something of the serenity that had been his most precious memory of her seemed to flow out from her, soothing his restlessness, allaying the vague fears that haunted him . . .

"Come along," she said at last, taking his coat from a chair and holding it out to him. "Come down and see Billy. That will make it real."

The group round Arthur under the cedar tree was discussing the terms of the recent peace.

"Too generous, by Gad!" said Colonel Fortescue, a retired veteran with white side-whiskers, a face yellowed by long service in India and eyes of a fierce and startling blue. "Three millions for rebuilding their farms! Demme, it's a new idea for the victors to pay the war damage. And then Botha and De Wet come over squealing for more. Demmed impudence!"

"Kitchener was responsible for the generosity of the terms," said Arthur. "He insisted that we shouldn't tax them and that we should rebuild their farms. It's largely due to him and to Campbell-Bannerman's stand about the concentration camps that there's so little bitterness on the whole."

"Demme, I'd teach 'em a lesson," said the Colonel.

"I think they've been taught it," said Arthur.

Billy wandered about among the guests, his small face almost hidden by his father's sun helmet, his father's shabby discoloured khaki tunic trailing at his heels. He had fetched them himself from Arthur's dressing-room and his nurse had found him proudly parading in them on the terrace. She had tried to take them away, but Arthur, drawn to the scene by Billy's screams, had said that he might keep them, so Billy strutted to and fro, his face wreathed in smiles, his minute form almost eclipsed by its burden, to the amusement of the onlookers.

"Your husband doesn't look well, Mrs. Weatherley."

"No, he's had enteric fever very badly. He needs rest . . ."

She threaded her way through the guests towards the end of the lawn, where tea was being set out by the servants on a long buffet table.

"You agree with me, don't you, Mrs. Weatherley?" Sir Bruce Evesham appealed to her as she passed.

Sir Bruce was the squire of a neighbouring village — a short thick-set man, with weather-beaten, mahogany-coloured face and a straddling horseman's gait. His mother, a frail wisp of a woman with white hair, dressed always in trailing black, to whom he was passionately devoted, hung on his arm, and gazed with dim reproachful eyes at Miss Clorinda Mavers, who was venturing to disagree with him. Miss Clorinda Mavers had a tall angular body, on the top of which a tiny bird-like face gave the impression of a miniature ornament on a long column. A shapeless garment of hand-woven, hand-dyed material hung about her. A long string of blocks of uncut amber almost reached her knees. A hand-plaited rush hat engulfed her small head but failed to quench the eager brightness of her eyes or control the disintegrating "bun" of hair that sent out tails in all directions. She was about fifty years old but had looked more or less like that ever since anyone remembered her.

"Look at the Education Act!" she was saying. "What a triumph for Progress, for Democracy!"

"A triumph for Democracy!" exploded Sir Bruce. "What does the Education Act do, madam? Spews up a mass of half-educated nitwits whose sole mental demand is for debased journalism."

"Oh, no, Sir Bruce! We're *raising* the people."

"Raising the jackasses!" growled Sir Bruce. "Look at this new Labour Party. *Labour* Party, by Gad! If this country's come to such a pass, madam, that it has to be governed by the working classes, we may as well give up all hope of it, as I, for one, have done.

Income Tax up to one and three in the pound! What's this fellow Hicks Beach thinking of?"

"We must pay for the war, Sir Bruce."

"Blundering nincompoops! Pandering to the lowest elements in the community! Betraying their own class and all it stands for! Progress indeed! No, madam, the world does not progress. It goes round in crazy circles."

Mr. Crabbe, the local M.P., and his wife joined the group, and Helena left them to greet some newcomers.

The Crabbes lived in a select quarter of Mayfair and only visited their constituency on rare occasions, which they invested with all the ceremonial of a royal progress. Mrs. Crabbe was closely connected with the aristocracy, and, after twenty years of married life, her husband was still acutely sensible of the honour she had done him in consenting to be his wife. No conversation could be started on any subject that he could not lead round — not with ostentation, but with an air of deep humility — to his wife's connections. She was a tall desiccated-looking woman, with a sharply aquiline nose, baggy eyes and a pursed mouth, hung round generally with quantities of priceless old lace and jewellery. Her face and figure suggested the tiara so strongly that, even in the daytime, she looked undressed without it. Her husband was short and rotund, with a chubby babyish face on which a bushy black moustache looked strangely incongruous.

"London's worn out," said Mrs. Crabbe in her languid monotonous drawl. "Simply worn out. First the Queen's Funeral, then the King's Illness, then the Coronation, then the Peace Celebrations . . . I've never known such a year. We're all exhausted."

"So many of my wife's relations are connected with the Court," explained Mr. Crabbe, "and, of course, she has been expected to Play her Part."

His wife was obviously going to elaborate the theme when Dr. Bellingham, a shaggy individual with a loud voice and brusque manners, who systematically bullied his patients into recovery, came up to the group and shouted,

"Don't like this alliance with Japan, Crabbe."

The M.P. cleared his throat, lowered his voice, and glanced round cautiously, as he always did when about to utter a political pronouncement. This was merely a nervous habit and meant nothing.

"We cannot stand alone indefinitely," he said in a confidential tone. "We have had no ally since the Crimean War."

"Just what Lord Kirkham said," murmured Mrs. Crabbe.

"My wife's uncle," explained her husband.

"But why Japan?" persisted the doctor. "Great Scot! If we must have an ally, why choose a yellow one? Why walk straight into the jaws of the Yellow Peril? Germany's our obvious ally, one would think."

Dr. Bellingham had in his youth been engaged to a flaxen-haired German girl, who had died a week or so before the date fixed for the wedding. He had never visited Germany, but was romantically attached to it as the native land of his Lotte and anxious to improve its relations with his own. Germany stood to him for the Schubert songs his fiancée used to sing so sweetly, the Beethoven sonatas she played so trippingly, and the picturesque forests of which she showed him so many photographs.

Mr. Crabbe cleared his throat again.

"It's not as simple as that, my dear doctor. Both Japan and ourselves are concerned with holding in check the power of Russia, and putting a stop to her encroachments. Germany, of course, has an interest in that, too, and, as you know, we made the Yangtse Agreement with her with the same object, but, when the need arose, Germany simply refused to implement the terms of the agreement."

"Germany's jealous of our naval power, isn't she, sir?" said Clive, who had joined the group.

"Well — er — without being indiscreet, I think I may say that that is a generally accepted view. Chamberlain has tried three times——"

"*Quite* three times," put in his wife.

"—*quite* three times to form an alliance with Germany in recent years, only to be snubbed and betrayed at every turn."

"That telegram the Kaiser sent to Kruger was a pretty mean trick, wasn't it, sir?" said Clive.

"I'm afraid it was, my boy. The Kaiser has shown great duplicity, too, over this alliance of ours with Japan — congratulating us on it and at the same time warning Russia against us."

"The man's abnormal," growled Sir Bruce. "The whole demmed lot of them are abnormal. This Berlin to Baghdad idea! Crazy! Stark crazy!"

"They are a dangerous element in Europe, all the same," said Mr. Crabbe. He glanced round again and lowered his voice. "I have it on the best authority that Chamberlain himself said that ever since Bismarck the policy of the German Empire had been one of undisguised blackmail."

"Soldiers, by gad, but not gentlemen," summarised the Colonel, twisting his long white moustaches. "I've always said it."

"Yes, yes, yes," boomed the doctor, "but you can't judge a whole nation by Bismarck and the Kaiser. Think of Schubert and Beethoven and — and all the rest of them. And, in any case, why the *Japs*? Cageful of yellow monkeys!"

Helena threaded her way through the guests to the end of the lawn. Isolated snatches of conversation reached her as she went.

"Well, my dear, he's the King now and one must be loyal, and, after all, the poor man's been terribly ill and may have reformed, but a sister of George's cousin says that she knows for a fact . . ."

"Clarence has bought one of those new basket-chair trailers for his bicycle, but I simply daren't go in it. He's such a reckless rider."

"*Have* you read Marie Corelli's latest? It's simply divine!"

"Yes, he went actually up in a balloon. He says it's such a thrilling experience."

Before Helena reached the tea-tables, a minor sensation was caused by the arrival of the Harmers, so swathed in motor hats, motor veils, goggles and "dust coats" as to be unrecognisable. Their motor-car was a recent purchase, and they described the journey in an excited chorus.

"We got along wonderfully at the beginning."

"*Quite* thirty miles an hour on the main road."

"Fortunately when it broke down we were just near Brooks' farm and could take his wagonette."

"Every single horse we met shied at us. After all," modestly, "we *are* the first in the district, aren't we?"

"We're simply *thick* with dust, Helena darling. May we have a wash before we have tea?"

"Nasty, noisy, smelly things!" said Sir Bruce, when the Harmers had vanished indoors. "Ought to be forbidden by law. They'll drive horses off the road, and then what will become of us?"

"Quite a lot of the best people in London have them now," said Mrs. Crabbe. "It's generally thought that they will eventually take the place of carriages altogether."

The colonel snorted.

"Impossible, my dear madam, impossible. They'll be saying next that the things will replace cavalry on the battlefield. Can you see our fellahs chargin' in motorcars? Ha! Ha!"

"We've no idea what changes are in store for us," said Lady Evesham in her thin ghost-like voice. "With Gladstone and the old Queen dead, I'm afraid that things can never be the same again."

Chapter Four

The silver urns had been brought out, and tea was being carried about among the guests — silver salvers with tea cups, cream jugs and sugar basins, cake-stands laden with cakes and sandwiches, trays of creams and jellies. The barrels of ice-cream were set beneath the cedar tree to keep cool, as they always were at Hallowes garden parties. Passing by the tree, Helena heard one maid say to another, "We'd got to keep a sharp eye on the ice-cream, d'you remember, when Miss Lilian were a little 'un."

Her thoughts went, with a sudden unexpected stab of compunction, to Lilian. Where had she gone now — urged by a restlessness that spared neither mind nor body? Had she come to them for help and been driven away by their lack of sympathy, their obvious absorption in each other? Then she hardened her heart. Lilian had blurred the peace of Arthur's home-coming, and for that she could not be forgiven. She was selfish, reckless, perverse — beyond help or restraint . . .

Her eyes wandered round the garden in search of Arthur . . . and found him standing a short distance away, talking to the Crabbes. Their eyes met in the half-smile of intimacy that they had always exchanged in crowds. A rush of thanksgiving seized her, and her eyes filled suddenly with tears. That intimate half-smile had been among the memories she had treasured during the years of his absence . . . She watched him anxiously, striving to reassure herself. Yes . . . there was more colour in his cheeks, his eyes had lost that burnt-out empty look. He would soon be his old self.

"You were with the Dundee column in the withdrawal from

Reitfontein to Ladysmith, weren't you, Major?" Mrs. Crabbe was saying.

"Yes . . ." said Arthur.

The sunny garden faded away, and he saw a wearied, starving column of men going at snail's pace, sodden with rain, knee-deep in mud, crawling on all-fours when they could no longer stand, falling asleep from sheer exhaustion, but still floundering on in their sleep through the mire . . . saw them, tottering, mud-caked, make a supreme effort to re-form their ranks as they neared Ladysmith, heard their thin quavering voices upraised in a popular music-hall song of the day as they stumbled into the town . . .

"You must have been through some very interesting experiences," said Mr. Crabbe. "Is it true, by the way, that at the battle of Talana Hill our men were driven from the crest by our own artillery?"

"Yes," said Arthur. "That happened several times . . ."

"We mustn't talk to Major Weatherley about the war," said Mrs. Crabbe. "I'm sure he wants to forget it . . . I love the fragrance of these late summer days, don't you?"

Arthur agreed, smiling fixedly. His nostrils were full of the stench of death . . . He heard the scream and crash of shrapnel, the stampeding of horses, the cries of the wounded. His hand started to his cheek as if to ward off that warm piece of human flesh . . . Panic swept over him. He felt that he was imprisoned in those dark years of war and must carry his prison with him, even in this peaceful sunny garden . . . Then, across the crowd, he met Helena's eyes, and she gave him that swift half-smile that he had remembered so often and with such an agony of longing in his exile. It had seemed the symbol of their love — deep, comprehending, unemotional. With that exchange of glances the horror faded from his mind like something being wiped off a slate, vanishing as completely as if it had never been. He was in his own home, with Helena and his children . . . His eyes roved round in search of the children . . . There was Clive, carrying a plate of sandwiches among the guests. He was a good-looking, well-mannered boy, and one should be proud of him. Helena had given an excellent report of his conduct. He had never caused her any trouble or anxiety, had tried conscientiously to fill his father's place in the house and towards the younger children. What was there about him that — ever so faintly — irritated one? He had read that faint irritation even in Helena's report, though she had tried to hide it. Was it that he was too sure of himself? Not exactly. There was a sincerity and humility about the boy, and he had no affectations. But the thought of him left that faint irritation in one's mind. Perhaps subconsciously one resented his lack of faults, would have preferred a more normal young savage for one's son. He dismissed the problem with a shrug and looked round for Anthea. There she was — the little monkey! — with a group of young people. She was imitating somebody — Miss Clorinda Mavers, he believed — and the group around her was laughing helplessly. She had been a wonderful mimic even as a tiny girl. Jove, how she'd grown up in these three years! When first he saw her yesterday, her likeness to Lilian had shocked him, but it was only her looks, of course — the red-gold hair, blue eyes and clear pale skin.

A nurse passed, leading Billy by the hand.

"I've taken your helmet and tunic up to your room again, sir," she said. "Billy found it too hot in the end, didn't you, Billy?"

"I was a soldier," said Billy proudly.

"But you're a sailor," said Arthur, smiling down at the miniature sailor suit.

"I'm bofe," said Billy.

"You know who this is, don't you, Billy?" said the nurse.

"It's Daddy," said Billy, and shouted for joy as Arthur swung him up to his shoulder so that he could look over the crowded lawn.

Helena had been nervous lest the child should be shy of him, especially as Arthur now bore little likeness to the photograph that he had been taught to call "Daddy", but he had accepted the newcomer as contentedly as he accepted most things, provided that his own private concerns were not interfered with.

"I'm taking him in now for his tea, sir," said the nurse.

Arthur put him down, and Billy trotted off happily, holding the nurse's hand. Arthur watched him, his worn face softening . . . He was surprised by the deep love he felt for this youngest child of his, whom he had seen for the first time yesterday. It had its roots, of course, in his love for Helena, which was the mainspring of his life. The boy resembled Helena, too, had the same honey-coloured skin, brown eyes and shining golden hair. He was sorry to have missed Billy's babyhood, but he and Helena would have other children, please God!

He saw Miss Berry, Anthea's governess, small and grey-haired, in a plain dress of grey silk with a black bonnet, standing by herself a short distance away. Miss Berry was the daughter of a former Vicar of Cokers End, who lived in rooms in the village and came to Hallowes every day to give Anthea her lessons . . . Arthur did not share the slightly contemptuous attitude to governesses shown by most of his contemporaries. He had determined to engage a woman of culture and breeding as his daughter's governess and had been fortunate to find one within easy reach of his own home. Having found her, he treated her with punctilious courtesy and insisted that the rest of the household should do the same.

"Come and sit down, Miss Berry, and let me get you some tea."

"I have had tea, thank you, Major," said Miss Berry, but allowed him to lead her to one of the ornamental iron seats that stood in the shade of the trees at the end of the lawn. She sat very upright, her hands, in black silk gloves, folded on her lap.

"You must be glad to be at home again, Major," she said.

"I am, indeed," he replied.

"And it must be a comfort to Mrs. Weatherley to have you back. So much responsibility has fallen to her lot during your absence."

"You have assisted her with that," said Arthur. When with Miss Berry, he always found himself falling into the stilted old-fashioned manner of speaking that she used herself. "Tell me about your pupil. How is she progressing?"

Miss Berry looked over to the group of young people, still dominated by Anthea's gaiety and high spirits. Arthur followed her eyes and smiled.

"She looks happy enough," he said.

She's always happy when she's in the limelight, thought Miss

Berry, and when she isn't she's miserable herself and makes everyone else miserable . . . but she knew that one does not say such things to parents.

Anthea had been in her worst mood that morning. She was angry because, in order to keep her occupied and the rest of the household quiet, Helena had decreed that the schoolroom routine should go on as usual till lunch-time. But the trouble went deeper than that. Anthea was, without knowing it, jealous of both her father and her stepmother, jealous of everything that removed her from the centre of the stage. The whole house revolved round its newly returned master, and he and Helena had eyes only for each other. The position of unimportance to which Anthea was thus relegated was unendurable . . . and the solution was obvious. Flagrant naughtiness, she had found, could generally restore her to the centre of the stage when all else failed. (Outstandingly good behaviour had the same effect, but was more difficult of achievement.) So she was flagrantly naughty — impertinent, defiant, disobedient, hoping that Miss Berry would be forced to send her to her stepmother or lay a formal complaint that would bring her to her father's notice. Miss Berry, however, had remained quiet, unmoved, remote, through the succession of one sided "scenes".

"She's an intelligent child," said Miss Berry, "and a quick learner."

"Of anything that interests her, I suppose," smiled Arthur.

"Yes," admitted Miss Berry, and, encouraged by this proof of understanding, continued, "It *is* a little difficult to get her to apply her mind to subjects she dislikes. Sometimes I wonder . . ." She hesitated.

"Yes?"

". . . whether a boarding school would be better for Anthea. Competition with other children——"

But Arthur shook his head.

"No, Miss Berry," he said firmly. "I don't agree. For a boy, of course, a boarding school education is essential. He has to be fitted to take his place in the world — in business or a profession. But a girl's place is at home both before and after marriage, she needs home influence for her development. Besides — one must be so much more careful of a girl's friends than a boy's, and at a boarding school, however carefully chosen . . ." He left the sentence unfinished and went on: "My wife and I discussed the subject before I went out to South Africa and were in complete agreement."

"I see," said Miss Berry with a faint sigh. In some ways Major Weatherley had seemed enlightened and understanding, but she realised that it would be impossible to move him from this decision.

"I have every confidence in your management of Anthea," he said. "I hope that you yourself do not wish to give up your charge."

"No," said Miss Berry, "but I feel that perhaps more modern methods . . . They have organised team games at these schools, you know. It serves to take the child's interest from itself and focus it on the community."

"I've seen pictures of them," said Arthur rather grimly. "Girls playing hockey! No, Miss Berry! They'll be playing football next."

There was a slight stir as the Vicar arrived, pushing the spinal carriage in which his invalid daughter lay, and Arthur made his way across the lawn to them. Miss Berry watched him, half smiling, half frowning. She understood that men who had known danger and uncertainty liked to think of their womenkind living sheltered guarded lives. Perhaps later, when he had seen more of Anthea, she would appeal to him again.

Anthea turned from the laughing group, and, seeing Miss Berry sitting alone on the iron seat, ran across to her. Her cheeks were flushed, her eyes bright, in the shade of the white-frilled cambric hat. She felt so full of happiness that she could hardly contain it. Everyone liked her, applauded her, paid her compliments. Mr. Frankson said she got prettier every time he saw her, Colonel Fortescue said that she'd be breaking a few hearts soon . . . They were silly things to *say*, but what they meant wasn't silly. She had even seen Mrs. Crabbe watching her and talking to her husband in a way that showed she was saying nice things about her. It was so lovely to feel that she was pretty, amusing, clever . . .

"Darling," she said breathlessly, slipping a hand into Miss Berry's, "I'm sorry I was so hateful this morning."

"That's all right, my dear," said Miss Berry.

She wondered whether to improve the occasion, and decided not to. The child would protest penitence without listening to a word she said. Already the bright — too bright — eyes were darting round in search of further conquests. One thing, however, Miss Berry had to say.

"Anthea dear, it isn't in very good taste, you know, to mimic your father's guests."

"Oh, I know . . ." said Anthea, but her lips curled irrepressibly into a smile at the memory. "People laugh and I can't help it . . . Oh, there's Philippa Duncan. I must go and speak to her."

And away she ran, her blue sash fluttering behind her.

Arthur had greeted the Vicar and the little invalid. The Vicar was a tall gaunt man, with cold grey eyes, deeply furrowed cheeks and a long, thin humourless mouth. Flora's small sharply-pointed face looked white even against the lace-trimmed freshly laundered pillow on which the silky golden ringlets were carefully outspread. She wore a short coat of pale-pink satin, elaborately tucked and ruched, and there was a gold bangle on the tiny blue-veined wrist.

A group of guests gathered round the carriage.

"Well, aren't you smart, Miss Flora!" said the doctor, looking down at the bangle and satin coat.

"Daddy gave me them," said Flora in her clear, rather shrill voice. "He's so sweet to me, and I must be such a nuisance."

The coldness left the Vicar's grey eyes as they rested on her.

"Daddy doesn't know what he'd do without his little angel," he said, "but we mustn't bore people by talking about that."

"The sun can never go in while this is out," said Colonel Fortescue gallantly, taking up one of the shining ringlets.

"The sun never goes in for me at all," smiled the Vicar. "I call her my ray of sunshine."

"Keeps you cheerful, eh?" said the Colonel.

"She does more than that," said the Vicar. "She helps and inspires me. Some of my congregation would be surprised if they knew how much of the good advice they get Sunday by Sunday comes from this little saint. She may be young in the ways of this world, but she is old in the ways of the other."

"Oh, Daddy," smiled Flora, "they won't listen to you on Sunday if they know I help you with your sermons."

"I think they'll listen all the more," said the Vicar. He laid a hand tenderly on her forehead. "Your headache gone, my pet?"

"Not quite," said Flora, flashing a smile at him, "but don't let's think of it. I'm so used to them that they don't worry me."

"You're a very brave little girl," said Miss Clorinda.

"Well, I can't be anything else," said Flora, "so I might as well be brave."

The Vicar's hand went to the pocket where he kept the notebook in which he recorded his little angel's more notable sayings, then, as he remembered where he was, withdrew. He could put it down later . . . Flora's sharp eyes had seen and understood the movement. If he forgot to put it down later, she would remind him. He didn't often forget, but when he did she reminded him . . .

Someone took Flora's chair to wheel it over to the tea-tables, and the Vicar was left dilating on Flora's goodness and courage and industry and cleverness . . .

"His devotion to that child is really beautiful," said Miss Clorinda, with tears in her eyes, to Dr. Bellingham.

"His devotion to that child is demmed morbid," growled the doctor.

"Is Ronnie coming, sir?" Clive accosted the Vicar.

"No," said the Vicar shortly, "the boy was troublesome over his lessons this morning, and I said he must stay in and do them again."

A light seemed to fade from his face as he spoke, leaving it cold and hard. Then he began to talk of Flora and the light returned to it.

"I say, Clive," said Anthea, as he crossed the lawn, "Flora keeps asking for you. Do come to her."

"I can't now," said Clive.

He always avoided Flora, who made him feel embarrassed and ill-at-ease. He hated the way her small white hand clasped his when he greeted her, and the way her pale-blue eyes watched him. Though she lay there helpless, she seemed to be clinging to him

. . . Last holidays when he had kissed her carelessly at the end of one of her visits, thinking of her as a child, she had turned her head sharply to press her lips on his. The thought of her now filled him with revulsion and panic.

"I'm going to the Vicarage to see Ronnie," he said. "Don't tell anyone. I won't be long."

The Vicarage was a bleak gloomy house surrounded by trees that grew close up to the windows, keeping out light and air. It had a derelict appearance, the paint-work scaling away, the windows dusty, the doorstep uncleaned. Knowing that the housekeeper was too deaf to hear the bell, Clive looked in at the sitting-room window, meaning to attract Ronnie's attention. Ronnie was sitting at the round table in the middle of the room, his lesson books strewn around him, his head on his outspread arms. At first Clive thought that he was asleep, then saw by the faint heaving of his shoulders that he was crying. After hesitating a few moments, he went round to the front door and knocked. It was a minute or two before Ronnie answered it. He looked red-eyed but otherwise as usual. He was even grinning in a determined tremulous fashion.

"*Clive*! How ripping of you! Come in. I thought it was someone for Father, wanting to be buried or married or something. Why have you left your party?"

"I wanted to come and see you."

"Are Father and Flora there?"

"Yes."

"I bet she's showing off, isn't she?"

"Well——"

"I bet she is. Did he tell you he wouldn't let me come?"

"Yes."

"It was beastly of him. I simply couldn't believe it at first. He knows how much I've been looking forward to it."

They had gone into the cheerless, shabby sitting-room, and Ronnie had taken his seat at the table in front of the chaotic jumble of books. He was a pathetic little object — inky, tear-stained and untidy — and the old paternal affection stirred again at Clive's heart.

"What was the trouble?" he said, drawing another chair to the table.

"Those beastly Latin verbs," said Ronnie. "Flora can remember them, and I can't. Flora can remember anything. She's only got to read a thing through once or twice, and she knows it, and I don't, and he gets in a bait with me. He says I'm stupid and idle and all the rest of it."

"Was he angry with you about yesterday?"

Ronnie nodded.

"Yes. He'd have given me a thrashing, but Flora begged me off. He made me thank her and kiss her. I hate kissing her. I'd rather have had the thrashing."

Suddenly he put his head on his elbow and began to cry again.

"Cheer up, old man," said Clive, putting an arm about his shoulder. "Tell me what you've got to do, and I'll help you."

"It's not that," said Ronnie, checking his sobs and wiping his tears away with inky fists till Clive offered his pocket-handkerchief. "I'm sorry I blubbed like that, Clive. He said I hadn't to have any dinner either, and, when you're hungry, you sort of want to cry. It — it came over me that perhaps I really *am* as bad as he says I am. I — I *do* hate Flora sometimes. I did today and yesterday. It makes me mad when she tries to be what she calls my "little mother" and starts messing about with my tie and my hair and things. I can't stand it and I'm rude to her, and then he gets in a bait. . . but, Clive, she *is* brave and she does have a lot of pain, and it's wicked of me to feel like this, and, if I died tonight, I know I'd go to Hell, and you never know you're not going to die tonight . . . All right," unsteadily, "I'm not going to blub again. You must think I'm a fool. I don't often get like this."

"I know you don't," said Clive. "Now tell me what you have to do and I'll help you. I won't do it for you, of course, but I'll help you. Your father wouldn't mind that, would he?"

"No," said Ronnie, who did not in any case intend to tell him . . .

As they worked, Clive wondered whether to go home and fetch Ronnie some sandwiches and cakes, but decided that Ronnie ought to take his punishments, even when they were as unfair as this one. Had he cared less for Ronnie, he would have done it.

Ronnie worked hard and with eager gratitude. Occasionally Clive glanced down at the small figure with affectionate amusement. It looked sodden with ink and tears . . .

"I say," said Ronnie, his voice still a little snuffly, "your hanky's getting in an awful mess. I'm frightfully sorry."

"That's all right. Now, you see, once you've got the principal parts into your head, you can get all the rest, can't you?"

"Yes . . . You'd make a ripping schoolmaster, Clive."

Clive considered.

"Sometimes I think I'd like to be one."

"You'd make a *ripping* one. What's Walsh going to be?"

"I don't know. We're both going to college first, anyway. We've always said that we'd try to keep together. If we were both schoolmasters, perhaps we could be on the same staff."

Ronnie sighed wistfully.

"It would be ripping for you . . . When do you go back, Clive?"

"Tomorrow."

"Blow! I'd hoped you'd come to tea tomorrow. I know Father would have let me ask you, because Flora likes you. She's always wanting you to come."

"I'm sorry I can't," said Clive uncomfortably.

He disliked going to tea at the Vicarage. The Vicar's habit of shooting sudden questions at Ronnie every few minutes ("What is the Ablative of 'tristis', Ronald?". . . "What are the principal parts of 'vinco'?") and, on Ronnie's failure to answer correctly, turning triumphantly to Flora, who never failed, embarrassed him almost as much as the cloying sweetness of Flora's glances and the clinging pressure of her hand. Ronnie, of course, was so much accustomed to the depressing atmosphere of his home that he took it for granted.

"You will when you come home next holidays, won't you, Clive?"

"Yes . . . That's all you had to do, isn't it?"

44

"Yes . . . Clive, you have been decent to me. Would you——" he hesitated.

"Yes?"

"You're the only person in the world I really care for. *Really* care for. And you're the only person in the world who's been decent to me. Would you think it frightful cheek if I asked you to be my blood brother?"

"Whatever do you mean?"

"You both make little cuts on your wrists and put them together and then you're blood brothers and all your lives you'll do anything on earth to help each other. I think Red Indians used to do it."

"All right," said Clive, amused.

It was rather a messy business, but was finally accomplished to Ronnie's satisfaction. He sat there, gazing into space — rescuing Clive from unbelievable dangers, diving into rivers for him, scaling cliffs, fighting wild beasts, jumping from trains . . .

Clive rose and stood, looking down at him, with that affectionate amused smile. Blood stains were now added to the general effect of ink and tears.

"I must go now, Ronnie . . . and you'd better have a good wash before they come back."

PART II

1908

Chapter Five

Clive's Twenty-first Birthday

Billy, a slender long-legged boy of nine, came running round the side of the house, took cover for a moment behind a variegated laurel, darted out again, fired an imaginary pistol at an imaginary pursuer, leapt down the terrace steps, four steps at a time, threw off his pursuers by dodging round the cedar tree, then, keeping warily in the shelter of the bushes, made his way to the summer house, where the mysterious X, cloaked and masked, awaited the secret document that he carried.

He was glad that Clive had gone to the Vicarage. No one else was interested in his activities, but Clive embarrassed him by asking kindly questions about them and even — worst of all — offering to join in them. Old Quimp was much more satisfactory. He just went on gardening and let Billy play around him, taking the part of friend or foe or inanimate object in the drama without knowing or caring anything about it. His only contribution was an occasional, "Now get 'ee out o' my way, Master Billy, do," or, "Now stop 'ee rampagin' round o' me like that, Master Billy, for the Lard's sake."

Clive, of course, was terribly kind, but his kindness gave one a *hunted* sort of feeling, made one want to hide from it. This business of going to school, for instance . . . Secretly Billy was delighted at the thought of going to school next term. He considered himself much too old now to be taught by Miss Berry, though he liked her and enjoyed her lessons. But with Clive he pretended not to care. When Clive said, "Aren't you looking forward to it, Billy?" he shrugged and answered, "Not particularly. I shall miss home, I expect," and then Clive began to encourage him and reassure him, telling him how much he would enjoy the games and lessons and companionship of other boys . . . You had to head Clive off onto something that didn't matter to you, and then it was all right.

Billy carried in his pocket now a book that Clive had given him yesterday, *Stories of Robin Hood*. He was enjoying it more than any book he had ever read, but he was careful not to let Clive see him reading it or guess how much he liked it. Clive would never have stopped talking about it — discussing the characters, asking how far he had got — and it would have been spoilt . . . He even resisted Clive's attempts to induce him to start a stamp collection (though he would have liked to collect stamps), because it would have been Clive's collection, not his. Everything Clive helped you with became Clive's . . .

What made things worse was that Clive never got cross like other people. Even when Billy was naughty and bad-tempered, Clive remained kind and patient. Sometimes Billy lay awake at night, oppressed by a feeling of shame because he did not love Clive as he ought to. His father was frequently irritable and unjust and displayed only a slight interest in Billy's doings, but Billy adored him.

Clive had been staying with a college friend called Joe Bentham and had come home yesterday, because tomorrow was his twenty-first birthday, and there was to be a dance in the evening. Anthea, of course, was wildly excited about it. She loved dressing up and showing off. Billy knew that people called her pretty and charming and clever, but he had a deep contempt for her. Though she was grown-up, he had heard her crying out loud like a baby just because a new dress that had come from the dressmaker did not fit her properly. She was kind to Billy when in a good temper, but, when put out, would snap at him or box his ears on the slightest provocation. To do her justice, her tempers never lasted long, and she was generous with sweets and pennies. Still — she was a girl and, like all girls, soppy, and the young men she brought home with her were almost as soppy as herself. Billy particularly disliked the admirer in favour at present — a lackadaisical young man called Gerald Oxley, who spoke with a drawl and generally referred to Billy as "our friend, the Human Boy". The only one of her admirers whom Billy liked was Jim Harborough, a slow silent youth, good-looking in a large clumsy fashion, whom Anthea consistently ignored or snubbed.

But he had more important things to do than thinking of Clive and Anthea. X had given him another secret message to deliver, and his enemies were already on his track. He hesitated on the edge of a gravel path, which was in reality a crocodile-infested river, then dived into it, stabbed a crocodile under water with a penknife, swam for half a mile, then scrambled up onto the opposite bank. Looking back, he was pleased to see several of his pursuers being consumed by crocodiles. Cutting across a stretch of open country, he plunged into a trackless jungle . . .

Ronnie saw Clive at the gate of the Vicarage and came down the drive to meet him.

"Hello, Clive! I wasn't sure when you'd be back or I'd have come round to see you."

"I wasn't sure myself," said Clive. "Are you doing anything? I wondered if you'd care for a walk."

"I'd love to," said Ronnie with slightly overdone heartiness. He was always afraid of letting Clive see that something of his old adoration had waned. But Clive's manner never altered. It remained affectionate and slightly avuncular, though the two years that separated them now made them almost contemporaries.

As Ronnie closed the gate, he turned back to look at the old house, which seemed gloomier, more overgrown with trees than ever.

"I wish I could do something about the old man," he said, "but there doesn't seem anything to do . . ."

Flora had died when Ronnie was fourteen, and since then a godmother had paid his school and college fees. He spent most of his holidays with the godmother or with friends, but occasionally his sense of duty forced him to spend a week or two at home. His father hardly seemed to notice his presence. On Flora's death he had begun to write the book, composed chiefly of Flora's sayings, that was to immortalise his "little angel's" memory. As he wrote, Flora herself seemed to be speaking, adding to what she had said in her lifetime, and what he called "automatic writing" began. He sat up night after night, writing pages of dreary platitudes — direct messages, as he believed, from Flora. His delusion had increased with the years. He seldom left the Vicarage now except to take the Sunday services, through which he hurried as quickly as possible in order to get back to the dark, comfortless old house, in which, he was convinced, his darling awaited him. He had grown thin and scarecrow-like, his person untended, his face grey with fatigue, his eyes blazing with a fanatical light. The desk and floor of his study were strewn with papers on which he had inscribed the "spirit messages". He was striving now to attain clairvoyance and clairaudience, so as to see and hear his darling. He fasted by day and prayed by night, for his religion was so closely intertwined with his delusion that they could not be separated. He would pass Ronnie on the stairs without seeing him, sit with him in the same room, mumbling to himself, without knowing he was there. The old housekeeper, deaf and slovenly, made no effort to rouse him or improve things.

"He's slowly going mad, you know, Clive. I don't know what to do about it. It's no use my saying anything to him. He doesn't even know I'm there. I don't believe he ever sleeps. I'm in the next room, you know, and I hear him talking all night . . . talking to Flora . . . begging her to let him see her and hear her . . . praying and almost crying. It would send me crazy if I stayed here long."

"Have you talked to Dr. Bellingham?"

"Of course. He does what he can, but the old man doesn't take any notice."

"You can't do any more," said Clive. "What sort of a term have you had?"

Ronnie gave him a somewhat stilted and expurgated account of the term's doings. So gradual had been his realisation that he and Clive had fundamentally very little in common that the knowledge still caused him a pang of disloyalty whenever he faced it . . . and he avoided facing it as far as he could. Clive was a bit difficult to talk to because — well, it wasn't, of course, that he had no sense of humour. It was that he had a — different sense of humour, and when you can't laugh at the same things it makes intercourse a little strained at times. Clive himself considered that he had a keen sense of humour, and would repeat the current *Punch* jokes with gusto to anyone who would listen to them. Guiltily Ronnie acknowledged to himself that many of the jokes he and his friends enjoyed were not "drawing-room" enough to be repeated to Clive. Clive was very particular about that sort of thing . . . and rightly, too. Dear old Clive! He was a grand chap — the grandest chap in the world.

Clive, watching him, thought how little he had changed with the years. The momentary look of anxiety that had clouded his blunt good-humoured face had vanished now, and it might have belonged still to the schoolboy of six years ago. It was difficult, indeed, to imagine Ronnie's face expressing anything but that radiant, slightly mischievous cheerfulness. If I had a son, thought Clive, I'd feel to him something of what I feel to Ronnie. And in a way, of course, Ronnie *was* his creation. He had guided him throughout his childhood, helped to form his tastes and standards. Ronnie's affection meant far more to Clive now than it had meant in their boyhood. His world would have been left dark and empty when he lost Paul's friendship had it not been for Ronnie. And now this last curious affair at the Benthams' . . . It was good to get back to Ronnie's uncritical devotion.

"Quite an uneventful term, on the whole, you see," ended Ronnie. "Just this and that . . ."

"Pity we aren't at the same university," said Clive, "but your godmother had this incomprehensible craze for unknown and out-of-the-way educational establishments."

Ronnie smiled dutifully at this reference to Oxford, aware of a guilty feeling of relief that they were not at the same university. He would have been a little too much under Clive's eye. Already Clive had warned him against several of his friends, and had afterwards taken for granted that Ronnie had dropped them. Actually they were still Ronnie's friends, though he never mentioned them now to Clive. Clive liked serious-minded people, and very few of Ronnie's friends were serious-minded . . .

"Yes," he agreed, "but you'd have been in a senior year, and, of course, you'll be going down soon. I suppose you're sure of a first, lucky beggar!"

"With reasonable luck," agreed Clive.

"You must swot a frightful lot," said Ronnie.

Clive smiled.

"It isn't what you'd call swotting," he said. "I really enjoy it, you see."

"I wish I did," said Ronnie enviously.

They had reached the outskirts of the village now.

"Which way shall we go?" said Clive. "Up the hill or along the valley?"

"The hill," said Ronnie without hesitation.

He didn't want to go into the valley with Clive. It was in the valley, sitting on one of the big fallen rocks, that Clive had told him about Walsh . . . and the first dim feeling of disloyalty had clouded his adoration.

Clive, made head prefect of his house, had decided to put down the bad language and gambling that had long been rife among the elder boys. He had addressed them firmly and courageously, reminding them that swearing and card-playing were forbidden and warning them that he would report the matter to the head master, if they continued. They continued, and Clive conscientiously reported to the head master any instance that came to his notice. He had never been popular, and his unpopularity increased. The damning epithet "sneak" was, of course, applied to him, though he could never be accused of deliberately spying or listening to tale-bearers. The ringleaders were expelled, and the ring-leaders' friends sent him to Coventry. As time went on, he was studiously "cut" by an ever-growing number of his contemporaries, and the younger boys did all they could — which was not a little — to make life uncomfortable for him. The strain of it told on Clive physically, but he did not falter in his task, and Walsh stood by him loyally.

"It's all very well to talk like that," he said hotly to Clive's detractors. "He's got more guts than you have — or than I have.

I bet you wouldn't go through with it, even if you felt it was your duty, and I know I shouldn't. You don't suppose he's enjoying it, do you?"

Certainly not even Clive's bitterest enemies could suppose that he was enjoying it, and that was their only consolation.

"And you can't say he's not just," went on Walsh. "You've all been as stinking to him as you can be, and he's not done anything mean or spiteful to any of you, even when he's had the chance."

With that, too, they had to agree, but, strangely, it did not endear him to them.

It was towards the end of his last term at school that Clive came upon Walsh smoking a cigarette surreptitiously in a secluded corner of the grounds.

"I'm sorry, Paul," he had said, "but I'm afraid I shall have to report it. It wouldn't be right to overlook it just because of our friendship."

"All right," said Walsh slowly, throwing away the stub of his cigarette. "Report and be damned to you! And you needn't let the thought of our friendship worry you, either, because it's over. I've stood by you till now, and it's not been easy, but I'm through with you now. I don't intend ever to speak to you again if I can help it."

Walsh kept his word. More than that, he openly joined the ranks of Clive's tormentors, and Clive left the school at the end of the term without a single friend to bid him goodbye. Even the head master took leave of him in an interview that was slightly lacking in cordiality. He was grateful for Clive's co-operation, but was growing a little tired of it.

Both Helena and Arthur had been concerned by Clive's looks when he returned home, but had put down his air of strain to overwork, and Ronnie knew that to no one else had Clive told the story of that term. Sitting on the rock, gazing fixedly in front of him, he had told it simply and straightforwardly, without self-pity or dramatisation.

"I don't see that I could have done anything else," he had said.

"I didn't really mind about any of the others, but I thought Paul would have understood . . ."

And, beneath Ronnie's flaming loyalty, beneath his stumbling expressions of sympathy and indignation, was a shamed torturing knowledge that, had he been there, he would have been among Clive's enemies.

They had reached the crest of the hill now.

"Let's sit down and have a rest," said Ronnie.

"Lazy little blighter!" smiled Clive, as they sank down onto the short firm turf. "You're out of condition."

Clive himself kept all the rules of physical fitness — early rising, cold baths, exercise, spare diet.

Ronnie grinned as he lit a cigarette, and Clive, who neither smoked nor drank, went on in half-jesting reproach, "And that won't do you any good, either."

"Don't be hard on a poor chap, guv'nor," pleaded Ronnie. "I've been on the river every day last term and I've trained like the dickens. Honest, I have!"

Clive looked thoughtfully into the distance and the smile faded from his face.

"A curious thing happened at the Benthams'," he said slowly.

"Oh, I was going to ask how you'd enjoyed it."

"I enjoyed it all right till— They'd taken a house on the river at Cookham, you know, and Joe and I went out sculling every day. It was an old thing, but he couldn't swim at all, and I could only swim a few strokes. We'd neither of us bothered to learn. Anyway, the day before yesterday, when we were out in the afternoon, the boat suddenly capsized. I managed to get hold of the upturned boat and hang onto it, but Joe was caught by the weeds, I think. Anyway, I hung onto the boat, and it drifted downstream . . ."

Ronnie's throat was dry.

"Was Joe——?"

"No. There were some people on the bank who could swim, and they got him out. One of them was quite a crack swimmer. They had to give him artificial respiration, and he's getting on all right now, but — his people were queer about it . . . as if they thought I might have done something to save Joe, but I don't see what I could have done."

"The blasted fools!" said Ronnie indignantly. He had glimpsed in Clive something of the same unhappy bewilderment as had assailed him when he lost Walsh's friendship, and all his boyhood's loyalty rose hotly in his defence. "What *could* you have done?"

"I don't see that I could have done anything. I want to be quite honest about it. I keep going over it in my mind. It's difficult to remember exactly what happened, but it's possible that just at the moment when I grabbed the boat, Joe may have been near enough for me to help him if I'd noticed, and I may have been too much taken up with myself to have looked for him." He considered the question, frowningly, conscientiously. "In that case I suppose I *was* a coward."

"Rats! What does Joe say?"

"Poor old Joe's too waterlogged to say much at present. It was evidently a pretty near shave. He just says he can't remember anything that happened. After all, I couldn't have saved him, even if I'd tried, and it might have meant two people drowning instead of one, which would have been stupid . . . Mind you, his people didn't *say* anything, and it may have been my imagination that they seemed a bit — queer. Stiff and quiet and not wanting to discuss it with me."

"They were probably just anxious about Joe," said Ronnie. He leapt to his feet. "Oh, come on! Let's forget it." There was, he knew, only one way of taking Clive's mind off his troubles. "By the way, we've been doing Pindar this last term, and his metres drive me crazy." For the rest of the walk, Clive patiently explained Greek metres to Ronnie, quoting examples, going over the points again and again, while Ronnie hid his boredom as best he could. He was relieved when they reached the Vicarage gate. It had been an uncomfortable walk.

Clive strode down the road, his face set and frowning. So often in the last two days had he gone over the details of the accident that his memory of it was blurred and confused. Perhaps he *had* deliberately saved himself, leaving Joe to drown. But what good

57

could he have done? Even if he had had time to consider the matter coolly and fully, surely he would not have been justified in risking his own life without the faintest hope of saving Joe. But did that attitude mean that he was a coward? And — *could* he have saved him? Was Joe near enough to the boat to have been helped to it if he had thought of him? His mind went round and round. How would Joe meet him next term? And that brought back the thought of Walsh and his desertion, the hurt of which had never quite healed. He could not have done anything else. Walsh should have understood that. His attitude had been simply incomprehensible. To have broken the friendship of years for a little thing like that . . . He had puzzled over it unceasingly. He still puzzled over it. He did not make friends easily and he had never made one to take Paul's place. Joe had been the nearest, and now— Well, thank God he'd still got Ronnie. But even the thought of Ronnie failed to banish his depression. Had Ronnie seemed quite the same this afternoon? When they reached the Vicarage, he had given him a set of enamel studs for his birthday present with hearty good wishes, but — had there been something faintly perfunctory in his expression of regret that he was leaving Cokers End that evening and so they would not meet again till next vacation? He couldn't face life if he lost Ronnie . . . He was not naturally introspective and seldom had much thought to spare from the matter immediately in hand, so that this heavy depression, this sudden unfamiliar distrust of himself, frightened and bewildered him.

As he turned the bend of the road, the pounding of hoofs startled him from his reverie, and he saw a horse galloping furiously towards him, the rider, a girl, struggling unavailingly to pull it in. Clive waited till it had come up to him, judged the exact second, seized the reins and tugged with all his might. The horse reared, then dropped, trembling. The girl dismounted, holding up the skirt of her riding habit with one hand and putting the other on the neck of the trembling, sweating horse. Her eyes, of deep violet blue, were fixed admiringly on Clive.

"How *brave* of you!" she said. "He'd have crashed into the wall at the end of the road if you hadn't been there. I should probably have broken my neck by now." Clive looked down at her, and the depression lifted from his spirit like fog clearing before sunshine.

"Nonsense!" he said, smiling. "You'd have pulled him in before then."

"I wouldn't. He's only just been broken, and we met one of those beastly motor-cars." She laid her cheek against the damp silky neck. "Poor old Tinker! Now don't start getting excited again." She patted and talked to him for a few moments, then looked again at Clive. "It *was* so brave of you. It was the sort of thing one reads about in books. He might easily have killed you. He didn't know what he was doing."

"He couldn't have done me any harm," said Clive. "Let me take him. He's still a bit nervous."

"Thanks." She raised both hands to her disordered hair. "I must look frightful. My hat blew off miles back."

"I'll get it."

"Let's walk back and get it on the way. I'd better take Tinker home anyway. He seems sorry already, doesn't he? He *hates* motor-cars. They *are* beastly things, aren't they? Daddy says he'd rather die than have one . . . My name's Lindsay Malvern. We've just come to live at Four Elms, and we don't know many people yet. Do you live here?"

"I live at Hallowes. My name's Clive Weatherley." The small lovely face lit up with pleasure.

"Oh, I know about you, of course. I've met Anthea, and your mother's called on mine . . . We're all coming to your dance tomorrow night."

"Good! Will you spare me a dance?"

Faint colour invaded the pale cheeks.

"As many as you like." She caught her lip in her teeth in a little rueful smile. "Oh, I shouldn't have said that, should I? But — it's such a thrilling way of meeting someone. I didn't know it happened outside books." They walked down the road, and to Clive everything about him seemed to bear a new and sharpened significance. The sky was bluer, the grass greener, the very sunshine more radiant than it had been half an hour ago . . .

"Are you quite sure you feel all right?" he said.

The girl laughed — a sweet childish laugh of eager happiness — as she gathered up the trailing skirt of her habit more securely.

"Perfectly all right. I never really felt frightened. It was as if I knew all the time that you were going to be there."

Chapter Six

"Germany seems to be supporting Austria in this outrageous annexation of Bosnia and Herzegovina," said Arthur from behind his newspaper. "The leader here says that there's no possible explanation of her policy except that she wants war."

Helena looked up from her sewing.

"War . . . Oh dear! I hoped we'd seen the end of war."

"I'm afraid we haven't, my dear."

"Anything good in the book reviews? Our Mudie's list is getting rather low."

"Let me see . . . Conrad's *Set of Six* and W. W. Jacob's new one . . ."

"*Salthaven*? I think we've got that down."

They were sitting in the library — the shabby book-lined room that Arthur loved. Nothing in it had been altered since his childhood. His father had refused to have gas installed when it was installed in the rest of the house, and Arthur had refused to have electricity installed. Though the servants grumbled, the room was still lit by oil lamps — the brass reading lamp on the writing table and the tall standard lamp, with its silk shade, by the fireplace. Even when the old-fashioned Venetian blinds were turned out of the rest of the house, they were retained here. This afternoon the windows were open and the sunshine poured into the room, dimming the log fire that burnt on the hearth and showing up with cruel insistence the pallor of Arthur's thin lined face.

Helena threw him an anxious glance as he turned over the pages of his newspaper. He had never really recovered from the effects of the African campaign. A succession of gastric ulcers had last year led to an attack of peritonitis from which he had not been expected to recover. He still had to diet carefully and was exhausted by any unusual exertion. It irked him to be compelled to lead the life of an invalid, but his deep attachment to his home and to Helena helped to reconcile him. He was happiest when, as now, alone with her in this room. The rest of the house was generally overrun by Anthea and her friends — noisy, high-spirited young people — and even Billy's exuberance soon wearied him, but the children were not allowed to enter the library, and there Arthur could always take refuge from the demands and upheavals of life. But its peace was only complete for him if Helena were there, too, and Helena was often torn between the claims of her household and the claims of her husband. There were times when to sit like this, sewing or reading aloud, with a hundred things needing her attention in other parts of the house, called for all her resources of serenity and self-restraint, but she gave no sign of restlessness and she knew by an unerring instinct when he needed her most. He seemed more her child now than her lover, and she was glad that there had been no other children. Billy, though affectionate, was very independent and demanded little time or attention from her, while her relations with Anthea and Clive were stereotyped. She gave what help they asked for and claimed little authority over them. With Anthea this arrangement had worked well, for the occasions on which Helena did exercise authority were so rare that she obeyed instinctively. Clive, of course, never needed help or restraint. Even as a child he had always been punctiliously polite and deferential to her. This attitude had an oddly wearying effect. She found an hour of Clive's politeness more exhausting than Anthea's tantrums or Billy's childish naughtiness.

"It's Clive's birthday tomorrow, isn't it?" said Arthur, lowering his paper suddenly.

"Yes."

"I must remember to make out the cheque. You've put the watch safely somewhere, haven't you?"

"Yes. I'll get it out tonight. Anthea couldn't resist showing him the dressing-case she'd got for him as soon as he came home. And she told him about Billy's inkpot, which made Billy furious."

"Where is he now, by the way?"

"Clive? I think he's gone to the Vicarage to see Ronnie,"

Arthur drummed his thin fingers on the arm of his chair for a few moments, then said:

"What's wrong with the boy, Helena?"

"Nothing's wrong with him," she said. "If you're thinking of that affair at the Benthams——"

"No, I'm not. There was nothing in it that the boy could be fairly blamed for, though he's quite capable of calmly weighing up the pros and cons and deciding that the risk of trying to save Joe wasn't worth it. He's too damned sensible."

She smiled.

"You ought to be glad of it, Arthur. I don't think that many men have sons who've caused them as little anxiety as Clive's caused you."

"I believe that's the trouble," he said. "Perhaps if I'd had to thrash him once or twice we might be fonder of each other. As it is, every time I meet the young jackass we might be strangers meeting for the first time."

"He's no fool, Arthur. He's doing extraordinarily well at college."

"Oh, he's got all the virtues," agreed Arthur wearily, reaching out his hand for his pipe. "Well, thank God Billy's a normal young devil, anyway."

Helena rose and folded up her needlework.

"I must go for a moment and see to things, dear," she said. "It's my At Home day, you know, though I don't suppose that many people will come because of the dance tomorrow."

His eyes followed her wistfully to the door.

"Don't be long," he said.

Anthea entered the drawing-room by the French windows, followed by Gerald Oxley. Her full ankle-length skirt, tightly waisted, with white shirt blouse, stiff collar and tie, suited her tall slender figure, and the flat cloth "motoring hat", so unbecoming to most of its wearers, had a jaunty tam-o'-shanter-like air, perched on her red-gold curls.

"Goodness!" she said, looking at the tea-cups ranged round the spirit kettle on the lace-edged cloth. "I forgot it was Helena's At Home day. I must fly up and make myself respectable. Sit down, Gerry . . .

"Mind if I smoke?" said Gerald, taking his stand on the hearth-rug.

"No, do . . ." She drew out the long hat-pins, took off her hat, thrust the pins into it, ran her fingers through her hair and sank down into an easy-chair. "Aunt Lilian smokes like a chimney, but she's in prison now, so I suppose she's had to give it up."

"Prison?"

"Yes, she's joined the Shrieking Sisterhood. The militant suffragettes, you know. She was brought up for assaulting a policeman and refused to pay the fine. Don't mention it when Father's about. He nearly has apoplexy whenever he thinks of it. Actually it's been a godsend to Aunt Lilian. She'd nothing to do before but run after young men or be run after by old ones and get drunk. It fills up her time nicely — interrupting meetings and going to prison." She stood up and began to fidget with the Goss china on the chimney-piece. "Gerry, must you really go up to London on Friday?"

"'Fraid I must," he said, smiling at her lazily.

"I expect you'll have a marvellous time there."

"I hope so."

"Going about with lots of girls . . ."

"None so pretty as you," he said, slipping an arm expertly round her waist and kissing her.

"*Don't*," she gasped in horror, pushing him away. "Not *here*, Gerry! Father or Helena might come in any minute, and there'd be a most *frightful* row."

"All right," he said, in no way abashed. "As long as it can be somewhere."

"You're pretty sure of that, aren't you?"

She wondered uneasily if she had "made herself cheap" by letting

Gerry kiss her. He was so unlike the other boys she knew. There was nothing shy or uncertain about his advances. He was completely sure of himself and took her response for granted, as he took most things for granted. It was she who, assured and imperious with the other youths of her circle, became shy and uncertain with him, afraid of betraying her lack of sophistication by any display of prudery.

Gerry's parents were in India, and he was subject to no authority, spending his college vacations wherever it pleased him and having an allowance of £500 a year paid into his banking account instead of the meagre pocket-money that was doled out to the other boys she knew. He wore suits of Savile Row cut, his cigarette-case was of gold, with his monogram in one corner, his shoes handmade, his socks of sheerest silk. He was spending some weeks with an aunt in the next village, and Anthea had only recently met him. He had singled her out from all the other girls of the neighbourhood for his attentions, and she felt flattered and excited. His good looks and easy poise of manner dazzled her. She was proud of her conquest, and would have felt unspeakably mortified had Gerry transferred his attentions to any of the other girls who were so eager to attract him, but there were times when she felt a little bewildered, a little apprehensive as to whither it was leading . . . For the first time in her life, she seemed to walk on shifting sands instead of solid ground.

"What will you do in London?" she asked.

He smiled at her quizzically through his cigarette smoke.

"Lots of things."

"The Harmers went to see Gerald du Maurier in *The Admirable Crichton*. Will you do that?"

"The prospect doesn't excite me wildly."

"What will you do?" she persisted.

"Little girls shouldn't ask questions."

She gave a laugh that was meant to sound worldly-wise and cynical.

"Oh, I know the frightful things young men do when they're on their own."

"I wonder if you do."

She changed the subject hastily, afraid of betraying her ignorance of the world in which he lived.

"Are you really going to get a motor-car?"

"That's one of the frightful things I hope to do. Will you risk your life with me when I've got it?"

"Oh, Gerry, it would be lovely! We never do anything exciting here. If I suggest a motor-car, Father snaps my head off. It's just like living in a museum." She swept her hand round the room. "We never even have any up-to-date furniture or new curtains, because Father doesn't like changes, and, anyway, everything was so good when it was bought that it will last till Doomsday. It's ghastly. We daren't even have the gramophone on while Father's in the house, and he's hardly ever out of it. We might all be in Madam Tussaud's. Clive, of course, was born in it."

"You'll have to kick over the traces," smiled Gerry.

He had grey-blue eyes, with laughter creases at the corners, fair hair, with a definite but not too obtrusive wave, and a cleft in his chin.

Anthea looked at him in silence, realising how deeply in love with him she was and how terribly it was going to hurt. She had been the accepted queen of her little circle, careless, selfish, heart-free. I wish I hadn't met him, she thought. Things won't ever be the same again. If only I knew whether he loved me . . .

"Kick over the traces?" she repeated.

"Marry someone or elope with someone," he suggested. "What about the solid Jim?"

He's saying that to hurt me, she thought. He wouldn't try to hurt me like that if he loved me. Or — could he be jealous of Jim?

"Jim!" She made a grimace. "I'd never marry Jim. Though"—she tossed her head — "I *could* if I wanted to."

"Who doubts it?"

"But I wouldn't — not if he was the last man on earth. Gerry," — she laid a hand on his arm — "you'll be coming back here before term begins, won't you?"

"'Fraid not. I shall go straight to Cambridge."

She was silent, seeing shadowy girls of incomparable beauty and charm, sitting with him in theatres, riding with him in hansom cabs, dancing with him in palatial ballrooms . . .

"I wish we weren't stuck here in this out-of-the-way hole," she said sulkily.

"Don't wish that," he said. "It's part of your charm. The modest violet, don't you know . . ."

Her face flamed with sudden anger.

"Why do you make fun of everything?" she said.

"You mustn't mind my teasing you," he said. "I can't help it. I only tease people I'm fond of."

She looked at him suspiciously.

"You're still laughing at me." She was silent for a moment, then went on: "I'm going to try to get Father to let me go to Cambridge to see Clive next term . . . Do you and Clive see much of each other?"

"I have the deepest respect for your brother," said Gerry, "but we move in different circles."

"Clive says that girl students come to the lectures."

"They do."

"I expect they're frightful frumps."

"On the contrary, most of them are very pretty and well dressed."

"I suppose you mean *one* of them is . . ."

"Perhaps."

Why is he always trying to hurt me, she thought miserably. Surely he couldn't have kissed me as he kissed me last night, unless he loved me . . .

The door opened and Helena came in.

"Good afternoon, Gerry . . . Anthea, haven't you changed yet?"

Anthea took her watch from her leather belt and looked at it.

"Goodness, I *must* fly, mustn't I! I was going to put on my new dress in your honour, Gerry."

"I must stay and see that," said Gerry.

Anthea's spirits swung skywards again.

"It's smashing, isn't it, Helena?"

Anthea had first begun to call her stepmother Helena in a fit of childish naughtiness, trying to hurt her by pretended devotion to her real mother, whom actually she hardly remembered. Helena had countered the move by calmly accepting the name and even persuading her husband that it was more suitable in the circumstances than Mother, and so Anthea had perforce to continue to use it.

"A Lewis Baumer straight out of *Punch*," said Helena, smiling. "Hurry up and put it on."

But Anthea still lingered, afraid that Gerry would go while she was upstairs.

"And put that skirt out to be brushed," said Helena.

Anthea inspected the patch of mud on the hem of the long full skirt.

"I wish we could wear trousers like men," she said.

"Don't be indecent," said Gerry.

"You're luckier than we were in my youth," said Helena. "At least yours clear the ground. Ours dragged on the ground, and we had to have one hand free to hold them up. We were always having to stitch fresh braid on the bottom, and when we went into the village to do shopping we used to put on little elastic bands to hold them up under our jackets so that we could have two hands for parcels."

"They'll probably creep up to the knee with the years," said Gerry.

"Who's being indecent *now*?" said Anthea.

Helena went to the tea-table to make some alteration in the arrangement of the cups, and Gerry watched her appreciatively as she bent over it. He liked the smooth coils of hair at the back of her shapely head, and the trimness of her figure in the plain dress of dark silk with the soft fall of lace at the neck. She dressed and behaved in so old a fashion that one was apt to forget that she was only a little over thirty. One was apt to forget, too, how pretty she was . . .

"You'll stay to tea, Gerry, won't you?" she said, looking up suddenly.

"'Fraid I can't," he said: "I only came to see Anthea home."

"But you're coming to the dance?"

"I hope so."

"He's going to dance every dance with me, aren't you, Gerry?" put in Anthea, stung by his obvious interest in her stepmother.

"As many as the solid Jim will spare me," he said.

"May I have the honour of this dance?" said Anthea, imitating Jim's slow voice and heavy formal manner. "If there's anything at all I can do to help with the preparations, Mrs. Weatherley, I trust you'll not hesitate to call on me."

Helena shot her a swift unsmiling glance, and she flushed. That was just like Helena, she thought mutinously . . . always trying to show one up, to put one in the wrong . . . making out that it was bad manners to jeer at Jim, who had been their friend all their lives and stood by them in every crisis, before Gerry, whom they had only known a few weeks.

In that exchange of glances the latent hostility between the two seemed to flare up. Anthea knew that Helena considered her and her friends fast and noisy and frequently ill-mannered, and she revenged herself for this by sneering at Helena as old-fashioned; but it was not a satisfactory revenge, and in her more honest moments she admitted to herself that right down at the bottom she liked Helena and wanted her good opinion.

The rather uncomfortable silence was broken by Clive's arrival. Helena looked at him with interest. He seemed — different . . . As if something that had always been asleep in him had suddenly awakened. His handsome, regular-featured face wore an unusual look of animation. He greeted Gerry perfunctorily, then turned to Helena.

"Do you know the Malverns, Mater?"

"The Malverns? Yes, they've just taken Four Elms. I called on them last week. They're coming tomorrow. Surely I told you."

"Probably. I don't remember. Did you see — Lindsay?"

"She's the eldest girl, isn't she? No, I only saw Mrs. Malvern, but she said they'd all be able to come."

"I met her at the tennis club," said Anthea. "Where have you seen her, Clive?"

"Just now. Her horse was bolting, and I gave her a hand."

So that's it, thought Helena, watching him . . .

"What's she like?" said Gerry. "Is she pretty?"

"Very pretty," said Clive.

"I didn't think her particularly pretty," said Anthea sharply. "In fact, I thought she was a silly little fool."

The interest in Gerry's eyes turned to amusement, and the now familiar sense of shame weighed down Anthea's heart. He's making me hateful, she thought, and he enjoys making me hateful. I didn't know being in love would be like this. I'm either wildly happy or wildly miserable all the time, and I seem to be miserable much more often than I'm happy . . .

"Where are you having the dance?" said Gerry.

"In here," said Helena, looking round the high spacious room, with its row of long narrow windows opening onto the terrace. "The men are coming early tomorrow to move the furniture out."

"And everyone's coming at eleven to help slide in the chalk," said Anthea. "Do come too, Gerry."

Then she bit her lip, realising how childish "sliding in the chalk" must seem to a man of the world like Gerry.

"Thanks so much," said Gerry, "but sliding isn't one of my accomplishments." He rose. "I really must go now, Mrs. Weatherley . . ."

"You can't. You haven't seen my new dress," said Anthea.

"I've no doubt you've got an equally smashing one for tomorrow night."

"Oh yes, I have. *And* ospreys for my hair. Well, if you must go, come by the conservatory. It's shorter, and you can inspect Quimp's hydrangeas . . ."

"I shall be delighted," he said, and again she was aware of the teasing light in his grey eyes and the faint note of mockery in his voice.

He knows I want him to kiss me . . . I don't care . . . She avoided Helena's eyes as she went out, and Helena looked at the closed door with a rueful smile. Poor Anthea! It's the first real thing that's ever happened to her, and she doesn't know what to make of it.

She's been so spoilt and — successful till now. Things have been too easy for her. Oh well, we all have to go through it. I remember the first time I was in love. He was old enough to be my father, and he never knew I was in love with him, and I nearly broke my heart, and all the time Arthur was waiting for me . . . Still — she's only a child. I hope she won't be hurt too much. It's a pity she lets him see so plainly. I wonder . . .

"What do you think of Gerald Oxley, Clive?" she said.

But Clive was gazing bemusedly out of the window and did not hear.

Chapter Seven

As Helena had expected, fewer people than usual attended the At Home, but the trains and large, heavily trimmed hats of the women seemed to fill the room. Anthea had put on her new dress of soft sage green, and bound her curls in a snood of the same material. She was talking to Jim Harborough, and Jim's round ingenuous face wore an expression of incredulous delight. Anthea's kindness was unprecedented . . . He could not know, of course, that his devotion mirrored for her a picture of charm and beauty that she was offering in thought to Gerald Oxley. If she was as Jim saw her, how could Gerald help loving her? She flirted shamelessly with Jim, shamelessly angled for compliments, even laid a hand carelessly on his arm to feel the faint tremor that ran through his thick-set frame.

"You'll let me have some dances tomorrow, won't you, Anthea?" he said hoarsely.

"As many as I can spare," replied Anthea, and her heart leapt as she imagined Gerald's arm around her . . . It was at the tennis club dance that she had first met him. He was a perfect dancer and held her in a firm expert clasp, unlike the shy fumbling touch of her other partners.

"You can sit out the lancers with me," she said graciously, "and perhaps a polka."

Anthea, like most of her friends, had enjoyed the romping element in both these dances till she heard Gerald refer to them contemptuously as "horse-play."

"Thank you, Anthea," said Jim gratefully.

Helena was making the tea at the low tea-table, pouring the

boiling water from the silver tea-kettle that simmered gently over its blue flame into the big old-fashioned silver tea-pot. Tea-making had been, in Arthur's childhood, a rite sacred to the mistress of the house, and he always liked to watch Helena perform it, insisting that the urn should be used only for large gatherings. He stood near her now on the hearth-rug, leaning his tall figure against the Adams chimney-piece, talking to Colonel Fortescue.

"I hear that your sister's joined the W.S.P.U.," Helena heard the Colonel say, and drew her brows together in a frown as she sent him a warning glance.

She had hoped that the subject would be avoided this afternoon. The mention of it always upset Arthur. He felt that Lilian had now finally and completely disgraced both herself and her family. Helena could not share his point of view. Perhaps she had known a little more of Lilian's way of life before she joined the Suffragette movement than Arthur had known . . . Lilian, drifting from one hectic love affair to another, flaunting her indiscretions, taking a perverse delight in shocking the respectable and defying convention. She had only escaped being cited as co-respondent in a recent divorce case because the man had managed to substitute for her name that of a woman of notoriously easy virtue who was in need of money. Arthur, of course, knew nothing of that and could not see that the activities of the Women's Social and Political Union offered Lilian a comparatively harmless outlet for her restlessness. She threw herself into it whole-heartedly and, the last time Helena saw her, had looked better than she had looked for years. Anthea turned round from where she stood talking to Jim.

"Oh yes, Colonel," she said. "Didn't you know? She's gone to prison. She and Christabel interrupted one of McKenna's meetings and were had up for assault and refused to pay the fine. I believe the bobby Aunt Lilian assaulted's still in hospital. She nearly scratched his eyes out."

"Don't talk such nonsense, Anthea," said Helena sharply, for Arthur's thin face had flushed and tautened.

"Unsexed hooligans!" he said angrily. "The whole thing's outrageous. They've lost their influence over men as decent women

73

and they've nothing to put in its place. This modern tendency to anarchy — strikers, Ulster volunteers, and now, Heaven help us! rebels in the House of Lords itself — is undermining the entire fabric of democracy . . . As for these women, they don't even stand by their own friends. They try to break up Grey's and Lloyd George's meetings as well as McKenna's and Asquith's. That fellow Keir Hardie ought to be jailed for encouraging them."

"I do so agree with you, Major," said Lady Evesham from her son's arm. "A woman's sphere is the home."

"But what about the women who have no home?" said Miss Clorinda, joining the fray with a warlike rattle of beads and rustle of hand-woven materials. "What about the thousands upon thousands of sweated women workers, whose lot no one troubles to ameliorate because they have no vote?"

"Violence never won anything worth having."

"After all, men got the vote by rioting."

"Surely an educated woman has as much right to a voice in her country's affairs as a man who can't write or read and is in any case willing to sell his vote for a pint of beer."

"They'll outvote the men, and then where shall we be?"

"Petticoats at Westminster! Good Lord, can you imagine it?"

Helena shrugged helplessly. The familiar argument was well under way, and nothing could stop it.

Clive wandered about the room, with a plate of sandwiches in one hand and a plate of cakes in the other. That strange sensation of moving in a world of clarified perceptions still upheld him. Even the walk that he had taken with Ronnie that afternoon was separated from the present by an immeasurable gulf of time . . . belonged to the old dim world that had ceased to exist . . . Paul . . . Joe . . . People he might have dreamed of, so shadowy and unreal were they. Impossible to believe that, only a few hours ago, the memories of them had darkened his whole spirit.

The usual hum of conversation rose and fell around him.

"What *is* to happen about the Vicar? Someone really ought to complain to the Bishop."

"Aren't I lucky, my dear! I've got both Marie Corelli's *Holy*

Orders and Mrs. Humphrey Ward's *Diana Mallory* from Mudie's. *Both* only just out!"

"It's all very well to say that the Kaiser doesn't represent the German people. I remember the same thing was said about Bismarck. It's curious that the Germans always have leaders to represent them who don't represent them . . ."

Clive replied absently when spoken to. The faces around him were blurred and indistinct. He saw only the pale oval face, violet-blue eyes and raven-dark hair . . . heard only that sweet eager peal of laughter . . .

Then Mrs. Malvern was announced, and Helena went forward to greet her and introduce her to the other guests. She was a short, dark, vivid little woman, somewhat swamped by an enormous hat, on which a large bird of prey had apparently just alighted. An elusive likeness to Lindsay made Clive's heart quicken.

She greeted Clive effusively.

"Lindsay's told me *all* about it, my dear Mr. Weatherley, and I'm *so* grateful to you . . . Do you know, Mrs. Weatherley, that this brave son of yours saved my daughter's life this afternoon?"

"I'm afraid I didn't really do that," smiled Clive. "She was managing very well by herself. I just provided the finishing touches."

"Oh, her account is quite different," said Mrs. Malvern. "She's convinced that you risked your life for her, and that, if you hadn't appeared just then, she'd have been dashed against the wall . . . and I believe her. I think that it's really *heroic* to tackle a bolting horse."

"Your daughter was tackling it herself magnificently."

"Oh, Lindsay's a good little horsewoman . . . It was that wretched motor-car. Not that I think them wretched really. I'd *love* to have one, but my husband gets furious if I even mention it. A lady, he says, should be content with her carriage; but I'm never allowed to use the carriage when it's raining, because of the coachman's rheumatism, and, when it isn't raining, my husband always wants it himself. So I generally have to walk. *My* rheumatism, of course" — she laughed, an infectious good-humoured laugh — "doesn't matter."

Animated conversation arose as on a much-worn but ever-engrossing topic.

"Well, we wouldn't be without our motor-car for anything."

"Yes, but you've got your carriage as well."

"Oh, that's just for Mother. She won't go in the motor-car."

"Of course, if you can run to a motor-car *and* a carriage, it's ideal, but otherwise——"

"Otherwise it means pensioning off the coachman and that's going to be expensive. Most of them are too old to learn anything else."

"The Gallophers have had theirs taught to drive a motor-car."

"Ours sulks for *days* if we even mention one."

"There's something *about* a carriage and pair. It's a question not only of style but of comfort."

"Oh, motor-cars aren't as uncomfortable as they were, with these new inflated seats. And, at least, you get some fresh air."

"A bit too much for my liking!"

"The horse, by gad, is man's best friend. The world's come to a pretty pass if we let him be driven off the roads by a bally machine."

Anthea yawned.

"I've been listening to this conversation for years and years," she said to Jim.

Mrs. Malvern looked with approval at Clive's handsome serious face as he brought her tea.

"Lindsay's so worried because she thinks she didn't thank you properly."

"There's nothing to thank me for . . . By the way, she said she'd like to read Rudyard Kipling's *They*. May I bring it round some time tomorrow?"

"Why not this evening?" said Mrs. Malvern. "Then she can set her conscience at rest and thank you properly. I've sent the carriage on to the town to call for some groceries and it should be back here any time now. But perhaps, as you're the hero of the occasion, you oughtn't to leave it?"

"I'm not the hero of this occasion," smiled Clive. "This is just my stepmother's At Home."

"I see. You don't start being the hero till tomorrow. But I think there should have been some birthday cake. I adore birthday cake. My husband says I'm much more childish than any of my children, and I believe I am."

"How many have you?" said Clive, trying to bring the conversation round to Lindsay again.

"Three girls. Lindsay's the eldest. She's eighteen. The other two are only eight. They're twins." Her eyes darted round the room. "I *am* enjoying myself. I love meeting fresh people and going to fresh places. Your stepmother's charming . . . and how pretty your sister is!"

"I suppose she is," said Clive. "We used to call her Carrots."

"She's *lovely!* . . . Well, everyone seems to be going, so I'm afraid I must go too. You will come with me, won't you? Now that I've met your family, I'm longing to show you mine . . . I'm afraid I must go now, Mrs. Weatherley. It's been a delightful afternoon. May I borrow your son? I won't keep him long, but he's promised to lend my little girl a book . . . and she wants to thank him properly for saving her life this afternoon."

"What did you think of our new neighbour?" said Helena to Arthur, when the carriage containing Clive and Mrs. Malvern, still chattering volubly, had driven away.

The other guests had all gone except Jim, whom Anthea had taken into the garden and on whom she was still practising the charms and graces intended for the ultimate enslavement of Gerry.

But Arthur was not to be diverted from the subject that was uppermost in his mind.

"When I think of my father's daughter," he said, "brawling in public . . . her name in the newspapers . . . bandied about . . ."

"Don't think of it, dearest," said Helena. "It does no good." She held out her hand. "Come back into the library with me and rest."

Four Elms had been built at the time when the French chateau style was in vogue, and was a rather pretentious affair of red brick and ornamental stone-work, but the pleasant shady garden in which it was set lessened its exuberance, and both brick and stone had mellowed with the years.

"Isn't it charming!" said Mrs. Malvern, as the carriage drew up before the front door. "As soon as I saw it I said to my husband that we must have it. We'd been looking for a house in the country and within reach of my husband's business for ages, but the minute I saw this I knew the search was ended . . . Come straight in. I may call you Clive, mayn't I? If I like a person, I can't bear to stand on ceremony, can you?"

Still chattering, she led him through a large hall into a drawing-room, which gave a general impression of white paint, chintz and silver tables. On a white fur rug in front of the fire lay two little girls in navy-blue kilted skirts and sailor blouses, their hair tied on one side with pink ribbons, their heads propped on their hands, reading . . .

"Well, my darlings!" said Mrs. Malvern, in a tone that suggested joyful reunion after a long parting.

They looked up, said "Hello, Mummy," and returned to their books. They were evidently as much accustomed to her effusiveness as she was to their lack of response.

"Come and say 'How do you do' to Mr. Weatherley, darlings," she went on. "This is Pat and Mab, Clive."

The little girls rose, straightened their crumpled skirts, advanced ceremoniously to Clive, shook hands, said "How do you do, Mr. Weatherley," and returned to their books.

"Where's Lindsay, darlings?" said Mrs. Malvern, but they had propped up their heads on their hands again, with the additional precaution of a finger in each ear, and did not answer.

At that moment the door opened and Lindsay came in. She wore a dress of yellow linen, with deep tucks at the bottom and a black velvet band at the waist. Her dark hair was parted in the middle, and brushed plainly back into a coil in the nape of her neck. As her eyes met Clive's in a shy level glance, her pale cheeks flushed slightly.

"You see, I've brought Clive back with me, darling, so that we can all thank him properly, and—"

There came the sound of the opening and slamming of the front door.

"Oh dear! There's Daddy," said Mrs. Malvern. She bent down and prodded the backs of the sailor blouses on the hearth-rug. "It's Daddy, darlings. Collect your things and run up to the nursery quickly. You know he doesn't like to find you down here when he comes home."

The little girls rose, picked up their books, said goodnight to Clive and went out, followed by their mother. Clive and Lindsay were left alone.

"I've brought the book," said Clive, taking it out of his pocket.

"Oh, thank you . . ."

Her low sweet voice struck soothingly on his ear after her mother's brisk staccato. The two seemed to have little in common except that faint physical resemblance. Lindsay, despite her shyness, was grave and gentle. It was difficult to imagine her flurried or excited . . .

"I hope you weren't——" began Clive, but the door opened and Mrs. Malvern entered, followed by a large man with a rubicund face, to which a thick upstanding thatch of black hair and bristling black eyebrows gave a startling air of ferocity.

"This is Mr. Weatherley who so kindly came to Lindsay's rescue," said Mrs. Malvern, giving Clive a proprietary smile.

Mr. Malvern greeted Clive shortly then took his stand on the hearth-rug and turned to Lindsay.

"Sorry to hear you've been making a fool of yourself in public, my girl," he said. "You ought to know how to handle a horse at your age."

Clive burst in hotly to defend her and describe what had happened.

Mr. Malvern listened without comment then turned to his wife.

"Did you get that tap mended?" he said.

Mrs. Malvern gave a peal of amused laughter.

"Now *isn't* that like me!" she said. "It went clean out of my mind."

"I saw to it," said Lindsay. "I got old Blake to put it right."

"Darling!" cooed Mrs. Malvern affectionately.

Mr. Malvern took out his watch.

"Dinner late as usual, I suppose," he said without any particular emotion.

"I must be going," said Clive uncomfortably.

"Oh, *must* you?" said Mrs. Malvern. "Well, if you *must*, you'd better go by the kitchen garden and take the short cut over the fields. Show him the way, Lindsay."

Mr. Malvern appeared to notice Clive for the first time.

"You live at Hallowes?" he said.

"Yes, sir," said Clive.

"What does your father think of this damned old-woman Government and its Old Age Pension tomfoolery?" he said, and went on, without waiting for an answer, "Pauperising the country . . . sapping its independence . . . cutting its guts . . ."

"Hush, dear!" murmured Mrs. Malvern.

Clive and Lindsay went out by the garden door and were crossing the lawn, when a loud voice, upraised on a raucous bellowing note, made Lindsay stop suddenly with parted lips and widened eyes.

"Oh . . . one minute," she said, and disappeared into the house again.

She came out a few minutes later with a little smile of apology and relief on her lips.

"I'm sorry," she said. "I thought that Daddy had got into a temper. He does sometimes quite suddenly . . . Mother doesn't mind. She just behaves as if it weren't happening. And I don't mind for myself but it frightens the children."

"And wasn't he in a temper?" asked Clive, remembering the loud bellow that had rent the air.

"No . . . He was speaking to Cook through the speaking-tube in the hall. He always shouts like that through the speaking-tube. They could hear him just as well in the kitchen without it . . .

He'd remembered that he'd brought some smoked salmon back with him and he wanted Cook to do something about it for dinner."

"Oh," said Clive.

They walked without speaking till they reached the high brick wall that surrounded the garden. Clive opened the door leading into the lane.

"Across the stile and over the fields," said Lindsay, "but, of course, you know the way . . ."

"Yes."

They stood looking at each other, and again that feeling of sharp delight seized Clive . . . It was Lindsay who broke the silence, speaking in a hushed breathless tone, as if afraid of disturbing someone.

"Goodbye . . . I'll see you tomorrow."

"Yes . . . Tomorrow."

PART III

1912

Chapter Eight

Joanna's Christening

Jim entered his wife's bedroom, tripping over the head of the leopard-skin rug that lay by the bedside.

"Clumsy!" said Anthea.

"I always fall over the darn thing, don't I?" said Jim cheerfully. "Are you nearly ready, darling?"

Anthea was seated at her mirror, holding up a handglass and inspecting with a critical frown what could be seen of her profile beneath the brim of her hat.

"Do you like this hat?" she said, "or shall I wear the one with the feathers?"

"You look lovely in anything," said Jim, gazing down at her with a smile of ingenuous admiration.

"Not exactly helpful, are you?" said Anthea.

Anthea had matured since her marriage. Her prettiness had deepened into beauty, and she wore a look of placidity and fulfilment — the look of a woman who is desired and beloved. Jim, at the end of two years of marriage, was as wholehearted in his devotion as he had been at the beginning. The birth of a baby daughter five weeks ago had put the final touch to his happiness, and his devotion now had a touch of reverence that Anthea professed to find amusing but that secretly gratified her.

"He'll hardly let me move," she had complained to Helena in the months before the baby was born. "You'd think no one had ever had a baby before. He rings me up a dozen times a day from the office to ask me if I'm all right . . . He's far more exhausting than the baby!"

But there was no exasperation in her laughter. She held the centre of the stage now without effort or fear of rivalry. Her every action was applauded, her every whim indulged. And Jim, because he was her husband, had lost all those qualities that she had once ridiculed in him. Because it was impossible that she should marry a man who was not handsome, clever and charming, Jim, by becoming her husband, automatically became handsome, clever and charming. She conveniently forgot the long torment of her love for Gerald Oxley, forgot the agonised fluctuations between hope and despair, the heart-sick suspense of the weeks when she had waited in vain for some sign from him, the wild excitement of his rare visits and letters, the burning shame of the advances she had made or yielded to . . . She even forgot the desolation of that morning when she had heard of his engagement to a girl in London whom she had never met, a desolation made blacker by the memory of a letter she had posted to him the night before, pleading her love and begging him to agree to an engagement between them. When she heard the news, her longing had turned to a blind fury. If he had been playing with her, he must be made to see — and everyone must be made to see — that she, on her side, had been playing with him. She met Jim that afternoon, led him on to make his often repeated proposal and sent him home, dazed with rapture, as her fiancé.

She went to her wedding, white-faced and stony, thinking only of Gerry, imagining Gerry by her side . . . But she could not retain the pose for long against Jim's tenderness and devotion and the excitement of being mistress of a smart up-to-date house, with as many new clothes and as much money as she wanted. Gradually, very gradually, the stony young martyr became the contented young matron, for she discovered in herself unsuspected abilities and was proud of her smoothly-running, well-kept home. The baby was the culminating point of the process, and she could not help in some degree sharing Jim's view that to have produced such a child — superbly healthy, weighing 8½ lb. at birth — argued outstanding merit on her part.

"I think I'll go in this one," she said. "Helena hasn't seen it, and she's seen the others. Has Nurse taken Baby to the car?"

"Yes, I've tucked them in. We're only waiting for you." Then, afraid that this might seem to convey a reproach, he added hastily, "No hurry at all, of course, darling."

Anthea stood up and surveyed herself in the cheval-glass, smoothing down the long "hobble skirt", buttoned tightly to the knees.

"I'm horribly shapeless."

"You're beautiful," said Jim.

"Well, for goodness' sake, mind my hat."

He kissed her with clumsy care, and she freed herself from him with affected impatience.

"Why must you always kiss me when I've got a hat on?" But she smiled at him as she spoke, tempting him to try again. "Now that's enough! Nurse hates to be kept waiting, and I told Helena that we'd be there by three, because of getting Baby home in good time."

"I bet Billy wasn't such a fine kid at that age," said Jim proudly.

"He was a boy, anyway," said Anthea, "and I know you wanted a boy, though you pretend you didn't."

"I'd like to have a boy, though I'm glad Joanna was a girl. We'll have a boy next time, shall we?"

"Yes," said Anthea carelessly, "or the time after that. We'll have one, anyway."

"We were so thrilled by this one that we've never discussed it," said Jim, "but you wouldn't mind having a largish family, would you, darling?"

"Me?" said Anthea lightly. "No, I'd love it . . ." She saw spacious sunny nurseries, nurses, nursemaids, little cavalcades setting off for walks with prams, troops of sunny-haired children playing in the garden. "It's fun having babies," she ended serenely.

"I suppose the house may seem a bit small later on," said Jim thoughtfully, "but we could always move into a larger one."

"No, let's not do that," said Anthea. "I like this house. Let's have a nursery wing built on, with separate bathroom and lavatories."

He gazed at her for a moment, speechless with admiration.

"You do have marvellous ideas, darling," he said. "I'll see Houghton about it at once."

"There's not all that hurry," she smiled. "Come along. Who's keeping Nurse waiting now?"

At the front door a uniformed chauffeur was holding open the door of a large car, inside which the baby, in long white satin coat and swansdown-trimmed bonnet, slept on the nurse's knee.

Anthea took her seat beside her, and Jim on one of the smaller seats opposite.

"Baby and I can sit there if you like, Mr. Harborough," said the nurse.

She spoke with easy conviction that the offer would be refused. Not only was Mr. Harborough "a real gentleman, if a little unpolished" (as she had written to a friend last night), but she basked, she knew, in the glory that was reflected from his wife and child. Nothing was too good for them, and therefore nothing was too good for her. Nursery meals were as well cooked and served as the family's meals, the night nursery was as comfortable as if it had been a guest-room, and everything she asked for was immediately supplied.

There were times when she found Mr. Harborough's devotion to his wife a little irritating. "It would drive me crazy," or "Some women have all the luck," she would comment, according to her mood.

"We want to arrange with Mrs. Weatherley about the christening," said Jim to her as the car drove off. "We thought it would be better to have it at Cokers End, so as to save Major Weatherley the journey, and, of course, it's conveniently near us and a good centre for the family."

"Yes, sir," agreed the nurse.

Jim bent over his sleeping daughter and tenderly patted her cheek.

"By *Jove*!" he said in a tone of awe, "have you ever *seen* such a marvellous kid!"

Jim insisted on taking the baby as soon as they dismounted from the car at Hallowes. The nurse carefully arranged the cape over his arm, the long coat reaching almost to his knees.

"Oyes! Oyes! Oyes!" he shouted as he entered the hall. "Make way for the sleeping princess!"

Helena came out of the library.

"Oh, the darling!" she said softly.

The sight of Anthea's baby stirred her heart, made her, in spite of herself, regret the children that she and Arthur might have had if the war had not shattered his health.

The nurse hovered round anxiously as the child was transferred from Jim's arms to Helena's with much rearranging of the heavy embroidered cape. "What with Jim and Nurse," said Anthea, "I hardly get a look in, but then I'm only the mother."

Arthur rose from his seat by the fire as they entered.

"Hello, hello, hello," he said. "Come along in. Let's see her!"

He looked older than his fifty-odd years, his face thin and lined, his brows set generally in a frown, but his smile banished the impression of severity as he welcomed the visitors. He was proud of his first grandchild and had always liked Jim — a plain straightforward fellow with no nonsense about him. He had been glad when Anthea "made up her mind at last and sent that bounder Oxley about his business."

He patted the baby's cheeks and made little whistling noises to her. She opened blue eyes and stared at him solemnly.

"Come to Grandpa," he said, holding out his arms.

"Goodness, Father!" said Anthea, "she's not old enough for that sort of thing yet." She smiled at the nurse. "Major Weatherley wants to start jogging her on his knee and throwing her up to the ceiling."

"Oh my!" said the nurse in horror.

"Don't believe her," said Arthur. "Babies always like me, and their mothers are always jealous."

"Come upstairs and take your things off," said Helena, and to Arthur, "We won't be long, dear."

The nurse, Anthea and Helena went out of the room, Helena

still carrying the baby, Anthea and the nurse looking at it over her shoulders.

"She's still awake, the precious!" said Anthea.

"She'll soon drop off again," said the nurse.

"Sit down, Jim," said Arthur, "and have a cigarette."

"I don't think I'd better," said Jim. "Anthea doesn't like me to smoke in the nursery, and Baby will be down here in a minute."

"I shall be smoking, anyway, so you might as well. Smoke your pipe if you'd rather."

"I think a cigarette would be better . . . Anthea doesn't really like pipes."

"You mustn't give in to Anthea too much, you know. She's a headstrong young woman and needs checking occasionally."

Jim was so shocked by this that he threw the match he had just struck into the fire.

"By Jove, sir," he said hoarsely. "She's marvellous! She's wonderful! She's — she's the most — the most——"

He stopped, choked by emotion.

"All right," smiled Arthur. "Have it your own way. Make your own mistakes . . . How's business?"

Jim had inherited from his father a flourishing wholesale ironmongery business. Despite his simplicity, he had plenty of commercial acumen and had already improved his position considerably.

Becoming calmer, he lit his cigarette and leant back in his chair, crossing his long thick legs, encased in the striped trousers on which Anthea insisted. She made him go to an expensive London tailor and preferred him to wear morning suits rather than tweeds, which, she considered, emphasised the clumsiness of his build.

"Business isn't bad," he said.

"Damned good, you mean," said Arthur.

Jim nodded.

"Yes, I've got something to work for now."

He thought of the nursery wing and the "largish family" on which he had set his heart.

"You're right there," said Arthur. "Anthea's not cut out for a poor man's wife"; then, afraid lest this should provoke another outburst, continued hastily, "What do you think of this Irish business?"

Upstairs, in Helena's bedroom, where a log fire burnt on the hearth, the nurse had taken off the satin coat and bonnet, revealing a small silky head and a voluminous robe of sheerest cambric with embroidered yoke and centre panel edged with Valenciennes lace. Anthea held the baby while the nurse took off her own things — long navy-blue cloak and straw bonnet with long veil — and laid them carefully on the bed beside the baby's. Suddenly the small face crumpled and a shrill whimper sounded . . .

"I'll soon get her off again," said the nurse, and took her to the armchair by the fire, rocking her to and fro. Gradually the whimper ceased.

Anthea stood at the dressing-table, tidying her hair and examining her figure, which, still graceful and supple, had lost its girlish lines.

"Aren't I fat?" she said placidly. "But Jim likes me fat, so I suppose it doesn't matter."

"You'll soon thin down," said Helena. "How do you think your father looks?"

"Pretty much as usual," said Anthea, taking up the hand glass to inspect her back hair. "My hair fell out a lot when Baby came, but it seems all right now . . . Why?"

"He had another heart attack last week and was in bed all the week-end. He really oughtn't to do anything, and it's so trying for him."

"And for you . . ." said Anthea, taking out a hair-pin and running it home more securely.

"Oh, that doesn't matter," said Helena, "but Billy's over for half term, and Arthur feels not being able to go about with him."

"I didn't know Billy was over. How's he getting on?"

"Very well. He's taking his Common Entrance next term . . . Oh, and Aunt Lilian's here, too. She arrived unexpectedly last night."

"She always arrives unexpectedly when she arrives at all, doesn't she? Where is she?"

"She's gone into the village. She'll be back for tea. Shall we go down now? Are you ready, Nurse?"

"I think we'll stay up here another minute or two, Baby and I, Mrs. Weatherley. She hasn't quite gone off."

Downstairs in the library they found Billy sitting sideways on a hassock in front of the fire, sharpening a piece of stick with a penknife. He was a tall thin child and had lately had what Helena called one of his "growing spurts", so that his wrists protruded bonily from the sleeves of his jersey and his knees from the legs of his knickers.

"Hello, Billy," said Anthea. "You over for the weekend? What are you making?"

Since her marriage the relations between Anthea and her step-brother had been formal and polite.

"Yes. Half term. I'm making some new arrows for my bow."

"Mind you don't let that stuff go on the hearth-rug," said Helena.

Helena loved this young son of hers passionately, but treated him with off-hand curtness, especially in his father's presence. Arthur was proud and fond of the boy, but quick to notice and correct any signs of "spoiling", and, though he was unaware of it, inclined to be jealous of Helena's affection for him. He was sensitive, too, on the score of his invalidism at an age when he would normally have been initiating his son into manly sports and sharing his activities, and apt to exert his authority with undue severity to restore the balance.

"Billy's the captain of the football team this year," he said to Jim.

He had been a keen footballer and cricketer in his youth and was anxious that Billy should follow his example. He discouraged the interest in literature that Billy showed and that Helena secretly encouraged. Billy had asked for a copy of Rudyard Kipling's poems for his Christmas present last year, and Arthur had contemptuously ignored the request and given him, instead, a new pair of skates.

Billy wrote poems himself — childish immature pieces, but with evidence of imagination and poetic feeling. At first Helena had shown them proudly to Arthur, but Arthur's face had flushed as if in personal humiliation, and he had said shortly, "For God's sake, don't let the boy go in for tommy-rot like that." He disliked even to see him reading. "Can't you find something to do out of doors?" he would say.

And so there was between mother and son an unspoken conspiracy that strengthened the bond between them. That both were devoted to Arthur and that Billy, with unchildlike sensitiveness and sympathy, avoided anything that could remind his father of his invalid state, made their understanding deeper and more real.

"It's all right, Mater," said Billy, picking up a piece of wood from the rug and throwing it into the fire. "I've kept most of it in the hearth, and, anyway, I've nearly finished now."

Jim had leapt up from his easy-chair and drawn it forward for Anthea.

"Sit down here, darling," he said. "I'm sure you're tired by the drive."

"Goodness!" said Anthea, sinking into the chair with a smile. "Jim seems to think I'm a permanent invalid just because I've had a baby. By the way, Billy, if you'd like to see Baby, she's upstairs in your mother's room with Nurse."

"Thanks," said Billy, moving a little to one side, as Jim's large feet now occupied part of the hearth-rug. "I'll wait till it comes down."

"It!" laughed Jim, giving him a dig with a well-polished boot. "Don't you dare call her 'it', young fellow!"

Billy grinned, gathered up his arrows and went from the room.

"Now about the christening," said Anthea in a businesslike tone. "We want to get it fixed up today. Will Sunday week suit you?"

"Yes, it will suit us all right," said Helena. "Will Clive and Lindsay be able to come over?"

"Clive said he could manage any Sunday."

"When's Lindsay expecting hers?" said Jim, looking carefully round to make sure that Billy had gone.

"In the spring," said Helena. "About April, I believe . . . She's such a child. I hope Clive's looking after her all right."

"Whom else ought we to ask?" said Anthea, who saw no reason why the conversation should be allowed to stray from herself and her baby to Lindsay and hers. "You'll fix up with the Vicar, won't you, Helena?"

"I'll arrange everything here," said Helena. "Just tell me how many people are coming to tea and I'll have everything ready."

"We must find out how many of Jim's people can come. Will Aunt Lilian still be here?"

A familiar frown of irritation contracted Arthur's brow.

"You should know by this time," he said, "that no one can ever predict your Aunt Lilian's movements."

"Anyway, she's not a militant any longer," said Anthea soothingly.

"Yes, she's quarrelled with that gang, I'm glad to say," said Arthur, "but I don't know that the one she's got in with now is much better."

"Oh, Arthur, it is," murmured Helena.

"What's the new one?" said Anthea.

Arthur knocked out his pipe against the fireplace.

"Some crazy tomfoolery I can't make head or tail of."

"She calls it Theosophy," said Helena.

"Reincarnation and — what does she call it? — karma and astrology and a whole lot of balderdash of that sort. She's got hold of some bounder — or rather he's got hold of her, who can — What was it she said he could do, Helena?"

"Go to other dimensions," smiled Helena, "and find out what people's other incarnations were and foresee the future and——"

"Let's ask him for the next Derby winner," said Jim with a loud guffaw.

"She says that he sees colours round everyone," went on Helena, "and can see right into their bodies and find out what's wrong with them——"

"Tut! tut!" put in Jim.

"Anyway, Arthur, it gives her an interest in life."

"Interest in life!" snorted Arthur. "Why on earth can't she marry and settle down? That would give her an interest in life."

"My dear Father!" murmured Anthea. "She must be thirty-six at least . . ."

"No woman ever had better chances," said Arthur. "She's simply thrown them away, one after another. I could tell you a dozen men who would have made her good husbands and who wanted to marry her . . . If she needs tomfoolery like this to give her an interest in life now, she's no one to blame but herself."

He was growing heated, as he always did when he talked of Lilian, and Helena, watching him anxiously, hastened to change the conversation.

"Ronnie's staying at the Vicarage," she said. "He was here to tea yesterday."

"He can come to the christening," said Anthea graciously.

"I've not seen the boy for years," said Jim. "What's he turned out like?"

"Just the same old Ronnie," said Helena with a smile.

The old Vicar had died suddenly in his sleep three years ago. He was worn almost to a shadow, and by his bedside lay a pencil and paper —the paper covered with the illegible scrawls of his "automatic writing". He died opportunely, as the scandal of his holding the living in which he took no interest and for which he did no work could not have been allowed to continue much longer. Ronnie's godmother, who believed in foreign travel as a formative influence for the young and liked Ronnie's companionship, took him abroad for most of his vacations, and the Weatherleys had seen little of him in recent years. The new Vicar, young, unmarried and modern in his views, with High Church tendencies that were not wholly approved by his parishioners, had housed Ronnie's few possessions at the Vicarage, and a friendship had sprung up between the two.

Jim looked round. He was not interested in Ronnie or Lilian, and he had come here to have his daughter admired.

"What's happened to the kid?" he said.

"She's still upstairs with Nurse," said Anthea, rising. "I'll go and bring them down."

She, too, felt that the real business of the day had not yet begun.

Lilian came slowly up the drive and round the house towards the side door. Though she had now severed all connection with her former suffragette friends, she still retained the style of dress that had been popular amongst them. She wore a dark perfectly-tailored coat and skirt — long in the fashion of the day but without the usual "hobble" effect — and a small close-fitting hat with a veil drawn tautly beneath her chin. She was tall and graceful and, despite her defiance of the prevailing modes, had a striking air of elegance and distinction.

Outside the library window she came upon Billy standing, legs apart, hands in pockets, looking into the room, whose thick lace curtains hid him from the view of its occupants. The baby lay on the sofa, its head on an embroidered pillow, its robe spread out to cover the sofa from end to end. Arthur, Helena and the nurse were bending over it. Anthea sat by the fire watching with a complacent smile. Jim hovered attentively between wife and child.

"Hello, Aunt Lilian," said Billy.

Secretly (for he was aware of his father's disapproval of her) he liked Aunt Lilian. She didn't "show off" and talk about clothes all the time, as most women did. She resembled his mother in that, but there was something exciting and adventurous about her that his mother lacked.

"Hello, Billy," said Lilian.

"Look!" said Billy. "They've brought that sickening baby down. I'm not going in there again till it's gone." As he spoke, Jim bent down to kiss the back of Anthea's neck. "The way those two go on . . . It's——" He uttered a sound expressive of acute nausea.

"The word is uxorious, Billy," said Lilian. "It's revolting, isn't it?"

Chapter Nine

Clive looked up from the letter he was reading and smiled at Lindsay across the table.

"Anthea wants us to go over for the baby's christening a week on Sunday," he said. "I suppose we could manage it?"

They were having breakfast at a gate-legged table by the window of the dining-room. Sunlight filtered through the net curtains, shining on the silver that almost covered the little sideboard and that still wore the brand-new look of wedding presents.

"Yes," agreed Lindsay, passing him his cup of coffee. "It would be lovely."

She took up her own letter, slipped a thumb under the flap, then, catching Clive's eye, smiled guiltily and reached across for the paper-knife that he always kept handy on the breakfast-table.

"It's from Mother," she said when she had read it. "They're going to the christening, too, of course, and she wants me to stay at home for the week."

"Not 'home', darling," corrected Clive gently. "This is home . . . Would you like to stay?"

Lindsay was silent for a few moments . . . The thought of the old easy-going home life — the twins leaving their things all over the place, Mummy's constant good-natured chatter, even Daddy's blustering short-lived tempers — filled her with a sudden nostalgia that surprised and frightened her. That she could endure to contemplate a whole week apart from Clive, whom she adored, that the prospect should give her this strange sense of relief, seemed incredible . . . *was* incredible.

It must be the baby that made her feel like this. People who were going to have babies had strange whims and fancies. It was just a — symptom, like the other queer sensations that she sometimes experienced. She was not quite herself these days . . .

"Yes, I think I would," she said, then, afraid lest he should be hurt, added, "Mummy seems to want me. She's missed me very much."

"I shall miss you, too," said Clive, "but I agree that you ought to go if your mother wants you. It's only for a week."

"Yes," said Lindsay, "only a week."

Clive neatly slit open another letter with the paper-knife and began to read it.

Lindsay looked at his kindly handsome face, and realised with sinking of the heart that the emotions it usually roused in her were signally absent. It was all part of the same thing, of course. She wasn't — quite herself. Everything would be all right when the baby came . . . Her mind went over their short married life. They had been engaged for two years, during which time they had, of course, met only in Clive's vacations, and the romantic element of their first meeting had thrown its glamour over everything. Lindsay had worshipped him as a hero— handsome, brave and chivalrous. His unfailing kindness and patience were in grateful contrast to the turbulent atmosphere of her own home. And when they were married, Clive had set to work, still with unfailing kindness and patience, to help her tackle the problems of housekeeping. Certainly she needed help. She had had little experience, and her mother's housekeeping had been erratic and incompetent. Often and with deep gratitude she had compared Clive's loving forbearance with the outbursts of temper which her father would have displayed. Only lately — since she had been not quite herself — had she begun to think that she would have welcomed an outburst of temper from Clive . . .

Clive folded up his table napkin, rose from the table, went to his bureau, slipped an elastic band round his letters and put them in his letter basket. On the top of the bureau was a little pile of books that Lindsay had brought from the Library the day before. He looked at them with a kindly smile.

"No trash, I hope, darling?"

"No," said Lindsay. "They're all from the list you gave me."

Since Clive knew about the baby he had been all the more anxious to fill up the gaps in her somewhat sketchy education.

He went to the window and stood looking out at the garden, his hands in his pockets. The house was a small modern villa, compactly and solidly built, with dining-room, sitting-room and a third box-like room that was used as Clive's study. It held his desk and book-shelves with difficulty, but Clive was so tidy and organised the smallest detail of his arrangements so meticulously that it never seemed overcrowded.

The front of the house faced the main road, the back overlooked the playing-fields of St. Michael's, the preparatory school to the staff of which Clive had been appointed immediately on leaving college. Beyond the playing-fields and shady garden could be seen the long rambling buildings, the turrets and gables of St. Michael's itself. It was a school with a good standing in the educational world and a constantly growing list of scholarships to public schools. Clive was proud of its reputation and had been anxious that Billy should be sent there, but, greatly to his disappointment, Helena had refused to agree to it. "I think it would be an excellent arrangement," Clive had persisted. "Knowing the boy at home, I could understand his difficulties."

"That would be the trouble," Helena had said cryptically.

The little garden that separated the house from the playing-fields was untidy and overgrown.

"I'll try to get back in time to tidy it up this afternoon," said Clive. "Did you ask Mrs. Parker about that gardener?"

"Yes," said Lindsay. "He's her gardener's brother. He'll be free at the end of the month, but he'd rather have a job nearer home."

They had had three gardeners since coming to St. Michael's, and all three had left without giving notice. The trouble was that Clive knew so much more about gardening than they did, and gardeners were notoriously "touchy".

"I shouldn't mind the gardening if I had more time," said Clive, "but the days seem all too short as it is."

Clive, who taught Latin and some History, was a conscientious teacher, spending hours sometimes over the preparation of a single lesson, delving to the bottom of any doubtful point, taking endless pains to make his lessons interesting. He would spend whole days in London in the holidays searching for prints or pictures to illustrate his lessons, looking up manuscripts in the British Museum, making copies of them . . .

"I know, poor darling!" said Lindsay. "You're horribly over-worked."

"Work never killed anyone, my dear," smiled Clive. "I enjoy it." He glanced at his watch. "I needn't hurry off yet . . . What about dinner?"

"The butcher's sending some chops, and I'll get some Brussels sprouts . . . I thought I'd make a caramel pudding for a sweet."

"Excellent!" said Clive cheerfully. "But I think your caramel pudding recipe is a bit extravagant. I was looking through your cookery books the other day, and I found another one that's much more economical. It's in the small red book. I've put a marker in the place."

"Thank you, Clive," said Lindsay after a slight pause.

"And I was looking through your accounts again last night. I see you paid fivepence a pound for macaroni, but I noticed in the town yesterday that it's on sale at Foulkner's for fourpence-halfpenny. It's quite worth while going to different shops for different things. It's a small sum, I know, but it mounts up . . . If you buy everything at one shop, you'll generally find that they begin to take advantage of you."

"Yes . . ."

Clive would query every halfpenny in her housekeeping accounts and was always checking her purchases to make sure that she bought things at the most reasonable prices, but he was not mean. He would buy her extravagantly expensive presents and, when they went to London, would take her to the Savoy for lunch and to stalls at a matinee as a matter of course. It was just, as he frequently explained to her, that housekeeping was a science and must be carefully studied.

"And what are you going to do today, darling?" he asked.

"I have to go to tea with Mrs. Holden," she said with a little grimace.

Mrs. Holden was the head master's wife. She gave large tea parties at regular intervals to the local parents (for, though the school was a boarding school, many of the boys' homes were in the immediate neighbourhood) to which she always invited the wives of the staff.

"I'd have liked to get out of it," she went on, "but I can't very well . . ."

"No, I suppose it's a sort of royal command, and she's not a bad old thing."

"When last she came here she was admiring your engravings. She said you had wonderful taste."

Clive looked round, with a gratified smile, at the carefully chosen engravings hanging on the plain cream-coloured walls, then seemed to remember something.

"Oh . . . I meant to tell you, darling." He stood on tiptoe and ran a finger along the top of one of the frames, drawing it away covered with dust. "She's not been doing them properly. I think you'd better speak to her."

"Very well," said Lindsay rather shortly.

"Why, darling," said Clive in a tone of surprise, "you sound as if I'd been reading you a lecture."

Lindsay smiled.

"Well, you know, you do rather make me feel like Dora in *David Copperfield*."

Clive was all concern.

"Sweetheart, you know I'd never dream of finding fault with you. To me you're absolutely perfect. We're just — learning this business of housekeeping together — you and I. I learn from you, and you learn from me. It's a big thing and worth taking a little trouble over. And — I like to think that we share everything, even to the smallest household worry. Don't you see, dearest?"

"Yes," said Lindsay.

He put his arms round her, and at his kiss all her irritation vanished, and the old delight of her love for him swept over her, so that for a moment she felt faint and dizzy . . . Never, never again would she let that demon of irritation enter her heart.

"And now," she said at last, gently disengaging herself, "you must go off to school, and I must go to the kitchen to see Gertrude."

"I'll come, too," said Clive, slipping an arm round her waist and going with her down the little passage to the kitchen.

She stiffened slightly in his embrace, and the familiar little demon of irritation tried again to raise its head. She disliked his accompanying her to the kitchen for her interviews with the maid. He made her feel uncomfortable and embarrassed — standing there, listening to every thing she said, adding comments and advice and not infrequently criticising afterwards the manner in which she had conducted the interview. But determinedly she stifled her irritation. They were, as he had said, learning the business of housekeeping together. She was fortunate in having a husband who was willing to share her burdens. . . .

The interview over (Clive duly pointed out to Gertrude the dust on the picture frame), he went to his study to collect his books for the day's work, and Lindsay stood in the doorway, waiting to see him off.

"Oh, by the way," he said, stacking a pile of exercise-books neatly into his case, "Mater said that Ronnie would be over for the christening."

"Ronnie?"

"Ronnie Hayes. Don't you remember him? He was the old Vicar's son."

She knit her brows. The time between her coming to live at Four Elms and her marriage was a blur in her mind — except for Clive. No one else had existed . . .

"I remember about him, of course, because you've often mentioned him, but I don't think I ever met him."

"He's a grand chap. I've always wanted to have him to stay here, but he's been abroad so much. Well, goodbye, darling. Take care of yourself . . . and see that Gertrude doesn't leave the kettle boiling its head off in the kitchen. It's a waste of gas and ruins the paintwork."

He set off briskly down the little garden and through the playing-field to the school. She waited for him to turn to wave to her from the end of the field, as he always did, then went in and closed the door, oppressed by a sense of guilt at the feeling of relief that descended on her. But it wasn't that she was glad he had gone, she assured herself. It was just that she had a lot to do and was anxious to start on it. Why, already — already — she was longing for his return . . .

Lindsay always dreaded these tea-parties of Mrs. Holden's, though she could not have told why. Mrs. Holden was a kind good-natured woman, specially kind to Lindsay, who was a favourite of hers, and the parents were pleasant and friendly. In spite of this, Lindsay generally went home unaccountably depressed. Perhaps it was that none of these people seemed to appreciate Clive as he should be appreciated. Probably, she thought with a wry little smile, all the masters' wives felt the same . . .

She put on the dark-blue silk dress that Clive had helped her choose (her pregnancy as yet showed hardly at all), brushed back and re-coiled her dark shining hair, secured her large be-trimmed hat by its two long hat-pins, drew on her white kid gloves, took up her silver mesh bag, and set off across the playing-field with the short tripping step that the narrowness of her skirt demanded.

St. Michael's had originally been built as a country residence by a financial magnate who had overreached himself several years later and vanished into obscurity. It featured the battlements, turrets and gables beloved of financial magnates, but it was solidly built and well-proportioned and had a picturesque air, set among its trees and playing-fields.

The front door opened into a large panelled hall from which a wide staircase with elaborately carved balustrades led to the upper stories. From the hall, doors opened into the head master's study on one side and his dining-room and drawing-room on the other. Opposite the front door, a green-baize door shut off the "boys' part", which had been built on to the original building and which consisted of classrooms, dormitories, changing-rooms and assembly hall. The school's classical "dare" was to run down from a dormitory by the boys' staircase, through the green-baize door, across the head master's hall, up his staircase and back to the dormitory. The moral ascendancy of a boy who had accomplished this successfully was secure for the rest of his school life.

The sound of voices and laughter and the clatter of tea-cups met Lindsay as she entered the drawing-room. All the women guests showed the modish shape of an inverted pyramid — from "cart-wheel" hats to skirts that were hardly wider than a trouser-leg at the ankle. All had white kid gloves and silver mesh bags. Mrs. Holden was a stout, florid motherly woman of about sixty, wearing a silk dress of roomy unfashionable cut ("Not for me, those hobble things, my dear, though I grant you they look smart"). She greeted Lindsay affectionately, putting an arm on her elbow and shepherding her across the room to introduce her to some new parents. Several people greeted her cordially as she passed. They're all so kind, she thought unhappily. I wonder why I hate coming here so much . . . And suddenly the idea occurred to her that perhaps it was because there was an element of pity in their kindness. She recoiled from the thought in horror, so black was the abyss of disloyalty it revealed . . .

The new parents were enthusiastic about St. Michael's and discoursed to her eloquently on the drawbacks of the school from which they had removed little Claude in order to send him there. Lindsay's eyes roved round the room as she made suitable comments . . . The Bullimers were there in the corner by the window. A faint flush dyed her cheeks as she noticed them. The unfortunate incident had happened last term, and she still shrank from the memory of it. Clive had had occasion to warn young Bullimer of the dangers of a sentimental friendship with another boy, and Mr. Bullimer had come to the school the next day in a raging temper, storming at Clive and threatening a law-suit. Mr. Holden had tried to persuade Clive to apologise, but Clive, who had merely performed a disagreeable duty conscientiously, had refused to do so, and Mr.

Holden had with difficulty smoothed over the affair. It made things worse that the Bullimers now ignored Clive at all school functions but went out of their way to be pleasant to Lindsay.

Some other parents had joined the group.

"Little beggar!" a man was saying with a laugh. "Came home for the week-end and pretended he'd got earache on Monday morning to dodge his History lesson. Took him back myself and bunged him into your husband's classroom . . ."

Lindsay gave a strained smile and her heart quickened indignantly. It was cruel of these people to talk as if Clive's lessons were dull, as if the boys tried as a matter of course to escape them. But probably she was over-sensitive about Clive. She knew how wonderful he was, and it infuriated her that other people should fail to realise it.

An eager little woman came up to her and said, "I'm so grateful to your husband, Mrs. Weatherley, for all he's done for Peter. Nothing seems too much trouble." And Lindsay was surprised and horrified by the rush of grateful tears that filled her eyes. Oh, she wasn't herself. She should have stayed at home . . . Home . . . Again that agony of homesickness swept over her. She saw the big untidy house as a lost paradise, heard her father's bellow of rage as if it were heavenly music . . . How silly I am, she thought. I shall be going there soon, and I shall hate it and long to get back to Clive . . .

Mr. Holden had come into the room and was moving about among the guests. He was a tall spare man with greying hair, keen eyes, a long humorous mouth and a jutting chin. He had a pleasant manner and a knack of getting on good terms with everyone he met that ensured his success as a head master. He could romp with the smallest boys without losing his dignity, and his classes were generally riotously noisy affairs which he could reduce instantly to order by a single word of command.

Lindsay watched him, wondering what he thought of Clive. He showed him unfailing courtesy and consideration, but he seemed to be on less familiar terms with him than with the other masters.

Clive, of course, was probably responsible for that. Clive had a punctilious formal manner and discouraged familiarity.

The hot room was making her feel faint, and she was glad the guests were now beginning to go. She took her leave of Mrs. Holden, received an affectionate motherly smile and a pat on the shoulder, and made her way to the door. At first she did not notice that Mr. Holden was accompanying her.

"May I see you across the field, Mrs. Weatherley?" he said. "A breath of fresh air will be very welcome after the atmosphere of the drawing-room. I wanted to open another window, but, whenever I do, people complain of the draught."

They walked along the path that wound between the flower borders towards the playing-field. He talked of the weather and school affairs, the prospect of the football season, the alterations to the chapel, and Lindsay replied shyly. She liked him but felt ill-at-ease with him. Between them was always the suspicion that he did not appreciate Clive . . . He threw her an occasional glance as he talked. Her youth and loveliness, even her shyness, moved him deeply, and he half regretted the sudden impulse that had made him seek this interview with her.

"Mrs. Weatherley," he said suddenly, "I believe that you have great influence with your husband."

She stiffened, and her heart began to beat more quickly.

"Don't think me impertinent if I ask you to use it in a certain direction."

Still she was silent, staring fixedly in front of her. Her face looked very pale in the shadow of her broad-brimmed hat. He went on in a gentle, almost apologetic tone.

"I've hinted at it myself and don't like to say more, because — well, advice from me is apt to have a boringly official air, but, if he happens to mention his dealings with the boys to you, I'd be so grateful if you could manage to convey to him in your own tactful way that it's as well sometimes to turn a blind eye on the little devils' devilment, and that constant fault-finding, however kindly meant and however kindly done, isn't the best way of dealing with them. It has an irritating or discouraging effect. He has so many excellent points as a teacher that——"

They had reached the gate now, and she swung round on him in a sudden gust of anger that surprised them both.

"I know that, Mr. Holden," she said, trembling, "and I shouldn't dream of interfering with his methods. You don't realise how hard Clive works and — and how *good* he is and — and——" Her voice quivered and she broke away from him, going quickly up the little path to the front door.

He watched her go, his face set in lines of compunction. Poor child! He didn't often make a mess of things, but he'd certainly made a mess of this. He walked slowly, thoughtfully, back across the field.

Lindsay closed the door and stood for a moment motionless in the hall. She was still trembling, but her anger had vanished, and with it the strange disquiet that had troubled her all day. There was no room in her heart now for anything but a burning love for Clive. It was not quite the old love — uncritical, worshipping. It held a new enriching element — a deep tenderness, a desire to protect him from everything that might hurt him. It was as if her coming motherhood embraced him as well as the child she carried.

She went slowly upstairs, her eyes, still wet with tears, shining triumphantly.

Chapter Ten

The drawing-room was fragrant with the scent of the log fire and the jars of white lilies that stood on either side of it and on the tall Adam chimney-piece above. The mahogany dining-table had been brought in from the dining-room and set by the windows. The deep lace border of the table-cloth swept the floor, and in the centre, surrounded by tea-cups and champagne glasses, stood the three-tiered christening cake, elaborately iced and surmounted by a miniature angel presiding over a miniature crib.

The maids hovered about, bringing in cream-jugs, sugar-basins and laden cake-stands, peeping at intervals out of the window, till one of them said excitedly, "There they are!" and they all clustered to watch discreetly from the shadow of the window curtains.

Jim, frock-coated and top-hatted, stepped down from the first car and handed out Anthea, wearing a green silk dress with the new pannier skirt, ermine stole, pillow muff and pudding-basin hat. Little of her face could be seen, as the hat came right down to her eyes, and her nose and mouth were obscured by a veil ("Isn't there *anything* I can kiss?" Jim had said when he saw her); then came Nurse with the baby, a sheaf of roses pinned across the satin coat; then Helena.

"Come straight into the drawing-room," said Helena. "There's a fire, and you can take her things off there." Nurse, throwing an approving glance round the room as she entered, sat down to slip off the coat and bonnet, revealing a christening robe of white China silk, the front panel covered with embroidery and lace insertion. A string of corals, Helena's gift, encircled the tiny neck, and a gold bracelet (from the staff at Hallowes) one dimpled wrist. Other christening presents — mugs, ivory-backed hair-brushes, silver fork and spoon sets, silver napkin rings, a brush and comb decorated with Sir Joshua Reynolds' cherubs in silver — were ranged on the grand piano . . . Jim's gift (a string of pearls) and Arthur's gift (an emerald bracelet) were safely housed at the bank.

Jim relieved his wife of muff, stole and gloves, then looked wistfully at the pudding-basin hat.

"Can't I take the meat-safe off, darling?" he said. "You won't be able to eat anything in that."

"All right," conceded Anthea. "You can take the veil off if you like. It unties at the back. My goodness, *aren't* you clumsy! No, don't take the *hat* off. I came in this hat so that people could *see* it."

"Well, they'll see it all right," said Jim, "but they'll wonder what's happened to *you* . . . Let's have a kiss before the general public arrives."

"If you mess up my hat, I'll never forgive you. That's enough, for Heaven's sake! I'll take Baby now, Nurse."

Her role was Young Mother with Child, and she did not intend that her most important stage property should be in someone else's hands. Nurse transferred the still sleeping Joanna to her.

"Sit down, dear," said Helena. "I'm sure you're tired."

"No, I'm not a bit tired," said Anthea. "I'd rather stand."

So that the first thing the guests saw, arriving in twos and threes from the church, was Anthea standing in front of the fire, the baby in her arms, Jim by her side.

Arthur arrived with Clive and Lindsay and Mrs. Malvern. He looked worried and put-out. Lilian, who had gone to London at the beginning of the week and given no warning of her return, had completely spoilt the service for him by appearing unexpectedly in the middle of it, accompanied by a bearded, Bohemian-looking man in open-necked shirt and sandals. She had not introduced him to anyone, and he had gone straight back to the station after the service. The familiar exasperation nagged at Arthur's mind. Always making an exhibition of herself . . . Perhaps it was too late to expect her to marry now, but other unmarried women didn't go about making such fools of themselves. Why couldn't she settle down quietly to embroidery or parish work or something? But the lines of irritation faded from his face as he bent down to kiss the soft rosy cheek of his sleeping grandchild. Helena was greeting Clive and Lindsay and Mrs. Malvern.

"So nice to see you again, darling," she said, kissing Lindsay. "You look rather pale, but I suppose——You're looking after her, I hope, Clive?"

"Clive is nurse and father and mother, all rolled into one," smiled Lindsay.

"And her *real* mother is going to have a hand in it now," said Mrs. Malvern, "She *says* she's coming for a week, but if I can manage it, I shall keep her for longer."

"Are you *sure* you don't mind my staying, Clive?" said Lindsay anxiously.

"I won't let him mind," said Mrs. Malvern.

"Mother-in-law already starts coming between man and wife," guffawed Jim.

Ronnie came in with the Vicar, and Clive greeted him with the old eager affection, leading him across the room to Lindsay.

"I don't believe you two have ever met," he said. "Lindsay doesn't seem to remember."

"I don't think we have," said Lindsay shyly.

"No," said Ronnie. "I don't believe we have. I wasn't over here much between the time you came to live at Five Elms and your wedding."

"And you didn't come to the wedding, you old blighter!" said Clive.

"I was in Egypt," said Ronnie.

Old Ronnie was growing up at last, thought Clive. His youthful exuberance was dimmed. Even his grin was less in evidence than formerly.

Cups of tea and glasses of champagne were being handed round.

"When does she cut the cake, Anthea?"

"She behaved beautifully."

"Ah, but she shouldn't have done. If they don't cry, it means that the devil hasn't gone out of her. I'm right, aren't I, Vicar?"

"She did just give one tiny little whimper."

"That's not enough. That only means that one tiny little devil's gone out. The others are still there."

"Do you know what I heard one of your parishioners say the other day, Vicar? It was old Mrs. Green at the shop. Someone asked if you weren't a bit too High Church for her, and she said, 'Oh, 'e antics a bit, but we likes 'im so well we puts up with it.'"

There was a roar of laughter in which the Vicar joined.

Having received the guests ceremoniously, Anthea had now sat down by the fire with the baby on her knee, its long christening robe sweeping the ground around her, and Jim standing behind. The Malvern twins — in frocks of *broderie Anglaise* with blue silk sashes, their fair hair tied with blue ribbons — knelt on either side, watching the baby, like small adoring angels.

Clive, the son of the house again, handed round cups of tea and plates of cake and sandwiches. Billy was sprawling on one of the window seats, his hands in his pockets, watching the group by the fireplace with an air of aloof disgust.

"Now, Billy," said Clive briskly, "hand some of these plates round."

He looked across the room to where Lindsay and Ronnie were standing . . . and a wave of happiness surged over him. The two people he loved best in the world . . . The only two people he really loved . . . He would have been bitterly disappointed had they failed to like each other, but obviously they were getting on together excellently.

Ronnie took a glass of champagne from a tray and handed it to Lindsay. Clive crossed the room, and laid a hand on her arm.

"Tea, I think, darling," he said gently.

She flushed.

"Oh yes, of course . . ."

He put back the glass on the table and brought her a cup of tea.

"She's not used to strong drink," he said to Ronnie, smiling.

Lilian entered, and there was a faint stir among the guests, as there generally was when Lilian entered a room. She was, as usual, immaculately groomed, and her plain dark coat and skirt made all the other women look over-dressed. Why on earth can't she dress like the others? thought Arthur . . . Well, at least she hadn't brought that bounder back to tea with her . . .

"I'm dying for a drink," she said, taking a glass of champagne from a tray that a maid was carrying about the room. "What a depressing ceremony it is! But it's something of a relief to realise how completely responsible one's godparents are for one's shortcomings. They renounced the devil and all his works for one, so, if it wasn't properly done, the responsibility is theirs."

Arthur watched her under frowning brows. She had drained one glass of champagne and taken another.

Everyone was drinking Joanna's health now, and Clive glanced across the room to make sure that Lindsay still had her cup of tea. He hated to see a woman drinking alcohol in any form. Aunt Lilian had been an object-lesson to him, and, with the baby coming, it was specially important.

As if embarrassed by the sudden publicity, Joanna woke up and began to cry. Anthea, Jim, Helena, the nurse and the twins bent over her solicitously . . . Gratified by this attention, Joanna stopped crying, and Anthea carried her to the table, placing her tiny hand over Helena's as she cut the deep wedges of cake. Clive filled plates for himself and Billy.

"Come on, Billy. Take this round. You can guzzle afterwards."

"There are enough servants to do it," grumbled Billy.

"Never mind that. It's your duty to wait on the guests whether there are enough servants to do it or not."

Wandering round with his plate of christening cake, Clive thought how like this party was to all the others he remembered at Hallowes. Room, servants, guests, practically unaltered through the years. He had inherited from his father a strong dislike of change, and the reflection pleased him . . . A few changes, of course, there had been. Lady Evesham had died last year, and Sir Bruce looked strangely incomplete on public occasions without the familiar wisp of black hanging onto his arm. Miss Clorinda Mavers, too, had succumbed to what was vaguely called "chest trouble", and, having been ordered to the South of France, was now astonishing the inhabitants of Mentone by her costume and views.

Dr. Bellingham, who, alone of neighbouring doctors, still went his rounds in a pony-trap, was giving Anthea advice on the upbringing of her baby.

"To the mother of an only child, in affluent circumstances, Anthea," he was saying, "I always counsel neglect. Aim solely at neglect, and you may achieve something."

"Here!" said Jim indignantly. "Not so much of the 'only child'! And neglect your own children!"

"I have done," said the doctor simply, "and they've turned out excellently. I've even written a pamphlet on 'How to Neglect Your Children', but no one will publish it."

The Crabbes had come over from London for the occasion, and, having paid their respects to its heroine, were holding their usual little court by one of the windows. Sir Bruce straddled up to it.

"Still letting slip all our chances of an alliance with Germany, Crabbe," he said severely.

Mr. Crabbe glanced suspiciously at a potted plant near him, as if afraid that it might harbour an eavesdropper, then, lowering his voice significantly, said:

"Not our fault, my dear sir, not our fault. Haldane has done his best, and so has Grey. The condition they invariably lay down for an alliance with us is 'benevolent neutrality in any war forced upon her'. Well, my dear sir, we know that all Germany's wars are 'forced upon her'."

"It's France they've got their eye on, I suppose," said someone, "and they want to break the Entente first."

"Exactly, my dear sir, exactly." He coughed as if to cover his indiscretion.

"Beethoven . . . Schubert . . ." said Sir Bruce. "Different from this beastly rag-time you hear everywhere . . ."

"Dunno what you fellows do with yourselves at Westminster,"

boomed Dr. Bellingham, "but we plain men in the street are getting a little tired of this perpetual atmosphere of political unrest."

"It's this wretched Balkan War."

"But that's nothing to do with *us*!"

"My dear lady, the Balkan States are pawns in the hands of Germany and Russia — Germany driving East in search of a continental empire and——"

"Berlin to Bagdad! Ha! ha!"

"It is no joke, my dear sir. Or rather it is a joke for which we may all yet have to pay dearly."

"But what has all this got to do with *us*?"

"The connecting link is the Dual Alliance, my dear lady. We could not stand aside and see the control of the Channel ports pass to a power like Germany."

"Why not?" growled Sir Bruce. "Never had any use for the Froggies. Was in a collision in a cross-Channel boat once, and the Froggies were the only ones that lost their heads . . . Now if we could have the same sort of Entente with Germany that we have now with the Froggies . . ."

"Impossible, Sir Bruce . . ."

Mrs. Crabbe raised her languid voice.

"A friend of my mother's, a Frenchwoman, was in a village occupied by the Prussians during the Franco-Prussian War"

"The Marquise de Pontiere," put in her husband.

"The Marquise de Pontiere," confirmed his wife graciously. "She told my mother that the cruelty and barbarity of the Prussians could not be conceived by normal human beings."

"Oh, these stories get exaggerated — Christening cake? Thank you, Clive — or else they're deliberately invented."

In the secluded scholastic atmosphere of St. Michael's politics were seldom mentioned, but, as he went from group to group with his plate of christening cake, Clive found the atmosphere of "political unrest" much in evidence.

"We must give up this crazy break-neck naval race with Germany. Lloyd George is quite right. It's suicidal."

"Winston Churchill doesn't agree."

"Oh, that fellow! He's sane enough on most points, but he's got a bee in his bonnet about the Navy. And about Germany."

"I *adore* his moustaches. The Kaiser's, I mean. I'm always trying to get my husband to turn up the ends of his."

"They say the King can't stand him."

"Of course he's tactless but I don't think he *means* any harm. He made quite a good impression at the Queen's funeral."

"My dear, this is a *fact*. A friend of a friend of mine was staying with some people in Berlin and she went out to dinner and sat next to an officer who knew every *inch* of her home village in Kent. Every stile and field path. She asked him when he'd been there, and it turned out that he'd never been to England at all. He said, 'Oh, that's my bit of England. We all have to know a piece of England so well that we could find our way through it blindfold.'"

"Ah, Der Tag! . . . But, you know, these stories are always at second hand."

Glancing around, Clive noticed that Ronnie and Lindsay were no longer in the room, and, going to the window, saw them walking round the side of the house with Billy and the twins. The twins hung on Lindsay's arms, and Billy walked next to Ronnie, his hands in his pockets. Ronnie was talking, and Lindsay had turned her head with a smile to listen to him. They were probably going down to the paddock to see Billy's pony. Billy always took favoured visitors there. As he watched them, that wave of thankfulness again swept over Clive . . . Wistfully he wondered whether he might slip out and join them, but his sense of duty restrained him. His place was here, helping to entertain his father's guests. He must see if he could get Ronnie to come and stay with them in the summer, after the baby had arrived . . .

Lindsay and Ronnie were leaning over the low paddock fence. Inside, the twins and Billy were feeding the pony with windfalls that they had fetched from the orchard.

"Do you know what I thought when first I saw you?" Ronnie was saying. "I thought, I wonder why she looks so frightened."

Lindsay spoke in a low dreamy voice, as if speaking to herself.

"I've always been frightened — I don't know why. Frightened of doing the wrong thing or saying the wrong thing. It doesn't seem to worry other people. They seem to do the right thing by a sort of instinct. Did you know I was going to have a baby?"

"No."

"I'm frightened of that, too. Terribly frightened. I've never told anyone before. Not of the pain, but of— failing it, somehow. It's so easy to fail people without realising you're doing it, and to fail your own child——"

"But Clive . . ."

She caught her breath.

"Oh, I couldn't face things without Clive. He's so — *good*."

"I know."

"Did he ever tell you how he met me?"

"I don't think so."

She told him how Clive had stopped her horse, but, so anxious was she to make him see the heroism, share the glamour of the memory, that she told the story lamely and stumblingly.

"I'd have been killed if he hadn't been there," she ended.

"Trust old Clive not to tell me about that," he said.

"He never thinks of himself . . ."

"I know . . . Look at Billy showing off to the twins."

"He rides well."

There was a long silence, then he said in a low voice: "You're so lovely . . ."

Her eyes were still fixed dreamily on the distance.

"Don't laugh at me, but that's another of the things that — frighten me. It makes people notice me, when I don't want to be noticed. And it makes them expect things of me that I haven't got. I'm shy and stupid and uneducated. I didn't realise how stupid and uneducated I was till I married Clive. There's such a lot I don't know and never shall know . . . I'm always making silly mistakes."

"You're not frightened now?"

"No . . . Not now."

Frightened? Her whole being was filled with a strange unfamiliar peace — a peace she had never known in her life before. There

116

was another silence, and Lindsay found herself dreading the end of it, because it would be the end, too, of that new-found precarious peace. It was as if till now — till she met Ronnie — she had been weighed down by some intolerable burden, and, with the easing of it, an ecstasy of lassitude possessed her, soul and body.

"You're staying here next week, aren't you?" said Ronnie suddenly. "May I come and see you?"

Her dark eyes dilated, and she gave a quick intake of breath. The peace was shattered, as she had known it would be.

"No, I'm not staying. I'm going home with Clive."

"You're frightened again . . ."

"No, I'm not . . . I ought to go in now . . . Please don't come with me. Please stay out with the children." He did not seem surprised by the pleading in her voice. It was as if the peace that had enclosed the two of them had, even in its departure, left them so near to each other that nothing she said or did could surprise him.

"Very well," he said quietly, and leant over the fence, calling out advice to the twins, who were now trying to ride together on the pony's broad stout back.

The guests were thinning when Lindsay reached the drawing-room.

"Well, darling," said Clive. He took out his watch. "I'm afraid I shall have to say goodbye to you."

"Clive, I don't want to stay. I want to go back with you."

He looked at her in surprise.

"But, my child, you've brought your things."

"I can take them back again."

"Oh, darling, you *must* stay," wailed Mrs. Malvern. "Daddy and I have been looking forward to it so much, and the twins would break their hearts."

"I know just how she feels," said Anthea. "I hardly left Jim for a second when Baby was coming. Not even when Rosy Birch asked me over for Goodwood."

"You look tired, dear," said Helena. "Don't you think a week's spoiling at home would do you good?" Lindsay's dark eyes seemed to gaze through them as if she did not see them. She felt bewildered and thrown out of her bearings. She could not believe that she had talked like that to a stranger, telling him things that she had never told to anyone before. He hadn't seemed a stranger. It had been almost as if she were talking to herself. But she mustn't stay here . . . mustn't meet him again.

Clive had slipped an arm round her. He was torn between pleasure at her decision and a feeling that these whimsical changes of plan at the last minute should not be encouraged.

"Well," he said, smiling, "I can't say that I was looking forward to going home without you, but I don't know that it's quite fair to your people to change your mind like this."

She leant against his shoulder as if for protection.

"Let me come back with you, Clive."

"What does your mother say about it?"

"Oh, very well," said Mrs. Malvern. "I won't be a possessive mother, but I *am* disappointed. You'll come another time, won't you, darling?"

"Yes. I'll come another time."

"Where's Ronnie?" said Clive, looking round. "Didn't he come in with you?"

"No. He's down at the paddock with the children."

"Come with me and say goodbye to him."

"There isn't time, Clive."

"Very well. Say goodbye to him for us, Mater, won't you?"

Arthur and Helena waved them off, then returned to the drawing-room, where the nurse was tying the broad white satin strings of the bonnet beneath the baby's chin, and Jim was carefully arranging the ermine stole over Anthea's shoulder.

"She behaved beautifully," said Helena, smiling down at the baby.

"What else would you expect of a child of ours?" said Jim.

"I must say I *am* disappointed," said Mrs. Malvern again. "I'd taken such a lot of trouble turning my things out of her bedroom and that sort of thing, but it's nice to see them still so much in love with each other."

"Still?" said Jim. "What about us after two whole years?"

"I didn't think she looked well," said Helena.

"Oh, she's never had much colour," said Mrs. Malvern.

"I didn't feel too well myself at three months," said Anthea. "Come along, Jim. It's time Baby was in bed."

Helena and Arthur returned to the drawing-room after seeing off the last guest. The room wore the dishevelled look that the departure of the last guest generally gives to the scene of a party. Lilian stood by the table, a glass of champagne in her hand. Helena sighed. Lilian had been drinking steadily ever since she came in, and Arthur was tired and irritable.

"Wouldn't you like to go upstairs, Lilian?" she said.

"No thank you, Helena," said Lilian, "and, if I do, I know the way, I was born in this house, you know. I expect I had my christening party in this room. I don't remember. Do you, Arthur?"

Arthur frowned, and Helena gave a good imitation of a yawn.

"I'm tired," she said, "and I'm sure you are, Arthur. Let's go to the library for a rest before dinner."

It wasn't any good. Arthur ignored her.

"Was it necessary for you to bring that bounder with you to the church, Lilian?" he said.

"Not necessary, perhaps," said Lilian, pouring out another glass of champagne, "but quite in character for me to turn up like the bad fairy at the christening, don't you think?"

"And having brought him," said Arthur, "you might at least have had the decency to introduce him."

"But why?" said Lilian, speaking with careful distinctness. "You wouldn't have liked him, and he wouldn't have liked you. He's a seer, my dear Arthur. He sees people's auras. Yours is red, he says, and Helena's is blue. I know that he doesn't wear top-hats and frock-coats, but he has helped me considerably. He has explained to me that the reason why I am unloved and unwanted in this life is that in a former existence I have refused to give out love. You may not realise it, but that *does* help. He's enquiring into yours and Helena's previous existences for me. It's interesting to have people explained who are otherwise quite inexplicable."

A dark flush had crept into Arthur's cheeks.

"Don't talk such damn nonsense," he said angrily, "and put that glass down. You've had quite enough."

Lilian put down the glass rather shakily.

"You occasionally forget that you have no longer any legal authority over me, Arthur," she said. "And I'm not drunk. Or not very. It may interest you to know that I haven't touched drink for the last six months, but the sight of you all today — so unbelievably smug — made me feel so sick that I had to do something about it. The sight of your daughter's domestic bliss is in itself enough to drive a bishop to drink."

"Lilian," pleaded Helena, "please remember that Arthur——"

"Hold your tongue, Helena," said Arthur. "You can sneer at a woman like Anthea, Lilian, who does her duty to her husband and——"

Suddenly the precarious mask of Lilian's poise slipped from her and she burst out:

"I've never been anything but a nuisance to you, have I? You've never cared two pins for me. I worshipped you when I was a child, but first it was Adela, then Helena. You hardly knew I existed. You always wanted me to 'marry and settle down' just so that you could wash your hands of me. It wouldn't have mattered whether I was happy or not . . ."

Her face worked painfully for a few minutes, then with an effort she readjusted the mask.

"I apologise for the exhibition," she said steadily. "You're probably right, Arthur, and I'm more than a little drunk." She went to a mirror and, taking a powder-puff from her bag, carefully powdered her face. "May I have the car to take me to the station? I have to be in London tonight."

PART IV

1919

Chapter Eleven

Ronnie's Home-coming from the Great War

The twins scrambled up the steep sandy path that led from the beach, gained the plateau of short smooth turf at the top, and stood there, surveying the sweep of the bay below.

Like most other families in England, the Malverns and the Weatherleys were enjoying their first seaside holiday for four years. So great had been the exodus from the towns this summer that hundreds of people had been turned away from every watering-place, but Mr. Malvern had taken the bungalow at Belton Sands immediately the Armistice was signed last year and moved his family down to it at the end of June. Fortunately the bungalow was a comparatively spacious one, but even so the Malverns seemed to fill every corner of it — Mr. and Mrs. Malvern, the twins, Leslie Torrance, a school friend of the twins, and Lindsay with her six-year-old daughter, Cherry. Clive, of course, could not leave St. Michael's till the end of the term, and had arranged to come down and join them later.

At first Arthur, who always disliked leaving home, had refused to consider Mr. Malvern's suggestion that he and his family should join the party. It was Lilian's illness that had decided him.

Lilian's official war work had been that of voluntary helper at a Red Cross depot, but she had given much time and energy to the more unofficial war work generally known as "cheering up the boys on leave". She had waltzed and tangoed and dined, gone to theatres and music-halls and night clubs, with a succession of young officers, most of them, as Anthea, her severest critic, put it, "hardly out of the nursery". Occasionally she would descend on Hallowes, dressed with the expensive simplicity she always affected, her beauty now haggard and a little coarsened, her latest conquest in tow. Arthur still disapproved of her, but Lilian was careful not to smoke or drink in his presence, and the officer, primed by her beforehand, asked intelligent questions about the Boer War, so that the visits generally passed off without untoward incident. Helena suspected that Arthur failed even to realise that the young officer was not the same on each occasion.

But in the spring Lilian had been attacked by the "Spanish influenza" that decimated Europe that year, and had been so ill that at one time there had seemed little hope of recovery. Arthur had insisted on her coming to Hallowes to recuperate, and it was a ghost of the old Lilian who arrived there, with drawn features, hollow cheeks and lack-lustre eyes. Her convalescence had been long and not very satisfactory. She seemed sapped of energy, content to lie all day on a sofa, her hands idle in her lap, gazing dully into space.

Arthur himself had stood the long strain and anxiety of the war better than Helena had feared he would. Jim had volunteered immediately on the outbreak of war and Billy on leaving school in 1917. Though Billy had been wounded in the leg and Jim had "got a blighty one" at Ypres, they had both come home after the Armistice little the worse, and Billy was now a somewhat self-conscious high-brow undergraduate at Oxford. It was partly the wish to assist Lilian's recovery and partly the wish to celebrate the safe return of his son and son-in-law by a family reunion that induced Arthur finally to agree to take rooms at the Belton Sands hotel for himself and his family — Helena, Lilian, Billy, Jim and Anthea and their four children.

Belton Sands was a small seaside village consisting of a few farms and cottages, a general shop, a group of bungalows built by people who had "discovered" the place shortly before the war, and the hotel — a long white rambling building whose front gate was only a few yards from the gate of the Malverns' bungalow and whose shady untidy garden straggled down to the beach. The hotel itself was an old-fashioned rather shabby place with few modern "improvements" but with a high standard of comfort. To Helena's relief Arthur was enjoying the change and the company of his grandchildren. He would go down to the beach every morning to watch them play and even assist in the building of the sand castles, and he liked the whole party to assemble at the hotel for tea every afternoon. There was a small Writing Room with deep easy-chairs, in which he could always take refuge when he felt tired or the demands of the children became excessive. Lilian had so far shown little interest in her surroundings.

The twins cupped their mouths to halloo to the party on the beach below. Lindsay was sewing in a deck-chair, Jo and Cherry were making sand pies and Piers, Anthea's five-year-old son, was putting the finishing touches to a castle surrounded by a moat. He gave it a final pat and took his stand on it, his long bare legs coated with sand, his bright hair gleaming in the sun.

"I'm the king of the castle!" he shouted.

The two little girls, busy with their sand pies, did not accept the challenge. They worked absorbedly, the dark head and the red-gold one almost touching.

"Lend us your spade, Piers," said Cherry, looking up suddenly, her small, usually pale face flushed with effort. "It digs better than ours."

Piers, who was tired of digging and whose castle was already showing signs of collapse, threw them his spade and went galloping off across the sand to the rocks that encircled the bay.

"The pies are all ready now. Mummy," said Cherry.

"Come to my shop first, Auntie Lindsay," pleaded Jo.

The twins crossed the lane and went up the sloping garden of the bungalow to the verandah that ran along the front of it.

Mrs. Malvern lay in a deck-chair, reading, a basket of mending by her side. Near her, on an upright chair, sat Leslie Torrance, a sketching block on her knee, her dark vivid face set in lines of frowning concentration.

Mrs. Malvern looked up from her book and inspected the twins in mild horror. Their short skirts and jumpers were covered with sand, their bare legs stained with green slime from the rocks.

"My darlings, what *states* you're in! You can't go to the hotel for tea like that."

The twins sat down on the low wall that bordered the verandah and, taking off their canvas shoes, began to empty the sand from them. Rock plants were supposed to grow in the wall, but the young people used it so constantly as a seat that most of the plants had by now given up the unequal struggle.

"We know we can't. We've come up to change."

"We've been to the end of the bay and right up the cliff. It was lovely."

"Oh, Mummy, it's a heavenly holiday. It's the nicest thing that's happened since the Peace."

"The Peace," put in Leslie tersely, "has so far proved distinctly disappointing."

"I know. We *lived* for the first Christmas after the war and it was *awful*."

"No sweets. No toys. No decent food."

"And bread and sugar rationed still — eight whole months after the Armistice."

"Oh, things are gradually getting back to normal," said Mrs. Malvern. "People are beginning to go to the Riviera again. The Morrisons said that all the sleeping berths to Cannes and Nice are booked up for months ahead."

"And the ghoulish are already going on personally-conducted tours over the 'Devastated Regions' in France," put in Leslie without raising her eyes from her sketch.

"Oh, poor Mummy! What a lot of mending!" said Pat, ejecting little cascades of sand from between her toes.

"She hasn't put a stitch into anything all afternoon," said Leslie. "I've been watching her. She hasn't taken her eyes from *The Golden Scorpion*."

Mrs. Malvern blushed and laughed, slipping *The Golden Scorpion* into her mending basket.

"Well, I don't know that it's as shocking as it's supposed to be," she said, "but it's certainly not fit for you girls to read."

"Then you can bet your life we'll read it," said Mab.

Pat had gone over to look at Leslie's sketch.

"Oh, Leslie, it's lovely! . . . Mummy, I wish Daddy would let us go to the Slade."

"He won't, darling. He's said so. He says that no daughter of his shall live alone in London."

"But there'd be two of us. And we could stay at the hostel where Leslie stays. Oh, Mummy, *do* try to persuade him."

"After all, it isn't as if we weren't emancipated now. If Lady Astor can sit in the House of Parliament, I don't see why Pat and I shouldn't go to the Slade."

"Well, you'll have to talk to him again."

"We will. We'll give him no peace till he lets us. It's so dull just living in the country. All the exciting things happen in London. Leslie was there for Armistice Night and Peace Day and Lady Diana Manners' wedding . . . It isn't fair."

"Aren't you touched by your children's disinterested love of art, Mrs. Malvern?" said Leslie.

"Come along and tidy yourselves, children," laughed Mrs. Malvern. "We shall never be ready for tea at this rate. You coming in, Leslie?"

"No . . . I want to finish this."

"Leslie doesn't need to tidy herself. She never has a hair out of place."

Left alone, Leslie went on working intently. In her sleeveless dress of fresh pink linen, with white stockings and white buckskin shoes, she wore an air of well-groomed neatness in sharp contrast to the twins' dishevelment. Her straight hair was combed back severely from her brow in a fashion that showed to best advantage her regular features and the clear-cut line of chin and brow. After a few minutes she heard footsteps coming round the side of the bungalow and, still without looking up, said "Hello, Billy."

"Hello," said Billy, sitting down on the wall near her and taking his pipe from his pocket.

He was dressed in the carefully careless fashion of the up-to-date undergraduate on holiday, in dark-blue pullover, pale-blue soft-collared shirt, with tie but no tie-pin, and narrow, pale-grey flannel trousers.

"I've come to collect you for tea."

"The twins have gone to tidy themselves."

"I bet they needed it." He lit his pipe, threw away the match and took a magazine from his pocket. "Thought you might like to see this. It's J. C. Squire's new monthly."

"The *London Mercury?* I've heard of it. I'd love to see a copy. Thank you so much."

"He's running the Georgian Poetry crowd. I know you're keen on them."

"Yes, I love them."

She turned over the pages, her face, as usual, frowningly intent, and Billy watched her, puffing at his pipe.

"It's luck to find you alone without the Zoo," he said.

Her rare smile flickered over her expressive face.

"The twins? . . . I'm fond of them, but they never seem to grow up . . . Oh, isn't this lovely!"

He listened to her low clear voice as she read aloud, his eyes fixed on the sun-flushed oval of her face in its frame of straight dark hair.

"I wish I were a man and could go to college," she said, looking up suddenly. She spoke with the vivid intensity that marked everything about her. "I've no ambition at all to go to college as a woman. It's not the same . . ."

"Well, there's a pretty queer crowd of undergrads at Oxford just now," grinned Billy. "Middle-aged colonels and majors who seem to think they're still in the Army. The authorities don't know quite what to make of them . . . Besides" — he took her sketch and looked at it — "why on earth should you want to go to college when you can do stuff like this?"

"It's rotten," she said contemptuously. "It's the sort of thing Victorian young ladies turned out at their boarding schools assisted by the drawing master. But at least I know it's rotten, and that's more than they did. Anyway I'm going through with the Slade course before I do anything else. It's conventional and I hate convention, but I suppose that discipline's good for one." She turned over another page of the magazine. "Thank Heaven, they've got someone who understands art. Nothing makes me feel so savage as the way people sneer at things they don't understand, just *because* they don't understand them. Picasso, Epstein and the others. Just because people haven't got vision themselves, they must throw mud at anyone who has. It makes me *rage* . . . They adore Academy problem pictures, of course. 'The Fallen Idol'." Her lips curved in angry contempt. "I feel sick when I think of them pawing over genius — real genius — with their foul little minds and daring to snigger at it." She stopped and went on rather breathlessly. "I'm sorry to get so heated. I don't talk like this to many people. One doesn't often meet anyone who — understands."

"As a matter of fact and to be quite honest," said Billy slowly, "some of the new stuff does seem a bit — odd to me. Cubists and Vorticists and the rest. But I've got just enough sense to realise that the fault lies in my own ignorance . . . When next I'm in town, will you take me to a show and help educate me?"

She looked at him, and the tenseness of her face relaxed. Billy, sitting there on the wall, his long legs sprawling out in front of him, his fair hair ruffled, his pipe in his mouth, his elbows on his knees, was a very personable young man.

"Yes, I'd like to . . ." she said, and for a moment seemed young and shy, losing her hard bright resilience.

The twins' heads suddenly appeared from the bungalow's only upstairs window. They had changed into clean dresses of butcher-blue cotton. Their hair was brushed and shining.

"Oh, Billy, you do look smart in your new sweater."

Billy picked off the head of a dandelion that, on the principle of the survival of the fittest, bloomed in the wall among the remains of the choicer rock plants, and aimed it at the twins' heads.

"It's called a pullover, if you want to know, you young idiots! And come along down or you won't get any tea."

Chapter Twelve

Prue, wearing a short gingham frock and sun-bonnet, her teddy bear tucked under her arm, came trotting through the open door of the hotel into the garden. She had stayed indoors for her afternoon rest and was now eager to join the others on the beach. Anthea and the nurse followed her, Anthea carrying a bucket and spade, the nurse a tea-basket.

"Let's just see that Baby's all right," said Anthea, and the two went across the lawn to where the baby Roger slept in his pram in the shadow of the tall hedge. They contemplated him admiringly.

"Hasn't he got brown since we came here?" said Anthea.

"Yes, he's getting on a treat," agreed the nurse.

Prue, having stood on tiptoe but failed to reach the latch of the gate, was battering at the gate itself with three-year-old impatience.

"Open!" she said imperiously. "Prue wants to go *out*."

The nurse unfastened the latch and they stepped out onto the beach.

"There's Mrs. Clive with Jo and Cherry," said Anthea. "She said she'd stay with them till you came out . . . All right, darling," to Prue, who was clamouring for her bucket and spade, "let's put Teddy in your bucket, then you can carry them all. Now off you go!"

Prue ran down to join the others, her bare brown feet flashing over the sand, her sun-bonnet falling back from her short fair curls.

"She's growing out of all her frocks," said Anthea, "but it really isn't worth while making any more now. They won't fit her next summer."

"I can let that one down," said the nurse. "It has quite a deep

hem. And I can finish that blue one I'm making. I have got it here."
She patted the tea-basket.

"I'll get on with it this afternoon. Shall I come in to help with
Baby after tea?"

"No, I'll put him to bed. You stay out with the children. There
are some oranges and bananas and bread and jam sandwiches and
a bottle of milk in the basket. If you want anything else, send Jo
back for it . . . I thought she was looking a bit pale this morning,
didn't you? We must remember to give her a dose tonight. And I
shouldn't let her paddle too much . . ."

"Just *look* at Piers!" said the nurse, pointing to where Piers
stood, balanced precariously half-way up the cliff.

"Isn't he a *monkey*!" smiled Anthea. "He's worn out all his
knickers on those rocks. It's a good thing we brought plenty of
stuff for patching . . . you'd better bring Prue in a little before the
others. She runs about so much and gets over-tired." She waved
to Billy, the twins, Leslie and Mrs. Malvern, who were coming
along the lane towards the front entrance of the hotel. "Well, I
suppose I'd better go in. I'd rather stay out with the babies, but
Major Weatherley likes us all to be in for tea."

Nurse made her way over the sands, and Anthea remained at
the gate, surveying the little party as a general might survey his
forces. And, indeed, Anthea's attitude to her family was not unlike
a general's. She loved to organise and plan for it, to marshal and
parade it, to draw up schemes of campaign, the benevolent despot
of her little world. To do her justice, she spared neither time nor
trouble on it, and was so deeply immersed in her nursery duties
that she had little interest to spare for anything outside them. She
was regarded generally as a shining example of the "perfect mother".
Jim, in particular, amazed by the competence with which she had
managed the household during his absence in France, could never
sufficiently express his admiration.

"By Jove, old girl," he would say, "you're wonderful! Simply
wonderful!"

He came down to the gate now and slipped an arm round her
waist. He had lost his air of boyishness and grown heavier and

more thick-set, but his round rubicund face was as ingenuously good-natured as ever. Anthea pointed to where Piers was scrambling monkey-like down the cliff.

"Anyone who didn't know him would think that he'd break his neck. He's never happy away from those rocks. He's hardly got a stitch of decent clothing left."

Nurse had put a pair of rubber rompers over Prue's frock, and she was running down the beach to paddle with Jo and Cherry, waving her arms and uttering shrill little screams of delight.

"By Jove, how that kid grows!" said Jim.

He was an indulgent father, almost fatuously proud of his healthy, spirited young brood, but deferring to all Anthea's nursery rules without question.

"Hello, Lindsay," said Anthea, as Lindsay came up to them. "It was sweet of you to look after the infants."

"I love it," said Lindsay. "I'm afraid Cherry's been splashing Jo. She got a little over-excited."

"Oh, that's quite all right," said Anthea graciously. "Only children are apt to."

They walked up together to the hotel, pausing for a moment to admire the sleeping Roger.

The two families were assembled in the hotel lounge for tea — all except Lilian, who had been out for a walk in the morning and, overcome by the exhaustion that the slightest effort seemed to cause her, had decided to spend the rest of the day in bed. None of the other guests were in for tea, and Lindsay, entering the room, thought that the whole scene might have been transferred straight from Hallowes to this shabby Victorian hotel lounge. Helena was pouring out tea, Arthur stood near her on the hearth rug, Jim and Billy were carrying round cups and plates, Leslie and the twins were ensconced in the window seat, Anthea and Mrs. Malvern in easy-chairs. Lindsay took her seat with the twins on the window seat.

"George had to go to London on business," Mrs. Malvern was

saying. "Poor dear! He didn't want to go. He said he'd join us here if he got back in time . . . Got the babies safely settled, dear?"

"Yes, they're all on the beach with Nurse."

"Piers hanging from the cliffs by one eyebrow as usual."

"Baby still sound asleep, bless him! He looks just like Jim when he's asleep."

"Heaven forbid!" said Jim. "But it's grand air, you know. Those kids have come on no end since we came here."

"Even Cherry's getting quite a colour."

"Anyone seen a paper today?"

"I believe they came this afternoon, but there's never anything in them nowadays."

"There's something about a new invention for making films talk."

"Oh, I know. It's done by gramophone records. I've heard of it. It's rotten."

"No, this is something quite new. There's a whole article about it in *The Spectator*."

"Oh, *The Spectator*! Pat and I never read *The Spectator*. We prefer *John Bull*."

"We've put a pound each in the Victory Bond Scheme."

"Bottomley's a scoundrel. You'll never see a penny of it again."

"We shall. He's *absolutely* honest. He always champions the under-dog."

"And makes a jolly good thing out of it."

"Nonsense! Just because he isn't high-brow——"

"He's certainly not that, but——"

The door opened, and George Malvern thrust his square rugged face round it. His grey eyes were twinkling.

"I've brought you a present from London," he said. "Guess what it is."

Then he stood aside and pushed Ronnie Hayes into the room.

"Ronnie!"

"Where *have* you sprung from?"

"It's ages since we heard anything of you."

"Ran into him in Piccadilly," said Mr. Malvern. "Found he was just back from the war and going to put up at a hotel, so I dragged him down here. Can't have our returned warriors putting up at hotels. Must give 'em a proper home-coming . . . We can squeeze him into the bungalow."

"Oh, they'll find a room for him here," said Arthur.

They looked at Ronnie with interest. Four years of soldiering had improved his physique. He held himself upright, with an air of alertness and assurance. His face was lined and in repose looked grave, but his smile still had in it something of the old schoolboy grin. Arthur, watching him, thought, the boy's grown up. He's moved in a larger world than ours, among men who count for something. You can see it even in his clothes.

"But, look here!" Ronnie was saying, "I can't barge in on you like this."

"Sit down, you idiot, and do as you're told," said Billy. "We're here till the end of the month, and you're here with us."

"Of course you are, Ronnie," said Helena. "Come and sit down here by me and tell me what you've been doing with yourself all this time. Sugar but no milk, isn't it?"

"You're as wonderful as ever, Mrs. Weatherley," said Ronnie, sitting down next to her and taking his cup of tea from her. "Do you ever forget anything?"

Lindsay had greeted him casually, but her cheeks had paled and her pulses were pounding in her ears. They had met several times during the war. Clive had insisted on Ronnie's spending part of his leaves with him, and they had met occasionally in London. She had resolutely refused to meet him alone, but it had been inevitable that they should be left alone together occasionally. They had spoken then only of trivial matters, or, more often, silence would fall between them — a silence fraught, to Lindsay, with all the peace and happiness of their first meeting.

At first she had tried conscientiously to conquer her love for him, but it seemed as much a part of her as the breath she drew, and the utmost, she felt, she could hope for was to hide it from Ronnie and even, if possible, from herself . . .

"But where have you been all this time, my boy?" said Arthur. "Do you say you've only just got back from France?"

"Eight months after the Armistice," said Billy. "Did you go to sleep in the trenches and has someone just woken you up?"

"Gosh! I could have slept for eight years, let alone eight months, at the end of it," said Jim.

"We often talked of you, Ronnie," said Helena, "and wondered where you were, but the war made us lose touch with so many people . . . We heard of you occasionally from Clive, of course. He told us that your godmother had died."

"She died at the beginning of the war," said Ronnie. "I'm afraid it's my fault that we lost touch. I'm such a rotten letter-writer."

"But where have you *been?*" said the twins in one breath.

"I've been at the Peace Conference," said Ronnie, "and it's only just packed up. At least, the big-wigs went some time ago, but we had to clear up the sealing-wax and bits of string they left behind."

"How on earth did you get mixed up with the Peace Conference?" said Billy.

"It was rather unfortunate," smiled Ronnie. "You see, my colonel had to attend it in an official capacity, and he discovered that I could spell, so he took me along with him and kept me there in the background. It was full of long words that weren't in the dictionary."

"What was?" said Mab.

"The Peace Conference."

"Oh," said Pat.

"Well, it's grand to see you again, anyway," said Billy. "I say, wasn't it odd how we kept running up against each other out there? Gosh! D'you remember those trenches at Arras? I still feel knee-deep in mud whenever I think of it."

"I minded the rats most," said Ronnie. "I was much more scared of them than of Jerry."

"I remember waking up once to find one of the blighters sitting on my face," said Jim.

Lindsay listened as they exchanged war reminiscences, thinking regretfully that this was a freemasonry from which Clive would always be shut out. At the beginning of the war he had decided, after careful consideration, that he was more useful to the community in general as a schoolmaster than he would be as a soldier and had never seen cause for altering his decision, receiving white feathers and veiled accusations of cowardice without resentment, taking on additional duties willingly, as other members of the staff left to volunteer, and doing what war work he could after school hours.

"What sort of a day have you had in London, darling?" said Mrs. Malvern to her husband. She was sick of the war and couldn't think why people wanted to talk about it . . .

"Damnable!" he replied. "Makes you long for the palmy days of war when you could get a seat in a bus and a meal in a restaurant. Can't move in the streets for the crowd. Dunno where they've all come from. I'd almost welcome another Zeppelin raid to clear the place . . . Full of people and those great dogs . . . What are they called? Continental sheep-dogs or something."

"We've decided to call them Alsatians," said Billy, "as a graceful gesture to our Allies, and you can't get a decent specimen under three hundred pounds."

"Great clumsy creatures!" growled Mr. Malvern. "Taking up the whole pavement. Ought to be stopped by law . . . What's this government thinking of? Keeps on that ridiculous D.O.R.A. that ought to have come off with the Armistice, and lets loose a pack of wolves on the London pavements . . . Not to speak of processions charging all over the place with placards about the League of Nations. Damned nonsense!"

"You've been in the thick of things, Ronnie," said Arthur, "so let's have some inside information. What do you think of this League of Nations idea? Can't say I'm keen on it myself. We've finished with the war, so, for Heaven's sake, let's cut clear of Europe and its muddles and enjoy a bit of peace."

"Have we finished with the war?" said Ronnie. "I sometimes wonder . . ."

"Well, we seem to have got enough trouble of our own on our hands," said Jim, "without borrowing any from Europe. Look at those poor devils of ex-Service men tramping the streets hunting for jobs."

"They can always join the Black and Tans if they really *want* work," said Mrs. Malvern comfortably.

"What's going to happen about Germany itself, Ronnie?" said Billy. "Will there be any trouble there, d'you think?"

"Well . . ." began Ronnie, but Mr. Malvern interrupted him with a snort.

"Trouble? Nonsense! Germany's had her lesson. The Hohenzollerns are done for, and the German people won't let the power pass out of their hands again."

"What are you going to do now you're back in England, Ronnie?"

"I'm going to see the Russian Ballet and hear Melba sing and watch Suzanne Lenglen play tennis——"

"She's beaten Mrs. Lambert Chambers."

"I know. That's why I want to see her play . . . And I shall join this crazy post-war rush for pleasure that I've read so much about in the papers."

"You'll have to learn the new dances," said Pat.

"The Ki-Ki-Kari and the Shimmy-Shake," said Mab.

Mr. Malvern gave a bellow of rage.

"No daughter of mine shall dance the Shimmy-Shake," he said.

"And I shall finish my interrupted training as an architect," said Ronnie.

A faint wail came from the garden.

"Baby's awake," said Anthea, and went out, followed by Jim.

The Malverns took their departure shortly afterwards. It turned out that there was a vacant bedroom at the hotel, which was booked for Ronnie. Lindsay stayed to help Anthea put the children to bed (the twins loved to put Cherry to bed without her help at the bungalow) then joined the others at dinner in the old-fashioned hotel dining-room, with the huge mahogany sideboard and the stuffed fish in glass cases along the walls. She hardly spoke to Ronnie, but she was aware of his nearness in every nerve. When it was time to go back to the bungalow he offered to accompany her, and it was with a strange dreamlike feeling of inevitability that she set off with him along the darkening lane.

A high hedge separated them from the plateau of turf that shelved sharply down to the beach, but a gate gave them a sudden glimpse of the whole sweep of the bay. Some children were still playing on the sands, and on the far horizon a faint puff of smoke told of a passing liner . . . In the twilight sea and sky seemed merged together in a deep intensity of blue . . .

Ronnie stopped at the gate, and Lindsay stood by him, surrendering to the ecstasy of happiness that possessed her .

"Lindsay," he said in a low voice, "we can't go on like this . . ."

She caught hold of the gate to steady herself.

"You love me, don't you?" he went on.

"Yes . . ."

It was the first time they had openly admitted their love.

"Right back . . . that day at Jo's christening . . . You knew then, didn't you?"

She nodded.

"It isn't anything sudden. We've — belonged to each other ever since we met. Clive must let you go."

She spoke in a voice so low and unsteady that he could only just hear her.

"There's Cherry. I couldn't—leave Cherry."

"Clive might let you keep her."

"I don't think he would . . . And — Clive loves me . . . and you. We're the only people he does love."

"I know." There came to him a sudden vivid memory of the dark shabby room at the Vicarage . . . and Clive watching him with loving amusement as he made the clumsy scratches in their wrists that sealed their "blood brotherhood". "If only it weren't Clive!"

She burst into tears, and he caught her to him, holding her closely, while she sobbed brokenly like a child against his shoulder.

138

Chapter Thirteen

It was the first day of the Autumn term, and Cherry was standing at the dining-room window, watching for Clive's return from school. Her dark curls were brushed and shining, and she wore a bib, embroidered with cherries — a present from the twins.

"Isn't Daddy coming yet?" said Lindsay, setting a bowl of roses in the middle of the gate-legged table.

"Not yet," said Cherry.

Lindsay had felt uneasy about Clive all morning, wondering how things were going with him. His unpopularity was now part of the school tradition, sanctified, as it were, by custom, handed on to new boys, together with the ever-growing tale of his crimes. Because of his habit of reporting trivial misdemeanours to the head master, he was a "sneak-pot." Because of his failure to enlist during the war, he was a "funk." The seat next Clive's was left empty at school lectures or filled reluctantly. When Clive was on charge during "break" in the grounds, he walked alone, whereas most of the other masters would have half a dozen small boys hanging on each arm. When it was Clive's turn to take the week-end cycling expedition, not a single boy put his name down for it. Only yesterday Lindsay, weeding a border in the garden, had heard two of the boys discussing him in the playing-field on the other side of the hedge.

". . . and do you remember the time he let Pollit's uncle tell him as a joke about Pollit robbing that orchard and then went and reported him to Holdy for it afterwards?"

"Yes, and the time he reported Fletcher for saying 'Damn!' in the Merston match, though Fletcher got four goals and won the match for us . . ."

She always feared some open demonstration against him, but the discipline at St. Michael's was good, and so far nothing of the sort had happened. Sometimes she wondered how far Clive realised or was affected by his unpopularity. He prepared his lessons as carefully as ever, told her of school events as pleasantly and with as great an appearance of interest, ignoring all evidences of his unpopularity. But he was beginning to look older than his years, and his tall thin figure had lost its uprightness. There were times when Lindsay's heart was wrung by pity for him, but Clive did not want her pity. That rush of protective maternal love for him that had filled her heart when first she realised Mr. Holden's dissatisfaction with him, had died for lack of outlet. Clive must be her teacher, guide and guardian. He would not accept affection from her on any other terms. He did not wish her to share his burdens. He preferred to bear them alone. She had struggled desperately to come closer to him, but there seemed to be an impassable barrier between them. Yet she knew that he loved her devotedly. And — he was maddeningly reasonable. Once, exasperated beyond endurance by his constant gentle fault-finding, she had flown out at him, and he had replied calmly that it was his duty to tell her of anything in her that displeased him, and he would be grateful if she, on her side, would do the same. She had done so, vindictively, unfairly, carping at everything he said or did for the rest of the day, and he had received her rebukes with patience and a touching humility. But — she knew him no better than she had done the day she married him.

"Here's Daddy," said Cherry suddenly, and Lindsay joined her for a moment at the window to watch him.

He walked slowly and looked tired, but the first morning of a new term was always tiring.

When he came into the room he greeted them with his usual pleasant smile, kissing Lindsay and patting Cherry's curls as he took his place at the head of the table and began to talk cheerfully of the day's doings, describing the new boys and masters and the changes in routine. Then he turned to Cherry.

"Like to play a game with Daddy?" he said.

Cherry nodded, gravely intent.

"Now listen very carefully . . . A man was going along the sea-shore and he found twenty shells, but he dropped one and two fell out of his pocket. Then he found five more but he gave two to a little girl . . ."

Lindsay listened, with lips compressed. She hated the way he insisted on teaching Cherry in season and out of season, setting her problems and asking her questions through every meal. She was a highly-strung intelligent child, eager to learn, humiliated by failure. The holiday at Belton Sands had done her good, but already her colour was fading and the peaked look Lindsay knew so well was returning to the small face. Clive was never cross or impatient, but his only conception of intercourse with her was teaching and questioning, and he was proud of her quick mind and memory. She knew the numerals in French, German and Italian, and could recite long poems by heart . . . When Lindsay remonstrated with Clive, he would say, "My dear, you must really allow me to know something of my own profession."

He had even begun to teach her Latin and had only desisted when convinced by Lindsay that this fresh tax on the little brain was preventing the child from sleeping.

"Get on with your pudding, darling," said Lindsay.

She could not bear to see that look of puzzled concentration on the little face.

But Cherry pushed her plate away fretfully.

"Don't want it," she said. "It *does* come to seven, Daddy."

"No, it doesn't," said Clive. "Now we'll go over it again very carefully . . ."

Lindsay was relieved when the arrival of the midday post put an end to the "spelling game" that had succeeded the arithmetic.

Clive opened a letter and read it through.

"This is from Mater," he said. "That holiday at Belton Sands was evidently a bit too much for Father, though he enjoyed it. He's not been well since . . . Aunt Lilian doesn't seem much better either."

Lindsay was absorbed in trying to coax Cherry to eat her pudding.

"Has it got *two m*'?s" said Cherry. Her voice already had that rather shrill note that told of over-strain.

"Yes, two, darling. Now spell it again for Daddy."

"Clive, do remember that she's been at school all morning and is going back there this afternoon."

He looked up from the letter he was reading.

"This is from Ronnie. He can come over on Friday. Isn't that grand!"

Lindsay put down her fork, and an icy coldness crept through her limbs. When she parted from Ronnie at Belton Sands it had been on the clear understanding that they should see no more of each other. He had promised not even to write to her. She knew that Clive had written to him, giving him a vague and general invitation to visit them whenever he could, but she had taken for granted that Ronnie would ignore it. And now he was coming over on Friday. Anger, fear and a wild ecstasy of joy swept over her.

"His train gets in at 3.30," Clive went on. "I shan't be out of school, but you'll be able to meet it, won't you?"

"Yes . . ."

"Now here's another one, darling. It's one we did yesterday. How do you spell 'people'?"

Lindsay sat staring stonily into space.

As he stepped down from the train, she noticed again that new look of manhood that he wore. His face softened into tenderness when his eyes fell on her, but she greeted him unsmilingly, trying to quell the delight that flooded her.

"Ronnie, you promised . . ."

"I know . . . I'll try to explain. I hoped you'd come to meet me, so that we could have a talk before I saw Clive. Let's get out of this place."

They walked out of the station and down the lane that led to the main road.

"Now listen, Lindsay," said Ronnie. There was a note of urgency and decision in his voice. "We've got to have it out with Clive. It's no use hoping that this thing that's happened to us will — die. It's not just that I'm in love with you. You're part of me. I don't really exist without you. God knows I've tried to. And you—" He glanced down at her. "Well, I've only got to look at you to see that it's killing you."

"But, Ronnie——"

"I know everything you're going to say. You said it all at Belton Sands. Now listen, darling." He took her hand, but she snatched it jerkily away. "I want to talk about Clive first. I know how you feel about it, and I know how I feel about it. When I think of all he meant to me when I was a kid, and of what I'm trying to do to him now, I feel sick, but — Lindsay, he's a queer chap. He doesn't seem human somehow. Do you think he'd really care terribly?"

"I don't know . . ."

"There's something else I want to ask you. If he agrees to let you go, you wouldn't want him to 'do the gentlemanly thing', would you? I mean, in these cases, it's fairly usual to arrange for the husband to be divorced with a 'woman unknown' as co-respondent. It's a wretched farce, and I hate the thought of it. What about you? Would you be willing to face the music with me if it came to it?"

"Yes, but——"

"Oh, I know there's a lot more to it than that. Cherry and — other things. But I wanted to get those two points clear before I spoke to Clive. You're not really sure that it would cut him up so terribly, and you're willing to face the music with me."

"Ronnie, if he let me have Cherry, you'd——?"

Of course. I'm as fond of the kid as if she were my own."

Had she known of Ronnie's coming beforehand she would have tried to stop him, but, now that he was here, the sense of inevitability had seized her again. Besides, with Ronnie walking there with her down the quiet country lane, it was difficult to do anything but yield to the peace and happiness his presence always brought. She remembered Billy's telling her that one of Ronnie's men had said of him, "I'd trust 'im blind . . ." That was the feeling he gave you. You could leave things to him . . . trust him blind . . .

When they reached the house, Clive was already walking across the playing-field, and they went down the garden to meet him at the gate. Seeing the two men together, Lindsay noticed how slack Clive's figure looked beside Ronnie's upright soldierly one. Clive greeted him with the old eager affection, and Lindsay had to harden her heart against the pity that tried to enter.

Tea was laid in the sitting-room, and Clive bombarded Ronnie with questions about the war, expounding his own theories and opinions. It generally caused Lindsay a vague embarrassment to hear him discussing the war with men who had served in it, as he loved to do. She could sense the slight contempt they felt for a man who had preferred the safe life of school mastering to the dangers and discomforts of warfare. But today there was no room in her heart for such feelings. She waited, her body rigid with suspense, her heart beating uneasily, till Ronnie should broach the subject he had come to discuss.

When the little maid had cleared away the tea things, and Clive had settled back in his chair for a fuller discussion of the retreat of the 5th Army in 1918, Ronnie rose to knock out his pipe against the grate, then stood, looking down at Clive, the muscles of his face taut, his eyes steady.

"There's something I have to tell you, Clive," he said. Lindsay's heart seemed to stop beating, and she clutched the arm of her chair. Ronnie threw her a quick reassuring glance before he went on, "Lindsay and I love each other."

Clive did not move or speak, but the colour drained slowly from his face, leaving it pinched and drawn. Lindsay turned her head sharply away, so as not to see him.

When he spoke it was in his usual pleasant, well-modulated voice.

"I appreciate your telling me this, Ronnie, and I know, of course, that these — infatuations do happen. I'm not small-minded enough to blame either of you. One doesn't — do these things deliberately.

I confess that I hadn't the slightest suspicion of it, but now that it's happened and is out in the open, I agree that the best thing is for the three of us to thrash it out together honestly and frankly."

Were it not for the ashen hue of his face, he might have been discussing some impersonal academic problem.

"It's not an infatuation," said Ronnie slowly.

"Of course, one never admits that," said Clive, and one corner of his mouth jerked up as if he were trying to smile. "I suppose that Lindsay thinks she's as much in love with you as she was with me when she married me? These things are incalculable. Lindsay's a pretty girl, and you've been invested with the glamour of a uniform during the war, and I suppose there's been a mutual attraction that will probably go as quickly and inexplicably as it came . . ."

"Lindsay and I were in love with each other before the war," said Ronnie. "We fell in love with each other the first time we met. I give you my word of honour, Clive, that we've both honestly tried to conquer it."

None of them spoke for some moments, then Clive cleared his throat, making a hoarse rasping sound in the silence.

"I needn't ask you whether—" he began, and stopped. He spoke almost casually, but something haunted and suspicious flickered in his eyes as they went from one to the other.

"No," said Ronnie, setting his teeth, "you needn't ask that."

"What do you propose to do?" said Clive.

"Will you divorce Lindsay?"

Clive leant back in his chair, drumming his fingers on the arm of it.

"That needs a certain amount of consideration," he said. "I might as well tell you at once that I shouldn't allow Lindsay to divorce me. I shouldn't mind the disgrace — indeed, I should be glad to spare Lindsay the disgrace — but, as a matter of principle, I couldn't put my name to an untruth."

"We've already discussed that," said Ronnie, "and neither of us would have agreed to it in any case."

Lindsay leant forward, her dark eyes dilated, the lovely line of her lips compressed.

"Clive," she said breathlessly, "may I have Cherry, if—?"

Clive shook his head and spoke kindly, as if reluctant to pain her.

"No, I should never agree to that in any circumstances."

"Could Mother have her?"

He shook his head again.

"That would come to the same thing, surely."

"We'll accept any conditions you care to impose, if you'll let us have Cherry," said Ronnie.

"I'd like to agree," said Clive, "but I must fulfil my responsibility to Cherry, and I don't consider that in the circumstances you could provide her with a suitable home."

"You're utterly wrong there," said Ronnie sharply, then continued more calmly, "Well, it's up to Lindsay. What do you say, Lindsay?"

Lindsay dropped her face in her hands with a long tremulous sigh. When she raised it, it was white and expressionless.

"I can't let Cherry go," she said.

"You choose Clive, then?"

"Yes . . ."

"Very well," said Ronnie. The lines on his face had deepened, but there was only tenderness and compunction in his eyes as he looked down at her. "I'm sorry you've had to go through this. Perhaps I was wrong to come . . ." She still stared in front of her without speaking. "Thank you, Clive. I suppose one couldn't have expected anything else. It means the end of our friendship, I'm afraid."

"There's no reason at all why it should," said Clive. There was a look of furtive shamed pleading in his eyes. "These things — pass, you know."

"This won't." He held out his hand. "Goodbye."

"Goodbye," said Clive, taking his hand. His mouth twisted into a grimace again as he tried to smile.

Ronnie looked at Lindsay as she sat there motionless, her face set and stony, staring in front of her. He said, "Goodbye, Lindsay," but she did not seem to hear.

Clive saw him off, then came back to the sitting-room and stood on the hearth-rug, looking down at Lindsay.

"I'm glad we've had this out," he said. "I shall never say a word of reproach to you, Lindsay, and I shall never feel reproach. We've all been honest, and that's the main thing. And you must let me help you fight this, darling——"

He sat down on the arm of her chair and put his hand on her shoulder, but she broke away from him, and he heard her going stumblingly upstairs to her bedroom.

Chapter Fourteen

Lilian sat on the window seat in the drawing-room, pretending to read a novel. She even turned over a page occasionally in case Helena were watching . . . She was still convalescent after her illness, and her convalescence seemed to be making little progress. A sense of frustration lay over her spirit like a dense fog. She had looked forward to taking up the threads of her old life after her illness, but, though her illness was now over, all the savour seemed to have gone from her old life. She had belonged to a set that had never professed loyalty to its members. If you could "stay the pace" — be witty, smart, tireless and modern — you were accepted. If you dropped out you were not even missed. Lilian had no doubt that she would be readmitted into her old set — or, at any rate, into one so like it as to be indistinguishable from it — but she lacked the energy to take any steps towards it. Every day she would toy with the idea of writing to some of her old friends and arranging a meeting at one of the London restaurants or clubs that used to be her daily haunts, but she was always prevented from doing so by the knowledge that she did not want to meet any of the old set or go to any of the old places. She didn't want to do anything or go anywhere . . . And time crawled on from second to second, from minute to minute, from hour to hour, each day interminable. She seemed to be cut off from the normal world by the black fog that engulfed her. Sometimes the old craving for drink would come upon her, but there was little opportunity of satisfying it here. I believe I'd feel better if I could get really drunk just once, she thought, turning over a page of which she had not read a word. I shall go mad if I don't do something soon. Shall I write to Bobby

— or one of the others — and ask him to meet me somewhere? No, I couldn't bear it. The very thought of him bores me to death. The very thought of anyone bores me to death . . .

Helena watched her anxiously, thinking how these last months had changed her. She was pale and nervy. The old bright gloss of assurance had gone. There was a set staring look in her eyes and her brows darted together in a quick nervous frown at every sound. Her pose, as she sat now, her fingers drumming on the arm of her chair, was unnaturally tense and rigid. For the first time in her life she looked slovenly and ungroomed, her greying hair carelessly arranged, her pale face without make-up, her dress crumpled and showing an edge of petticoat. "It's a difficult convalescence," the doctor had said. "It's almost worse than the illness. What she needs is something to take her out of herself . . ." Helena felt guiltily that she ought to be doing something towards this. She had made several suggestions — a cruise, a holiday abroad — all of which Lilian had pettishly negatived. Helena could do little beyond making suggestions, for Arthur had had several heart attacks since his return from Belton Sands and was still in bed. The doctor had insisted on her engaging a nurse, but Arthur would not allow the nurse to do more for him than he could help, and was fretful and uneasy if Helena left him even for a few minutes. He was asleep now with the nurse in attendance, but he would ask for Helena as soon as he awoke. The life of the house even outside the sick-room had to go hushed and muted, for any sudden sound might bring on another attack, and any attack, as the doctor had warned her, might prove fatal. Upstairs, Arthur's sick-room; downstairs, Lilian, nerve-racked and miserable . . . It was not a cheerful household, and Helena was glad, for Billy's sake, that he was going away tomorrow to spend the rest of his vacation with a college friend. Fortunately he was of a happy-go-lucky disposition and did not seem to find the atmosphere irksome, content to spend his time in walking and reading the highbrow books that Helena found so formidable. He was a good deal at the Malverns', where Leslie Torrance was still staying.

He came into the room now and stood by her chair, looking down at her.

"Why are you looking at me like that?"

"I'm thinking how nice you look."

"Nonsense! I'm middle-aged."

"I like you middle-aged, don't you, Aunt Lilian?" Lilian pretended to be absorbed by her book.

Helena laughed.

"What rubbish you talk!" She glanced at the clock. "You'll be in for tea, won't you? It should be here in a minute."

"No, I'm going to the Malverns' for tea. Walk down the drive with me. I don't suppose you've put your nose out of doors all day, have you?"

"I don't need to put my nose out of doors. And, as a matter of fact, I have been out to look at my roses."

Now that Helena could so seldom go further than the garden, she had taken the rose-beds at the end of the lawn under her special charge and would work there — hoeing, weeding, cutting off dead blooms — while Arthur was asleep. The window of Arthur's bedroom faced that side of the house, so that the nurse could call her in when she was needed.

She took Billy's arm and walked slowly down the drive with him.

"I'm worried about you, Mrs. Weatherley," he said.

"Why?"

"You don't have much of a life, do you — what with Daddy and Aunt Lilian."

"I love my life . . . I mean, I wish they were both well, but——"

"But you've got a ministering angel complex."

She laughed.

"I hope it's not so bad as that. But I've been thinking that it's not a very cheerful place for you, darling."

"Me? I love being with you. I often have a guilty feeling that I don't do enough for you. Well, it's more than a guilty feeling. It's a guilty knowledge. Here I am on my last day at home going off to the Malverns' instead of staying to have tea with you and help you cope with Aunt Lilian's megrims."

"You know I love your going out to see other people. Leslie's still there, isn't she?"

"Yes . . . She wanted to read this, so I'm taking it along."

She looked at the book he showed her without seeing it.

"You like her, don't you, Billy?"

"Yes . . . do you, Mrs Weatherley?"

She considered, a slight frown creasing her forehead . . . Leslie . . . clever, intelligent, honest, but — even her beauty shared the hard assurance of her whole personality.

"Y-yes."

He laughed.

"Now, Mrs. Weatherley, don't be jealous. You know she's devoid of all the things you hate in women — coyness, stupidity, mental laziness, deceitfulness. She's as clean and honest as the day. She has a mental and spiritual integrity that well, that makes me feel humble when I'm with her."

"And you love her."

"And I love her. That's why it's rather important to me that you should love her, too."

"Billy, darling, I'll try to."

"I wish you could sound a little more enthusiastic. You're not being a possessive mother, are you, Mrs. Weatherley? It's all out of character if you are."

She smiled — a crooked, tender little smile. "No . . . it isn't that I don't want you to marry. I've always wanted you to marry and to marry young. But I'd built up an imaginary wife for you and — it isn't Leslie."

"They never are, you know," he said.

"I suppose not," she sighed. "I suppose I'd built up a girl of my own generation, and Leslie's yours."

"I'd rather have mine."

He spoke teasingly, but there was something boyishly — almost shyly — pleading in the smile he turned on her. He looked so young, so confident, so — defenceless that a pang shot through her heart.

"If only I could be sure she'd make you happy!" she said tremulously.

"She'd make me happy, all right. But we're rather counting our chickens, you know. I can't marry for years, and, anyway, she may not have me."

"Are you going to speak to her?"

"Not speak with a capital S in the Victorian sense, but I'm going to throw out feelers. I'd like to know if there's any chance for me if and when I'm in a position to marry."

Helena sighed again. He seemed to her so perfect that she could not imagine any girl refusing him.

He laughed.

"I know exactly what you're thinking, but she doesn't see me through your rose-coloured spectacles, you know. She's a highly critical young woman, and she sees me as I am. *Your* invention wouldn't, I suppose, but Leslie will be much better for me. However, don't worry. She probably won't have me, and you'll be saddled with me for the rest of your life."

They had reached the gate now. She put her hands on his shoulders. "Good luck, darling . . . I shall love her if she's kind to you."

He bent to kiss her.

"Goodbye . . . and God bless you for everything."

She walked slowly back, up the drive and in at the open front door. The post had arrived and, taking up the little pile of letters from the chest, she went into the drawing-room. Tea had been brought in, and Lilian had poured out a cup for herself and put it by her on the window seat.

"Has Nurse been down?" said Helena.

"She just looked in to say that Arthur was still asleep."

Helena sorted the letters on the tea-table.

"Nothing from Clive," she said. "It's the day we usually get one from him, isn't it? But sometimes it doesn't arrive till the next morning."

Lilian looked up from her book.

"Do you remember the time when Lindsay forgot to post it, and he wired the next day to put you out of your suspense, and neither you nor Arthur had realised that you hadn't heard from him?"

"Don't remind me of it," smiled Helena. "It was dreadful of us."

She opened a letter and was reading it, when there came the sound of wheels on the gravel outside.

Lilian craned her neck round the window curtain.

"It's the station taxi," she said.

"Who on earth——?" said Helena.

Lilian craned her neck further.

"It's Lindsay and Cherry," she said.

Helena went to the front door.

"*Lindsay!* . . . Come in, my dear."

She led the two of them, Cherry holding Lindsay's hand, into the drawing-room.

"Why didn't you let us know you were coming? I'd have sent the car. You look tired out. Sit down . . ."

But Lindsay still stood there, gazing at Helena. There were dark shadows round her eyes and her white face wore a look of strain and exhaustion. Cherry stood, too, with an unchildlike stillness, clasping Lindsay's hand, as if aware of mysterious troubling forces around her, but not afraid as long as Lindsay was there.

"May I speak to you . . .?" said Lindsay.

"Cherry, darling," said Helena, "will you stay here with Aunt Lilian? Give her some tea, Lilian. I won't keep Mummy long, sweetheart. Come into the library, Lindsay."

In the library Lindsay sat down, and gusts of shivering swept over her, making her teeth chatter, so that at first she could not speak.

Helena put her hand on her shoulder.

"Tell me in your own time and in your own way, Lindsay," she said gently. "There's nothing to be afraid of here. What's happened?"

"It's — Ronnie," said Lindsay at last with difficulty.

"Ronnie?"

"We love each other. You didn't know, did you?"

"No. I never guessed that."

"He came over last week," said Lindsay. She still spoke through chattering teeth, drawing quick quivering breaths. "I said I'd stay with Clive . . . And — Clive's been so kind. He watches me all the time. He tries to help . . . and I hate him so much I can't bear him to touch me. I can't bear to be in the same room with him. I can't stand it any longer. I had to come to Ronnie .. . . I had to." She clenched her teeth for a moment, as if trying to control herself, then went on, "I haven't slept since Ronnie went . . . I couldn't bear it any longer . . . I had to come . . ."

"But, my dear, have you thought——?"

Lindsay interrupted, speaking with sudden stammering earnestness.

"And I couldn't leave Cherry with him. He doesn't mean to be unkind, but he doesn't understand . . . Will you take Cherry for me, Helena? *Please!* . . . She'd be happy with you, and you're Clive's mother. He'd let you have her."

"Lindsay darling, this house is no place for a child. Even now, though Arthur is asleep, I hardly dare go out of earshot of his bedroom. I must be ready to go to him as soon as he wants me. On the days when he gets up, I hardly leave him for a second. I have to dress him and sometimes feed him . . . And the whole place has to be kept as still as death . . . It worries me even when Billy's at home. It would be cruelty to have a child here." She had drawn a chair close up to Lindsay's and laid a hand tenderly on her arm. "I won't say anything about your leaving Clive. That's your business. I take your word that you — had to. It's Cherry we must think of. Won't Clive let you have her?"

Lindsay shook her head.

"What about your mother?"

"He says he wouldn't let Mother have her . . ." Helena considered, with frowning brows, her hand still on Lindsay's arm.

"There's — Anthea."

Hope leapt into the dark eyes.

"Oh! . . . Do you think she——?"

"Well," Helena smiled reassuringly, "you'd think that one more

154

or less wouldn't make any difference to Anthea . . . What are your plans exactly, Lindsay?"

"I've wired to Ronnie. He's meeting me at Paddington. He knows I'm bringing Cherry to you . . . I've told the taxi to wait."

"I'll ring up Anthea now."

She took up the telephone, and Lindsay went into the hall, closing the door behind her. Through the open door of the drawing-room she could see Lilian and Cherry sitting on the floor, and between them a line of the red and white ivory chessmen that were kept in the cabinet. Lilian had taken off Cherry's beaver-trimmed green coat and bonnet, and the firelight played on the dark glossy curls and bare dimpled arms. The white muslin frock, with Hungarian peasant embroidery, happened to be one that Lilian had sent her last Christmas.

Inside the library Helena was telling Anthea what had happened.

"Her leaving Clive isn't our business——"

"Why not?" put in Anthea sharply.

"—but Cherry is," went on Helena, ignoring the interruption. "We mustn't let Cherry suffer if we can help it . . . Anthea, surely it wouldn't be much extra trouble for you. She's just about Jo's age and——"

But Anthea broke in on a shrill aggressive note.

"And why should I make things easy for her? Once we start making things easy for women of that sort, there won't be much hope for *us*."

"Anthea, she's desperate."

"Let her be. I hope she is. She deserves to be. And, as I said, I'm not going to make things easy for her by taking the child off her hands . . . I'm sorry, Helena, but that's how I feel about it. I feel that it would be definitely encouraging immorality . . . No, I certainly wouldn't like Clive to have the bringing-up of any child of mine, but the solution of that problem is obvious. Let her stay and do her duty to Clive and to the child. She can't eat her cake and have it . . . Anyway, who knows how long that affair with Ronnie has been going on or what the child may have picked up? I don't want my children contaminated."

"*Anthea!*"

"Oh, yes, it's all very well for you. I notice that you aren't having the child yourself. I must say I think it's a bit — strange of you to support her against Clive. Does Father know about the attitude you're taking up? . . . No, I won't consult Jim. This is my business, and I've given you my answer . . . I'm sorry, Helena. I don't mean to be offensive, but I'm certainly not going to — pander to immorality. I suppose I'm old-fashioned."

Helena put down the receiver with heightened colour and quickened breath, and paused a moment before she went to open the door.

Lindsay turned to her.

"She won't——?"

Helena shood her head. She could not bear to look at Lindsay's white tortured face, and looked instead into the drawing-room. Lilian and Cherry were still playing with the chessmen. Cherry's sweet childish laugh rang out suddenly.

Lilian, seeing them standing there, rose to her feet and came into the hall. Her air of listlessness had gone. She looked alert, confident.

"What's the matter?" she said, looking from one to the other.

Helena told her shortly. Lindsay stared fixedly before her in a kind of stupor of weariness and despair.

"I can't let Clive have her," she said in a low toneless voice, "and I can't stay with him . . ."

"Lindsay," said Lilian. There was a new ringing note in her voice. "Let me have her . . ." She stopped, then went on, stammering with eagerness, "Lindsay, do let me have her. I'll be a real mother to her. I love her already. I've never had — anyone belonging to me before. It will make all the difference to me. She shall never want for anything, I promise you. I'll take entire responsibility for her — financial as well, of course. My life's been so — empty, but if you'll let me have Cherry" — her eyes filled suddenly with tears — "it will be like having another chance, another life . . . We're two unwanted people — Cherry and I — and we'd make each other happy . . . Lindsay . . ."

156

Lindsay looked at Helena.

"I suppose it will be for Clive to decide," said Helena, "but I think he'd agree."

"Yes," said Lindsay slowly, "I don't think he wants her. He —just doesn't want me to have her."

"Well, we'll keep her for the present," said Helena, "and I'll get into touch with Clive."

"The train's at five," said Lindsay. "I ought to go now . . . You've been so kind, both of you. I shall never forget." She glanced into the drawing-room, where Cherry was still intent on marshalling her chessmen army. "I can't say goodbye to her. I daren't . . ." She put both hands to her throat as if to stem the rush of emotion that threatened to overwhelm her and went on in a low deliberate voice, speaking with an obvious effort: "I'll go now. Goodbye, and thank you again with all my heart."

"Goodbye, darling," said Helena. "Write to me, and I'll let you know about Cherry."

"I'll come to the taxi and get her things," said Lilian.

Helena waited in the hall till Lilian returned, carrying a small suitcase. The sound of the taxi wheels on the gravel died away. A maid came hurriedly downstairs.

"Nurse says that the master is awake and asking for you, madam."

"I'll go to him," said Helena. "I ought to ring up Clive now." She turned to Lilian. "Lilian, we could put Cherry in the blue room. It's next yours."

"I'll see to that, Helena," said Lilian briskly. "I'll have the camp bed put up in my room, and I'll put her to bed myself now. The poor little mite's worn out."

The nurse appeared at the bend of the stairs.

"Are you coming, Mrs. Weatherley?" she said. "He's getting — uneasy."

"I'm coming now," said Helena, turning to the stairs.

PART V

1931

Chapter Fifteen

Cherry's Confirmation

Billy walked slowly down the road that led from the station to the garden city in which he and Leslie, and their two children lived.

It had turned colder today, so, at least, he thought with a wry smile, he would not find the children playing in the garden without any clothes on, as he frequently had done during the summer. Gavin was seven and Elaine five and, though Billy tried to be broadminded about it, he couldn't quite conquer his scruples.

"Do you think it's wise?" he had said tentatively to Leslie, and Leslie had explained patiently and earnestly how much wiser it was than the system on which both he and she had been brought up.

"You see, darling, it's really important for them to become accustomed to the differences between the sexes from their earliest years. Then they take them for granted, and it puts an end to all that mystery and nasty curiosity that was connected with sex in the old days. It makes them frank and honest men and women, interested in each other's personalities instead of in each other's sex. Gavin isn't in the least interested in the fact that Elaine's body is different from his, because he's so used to seeing it, and Elaine isn't interested in his for the same reason. They're very emphatic about that at Gorselands."

Gorselands was the co-educational school to which Leslie sent the children. It certainly lived up to its official description of "free". There were no rules, no restrictions, no punishments, and the pupils were allowed to do exactly as they liked. There were, of course, no organised games and the children ran wild over the countryside, giving unrestrained expression to their individualities. These methods, however excellent in themselves, were difficult to maintain during the holidays, but Leslie insisted that they must be maintained as far as possible, however great the inconvenience. "All the good will be undone if we go back to the old-fashioned methods in the holidays," she said. "When people say that free education is a failure, it generally means that it hasn't been given a fair chance. It does involve trouble and inconvenience, I know, and people are rather apt to lose patience . . ."

Billy was very apt to lose patience. Gorselands was an estate of forty acres. The children could shoot arrows and throw stones there without necessarily doing much damage. Holidays in the small house in the crowded garden city meant to Billy an endless stream of complaints from infuriated neighbours. Leslie was unperturbed by this.

"No, Billy, you mustn't forbid them to do it. It's fatal to begin to say 'don't'. I'll explain to them, and, of course, they must pay for the damage out of their pocket-money, but they mustn't be *forbidden* to do anything."

Billy had at first taken an interest in the little garden at the back of the house, but, during the children's first holidays from Gorselands, Gavin had slashed off all the heads of the flowers with a stick, and Elaine had pulled up all his newly planted cabbages. This, as Leslie explained to him, was not "naughty."

"You see, Gavin was feeling annoyed with Elaine, and he worked his annoyance off that way. It's a good thing he could work it off that way. Otherwise he might have hit Elaine, and that would have been definitely antisocial, while if he'd repressed the feeling it might have formed an inhibition."

And, in some way that Billy could not quite understand, pulling up his cabbage plants expressed Elaine's individuality. So the garden was now a trodden overgrown waste . . . At the bottom of it was the wooden studio where Leslie painted cubist and post-impressionist pictures and did sculpture reminiscent of Epstein. Leslie was a serious artist and despised popular taste, content that her work was accepted by people who "counted". She could, when she wished, turn out conventional work of a high quality, and had recently done a poster for the Underground—a lovely delicate painting of trees in autumn, the nearer ones flaming gold and red, the further ones veiled in mist. Had she wanted to make money by her art, she could have done so, but she despised money. She refused even to employ a maid, on the principle that it was degrading for one human being to perform menial tasks for another. She employed a morning charwoman to clean the house, insisting always that the woman's work was as useful to the community as her own and was careful to demand no personal service from her. She would look contemptuously at the "bell-case" in the kitchen, marked "Lounge: Bedroom 1; Bedroom 2; Bedroom 3", and say, "Thank God they've never been rung since we came here."

As for meals, Leslie magnificently ignored them. She considered "set meals" part of the bourgeois tradition against which she and her friends were fighting. People, according to Leslie, should eat only when hungry. She provided bread, milk, butter, salad, cheese and fruit for anyone who wanted it, and there, she considered, her duty as a housekeeper ended. Even the children had no regular meals. When hungry, they fetched food from the larder and ate it picnic-like wherever they happened to be. Billy often thought that it was a good thing they were healthy, sturdy little beggars, with strong digestions and no nerves. Leslie herself, when engaged on a piece of work, often forgot to eat at all. Billy compromised with this regime by having a good bourgeois meal in the middle of the day, making himself a cup of tea when he came home (Leslie never drank tea) and having a supper of bread and cheese.

On leaving college he had obtained a post on a morning paper, and he and Leslie had married on the strength of it. He had been full of hope and ambition, both of which had faded somewhat with the years. He lacked the popular touch that might have made him a successful journalist, and he lacked, too, that touch of distinction that might have given him a place in the world of letters. As he put it to himself, he wasn't good enough, and he wasn't bad enough. He fell between two stools . . . He had now almost abandoned the free-lance work that had met with so little success, and carried out the routine duties of his job without much interest.

Approaching the house, he saw that the children were in the garden. Gavin wore conventional flannel shorts with a cotton shirt and was carving a piece of wood with a knife. He had inherited Leslie's darkly-vivid good looks, together with something of her artistic ability. He loved to carve and model, and the results showed originality and promise. Billy glanced anxiously at the sharp knife that he seemed to wield so carelessly, but checked the impulse to advise caution, remembering that admonitions of every kind were discouraged by Leslie. She had not even allowed him to guide Elaine's unsteady footsteps down the steep uncarpeted stairs of the little house when first she began to walk. ("Let her fall, dear. It won't do her any harm, and it's the best way for her to learn.")

Elaine came trotting round the side of the house now. She wore a short gingham frock and over it a cardigan of Leslie's, with a skipping-rope tied round her waist. One of her bare plump legs was covered with red crayon, the other with blue.

"Hello," said Billy

"Hello," she replied.

She resembled Billy as strikingly as Gavin resembled Leslie. She had straight fair hair, brown eyes and a golden-pale healthy skin. Sometimes Billy thought that Helena must have looked just like that when she was a little girl . . .

"What on earth have you got yourself up like that for?" said Billy.

Gavin glanced up from his carving.

"She wanted to," he said simply.

Billy went into the house by the back door, and Elaine followed him, the handles of the skipping-rope clattering behind her. It was a small bare cupboard-like kitchen, with none of the comfort that had been associated with kitchens in Billy's childhood. He put on the kettle and took a tea-pot and cup and saucer down from a shelf.

"Is Mummy working?" he said.

Leslie had at first taught them to call her and Billy by their Christian names, but the children themselves had preferred the

"Mummy" and "Daddy" used by other children. This had worried Leslie as showing a "conventional mentality".

"No, she's got the talking people here," said Elaine.

Billy remembered that this was the afternoon when Leslie's "discussion group" met, and the lounge would be full of earnest young men and women discussing the problems of the day. He sighed. He so seldom seemed to get Leslie to himself. When she was not working, she was holding meetings in the interests of the Left Wing, of which she was an ardent supporter.

"The kettle's boiling," said Elaine.

"Thanks."

He made his tea and poured a cup out, sitting on the kitchen table. Elaine stood watching him solemnly, her skipping-rope trailing on the ground, her blue and red legs planted firmly apart.

"Tell me about when you were a little boy," she said. She loved to hear stories of his childhood, and, when she went to Hallowes, would eagerly identify the scenes of them, but it was difficult to make his childhood, spent against a background of nursery discipline, seem real to her.

". . . And I always used to go down to Gran after tea, you remember, and she played games with me."

"What sort of games? Ludo?"

"Yes . . . or Gran would read aloud to me."

"*Alice Through the Looking Glass?*"

"Yes, I loved that."

"I think it's nice too."

"I always felt cross when visitors were there. I had to say my piece to them."

"What piece was it?"

"'Meddlesome Matty.'"

"Why did you have to say it?"

"Miss Berry told me to."

Elaine wrinkled her brows.

"But why did you *have* to?"

Billy remembered Leslie's contemptuous definition of obedience as a "slave's virtue" and hastily changed the subject.

165

"Were there any letters this morning?"

"Yes . . . One for you."

Billy poured out another cup of tea.

"Would you like to go and get it for me?"

Elaine considered, then said "Yes". The answer "No" might have been given equally cheerfully and representing nothing but a statement of fact.

She clattered into the hall and returned with a letter. As she opened the door, Billy caught a murmur of voices from the lounge.

"Is it from Gran?" said Elaine. "It's the way she writes'."

"Yes, it's from Gran," said Billy. He opened the envelope and drew out the letter.

My darling Boy

Thank you so much for your letter. I always look forward to them so much and am always delighted to hear news of Leslie and the darling children. I told you that the doctor had suggested the Pisany treatment for Father, didn't I? The specialist agreed that it might do him good, and we're hoping to go there in about a month's time. He certainly seems a little better now, and they seem to think that he can stand the journey quite well. He himself is quite excited about it and very anxious to try the treatment.

He particularly wants to see you all before he goes, and suggests that you all come down to Hallowes for his sixtieth birthday on the 20th. I do hope that you can come. I'd love to see the children again. You must stay for the night, of course. We can easily put you up. I'm writing to Anthea by this post to ask them to come. I don't know whether I can persuade Clive to come. I wish I could. It would do him good. He hardly goes out at all.

The only thing that worries both Father and me is the thought of Cherry. Lilian has left her at school for the holidays for two or three years now, which is hard on the child. She's sixteen and wants to leave school next year, but I don't know what's to happen to her. Lilian really isn't fit to have charge of her. The last time I saw Lilian she had changed very much for the worse, and I hear that she's drinking heavily again. I was afraid that that "cure" would not be permanent. Clive, I believe, would have no objection now to her going to Lindsay and Ronnie, if they would have her, but now that they have children of their own, I don't suppose they want her. The obvious thing is for her to go to Clive. She's old enough to keep house for him, with a little help, and it would be more comfortable for him than living in lodgings. I must try to go down to see him and come to some arrangement before we go abroad. If I can't manage it, she must come to Hallowes, but I feel strongly that it's no place for young people now that Father's such an invalid. Anyway, I'm going down to St. Monica's for her confirmation next week. She was to have been confirmed last year, you remember, but got measles at the last minute. I'll have a talk with her then and see what she feels about it.

I went over to see Anthea the other week. Now that they are living in Hampstead and the children are older, she seems to get about a good deal. She's crazy on this new contract bridge. It seems very complicated. Father still enjoys a game of whist on his better days, and the Vicar and Sir Bruce are very good about coming in, but we've never troubled to learn even auction bridge.

The garden is looking lovely and I think my roses are better than they've ever been. We've had hardly any greenfly, which, I suppose, is owing to the weather.

Now, dear boy, you must all come down on the 20th and stay the night. Father and I will be most disappointed if you don't.

My love to Leslie and the children and my dearest love to you.

Your loving
MOTHER

X for Elaine.

"Is it from Gran?" said Elaine.

"Yes."

"Has she sent me a kiss?"

"Yes."

"Let me see."

He showed it her, and she smiled — a slow sweet smile of gratification.

"Will you let me make one back for her when you write?"

"Yes."

He folded up the letter, put it in his pocket, and carried his tea things over to the sink.

"What does she say in the writing?" said Elaine.

"She wants us all to go over there for Grandpa's birthday."

"I'll go," said Elaine promptly. "I like going to Gran's. There are nice things to eat. Gavin says I'm greedy and I *am*. I *like* being greedy."

Billy smiled a little ruefully. Certainly there was not much comfort in this house. Probably even the children felt that . . .

"Well, I'll go in to Mummy now."

"To the talking people?"

"Yes."

"I don't like them. They go on talking and talking."

"You're a chatterbox yourself."

"I know. I like being a chatterbox, but I don't like other people being chatterboxes."

She went out into the garden again. Billy lit his pipe and stood for a moment at the window watching Gavin, who was still intent on his carving. Billy's lips were still twisted into that somewhat rueful smile. He wasn't going to enjoy having a crank for a son . . . At first he had taken for granted that this co-education regime would last for their kindergarten days only, but Leslie had recently made it clear that it was to last till the end of their schooldays.

"Darling, all the good would be undone if we took them away before their education's finished."

"As far as I can make out," Billy had objected, "they don't seem to be learning anything at all."

"Education isn't book learning," Leslie had said. "Education's development of personality. They can pick up book learning at any time."

"I'd hoped that Gavin might go to a public school," he had said, but Leslie's eyes had filled with horror.

"*Billy*! A public school! The only teaching a public school gives is contempt for everything literary and artistic. It would *ruin* him."

"Oh, very well," Billy had agreed.

Going into the hall, he met Piers coming in by the front door, elegant in green flannel trousers and an open-necked salmon-coloured shirt. Piers was seventeen, belonged to the aesthetic set at his school and was going to Oxford next year. He had recently become an enthusiastic supporter of the Left Wing and a regular attendant at Leslie's discussion groups, much to the annoyance of Anthea, who made it quite plain how strongly she disapproved of Leslie and her circle.

"Hello, uncle!" he grinned.

"Hello, you brat!" said Billy, taking him by the back of his neck and propelling him in front of himself into the lounge.

The lounge was a large room, running the whole length of the house. It was the only "reception room" and was intended to be dining-room and sitting-room combined, but Leslie's *menage* did not include a dining-room and she spent most of her time in the studio, so that the room was used chiefly for meetings. Curtains of cubist pattern hung at the windows, and the furniture was of geometric design with a few of the steel tubular tables and chairs that had recently been imported from Paris. There were no pictures on the walls, and the floor consisted of bare boards, with two or three small hand-woven rugs. In a niche above the fireplace stood the plaster cast of a girl's head modelled by Leslie. Despite the deliberate impressionist distortion, it dominated the room by its vitality and craftsmanship, and Billy could never look at it without a thrill of pride.

The room was full of people — sitting on chairs, perched on tables or leaning against the walls. Leslie was sitting with the speaker at a table facing the room. She lacked the air of dowdiness that characterised many of the women present. Though she avoided frills and furbelows and had adopted the "Eton crop" fashion of hair dressing, she was always immaculately groomed and tailored. Her face was set in its usual lines of earnestness, her eyes were fixed on the speaker, and she did not notice Billy's entrance. He stood at the back of the room, his dark town suit conspicuous among the corduroy trousers and coloured shirts worn by most of the other men present. Looking round, it occurred to him that no one here would be willing to discuss with him the things he was really interested in — Sir Malcolm Campbell's winning of the speed record on Daytona Beach and the trial flight of the R 101 over London. He realised, not for the first time, how much less highbrow he was than he had once imagined himself to be . . .

A tall grey-haired woman was speaking on Pacificism. Whatever subject Leslie's discussion group started with, it always reached Pacificism before the end.

"Things are moving in the right direction," she was saying in a clear incisive voice. "Germany has been admitted to the League of Nations; we have at last a government with sufficient vision and common sense to suspend the building of the Naval Dockyard at Singapore and so prevent the waste of thousands of pounds that may be better spent on alleviating the lot of our workers at home; Armistice Day is to be de-militarised; the League of Nations Union and the Fellowship of Reconciliation have it on their programme to abolish the annual Air Display at Hendon. The O.T.C. in schools must be abolished next and the cuts in our armed forces made more drastic. We must prove our desire for peace to the world, and the world will not be slow to follow our example. One encouraging factor is that our writers no longer try to invest war with a haze of glamour. Such books as *All Quiet, Death of a Hero, Sergeant Grischa,* even the play running in London now, called *Journey's End,* show our young people what war really is . . ."

Billy set his teeth. He hated the flow of "de-bunking" war books that was flooding the press. War wasn't like that . . . It had its black side, of course, but — it wasn't like that. He had met dozens of men since the war, who, sickened by the cut-throat competition and disingenuous methods of commercial life, looked back with nostalgic longing to the comradeship and loyalty of the trenches. Surely there was still some value in the old virtues of patriotism, endurance and self-sacrifice. These people had — got things wrong. And God only knew what harm they were doing among the younger men, spreading their ideas so speciously and insidiously. He would have liked to say something himself on the subject, but he was inarticulate and would, he knew, only make a fool of himself.

A small woman, wearing a shapeless knitted suit several sizes too large for her, was now speaking.

"It is the women of England who must make a stand," she was saying. "We fought to win the vote, and we must fight to win peace. Never again in any circumstance or for whatever cause must we allow our country to be dragged into war. I did not bear my child to be killed by a bomb . . ."

A quiet humorous-looking woman who was standing next to Billy turned to him and whispered, "To hear these women talk, you'd think they'd borne their children to be immortal. If they haven't borne them to be killed by a bomb, they've borne them to be killed by cancer or consumption or some other disease if not by a motor-car. Death by a bomb is a cleaner and more merciful death than death by many so-called 'natural causes'."

A woman just in front of them, who had heard what she said, turned round and said fiercely, "You pretend to love your country, I suppose. Would you see it laid in ruins?"

"Buildings," said the woman who had spoken to Billy, "are only bricks and mortar. The free spirit of man that designed them can design them again — as long as it remains free. There might arise circumstances in which that free spirit could only be saved by the deliberate sacrifice of material things."

The woman in front turned sharply to Billy, as if to put him, too, through his paces.

"Would you see your children maimed and slaughtered?"

Billy considered, then, to his own great surprise, found himself answering, "If that were the only way of assuring that the children of the future should not be born slaves, yes."

She glared at him, but another speaker had risen, and the various arguments that were taking place all over the room died away. The speaker had a nervous jerky voice, and Billy did not hear much of what she said.

". . . and we have much to learn from the Weimar Republic . . . sun bathing, nudism, life in the open . . . We must try to get Youth Hostels on the German model . . . We must cherish the new ideal of Internationalism, which in the end will break down all divisions of race and creed . . . Our present economic system is radically unsound. The recent case of Hatry alone proves that . . ."

Across the room Leslie's eyes met his, and, though the tense, earnest expression of her face did not alter, a light seemed suddenly to shine through it. In that glance he was aware of the deep ineradicable love that united them, despite their many differences. He loved her dark vivid beauty, her quick uncompromising mind, her slim vibrant young body . . . He remembered his mother's once saying, when they were discussing marriage, "It's a great help if you can laugh at the same things." He and Leslie could not laugh at the same things. Life was real and earnest for Leslie, and few things in it gave cause for laughter, but, he knew that however great the divergences of temperament and outlook, their lives sprang from the same deep root of mutual love and he would have been maimed and crippled without her. She was now reading aloud a letter that she had received from one of the absent members, and her low clear voice seemed to flow along his nerves, soothing, wholly satisfying . . .

"We will meet again at the same time next week at Mrs. Clemshow's house," she ended, "and the subject for discussion will be 'Diplomacy — Open or Secret?'"

The meeting broke up into little groups of informal argument. Leslie made her way to Billy across the crowded room. The woman in front of him greeted her with some asperity.

"I don't think that your husband is quite wholehearted in the cause of peace, Mrs. Weatherley."

Leslie laid a hand on his arm. There was something protective, almost apologetic, in the gesture, as if she knew that he hated these crowds that she assembled in his house and wished to spare him. So undemonstrative and self-contained was she that her slightest touch had in it something of a caress.

"He's an old soldier," she said. "They're sometimes hard nuts to crack. But we won't give up hope of him. . ."

Chapter Sixteen

Anthea gazed with frowning concentration at her reflection in the mirror . . . and decided for the hundredth time that she looked much younger than her forty-two years. But the fact remained that she *was* forty-two, and the fact nagged at her spirit incessantly. All the restlessness of her adolescence had returned, and her mind was a ferment of imagined wrongs and grievances. No one seemed to want her any longer. She, who had queened it all her life, found herself suddenly dethroned. Jim was wrapped up in the children, paying to Joanna's charm and beauty the tribute he used to pay to his wife's. And Jo was proving as unsatisfactory as Jim. Anthea had looked forward to taking her about with her when she left school, but Jo refused to be taken about. She insisted, instead, on studying Economics at King's College and set off every morning with an attaché-case full of books, returning in the evening to do homework and write exercises as if she were still a schoolgirl. Jim was ridiculously proud of her and spoilt her abominably. Often, when Jo could spare the time from her lectures, they would meet in town for lunch, and after dinner she would still sometimes sit on a low footstool by his chair, as she had loved to do in her childhood. The affection and understanding which united them and from which she seemed to be excluded, gave Anthea a desolating sense of loneliness. They took her for granted — her looks, her charm, her efficiency. They wanted her there, of course, in the background of their lives; but a background had never suited Anthea. Often she looked back wistfully to the time when the children had been little. It had been the happiest time of her life . . . Piers was as disappointing as Jo. He had been her favourite, and now Billy and Leslie (she would never forgive them for it) were stealing him from her. He went to their house every week, making the most unsuitable friends there — dangerous and frequently quite common people, who filled his head with a lot of ideas that might land him in heaven only knew what trouble. And Jim refused to take it seriously. "The boy's all right," he said easily. "It's a harmless enough form of wild oats . . ." "Your mother's a bit old-fashioned, of course," she once heard him say apologetically to Piers, and she had been so angry that for the next day she would not speak to either of them. It was making Piers impossible. He had even refused to come to the garden party she gave this summer, saying that the sight of a lot of bloated capitalists stuffing themselves with strawberries and cream and ices, when whole families, whole villages, whole towns were on the verge of starvation, made him sick . . . That, Anthea replied shortly, was ridiculous, because everyone knew that people on the dole didn't want work and could easily get it if they did. Then Piers lost his temper and said quite a number of offensive things for which he apologised afterwards, but relations between them had been strained for some time. Her children shut her out of their lives, she complained bitterly to herself, as she examined the roots of her hair in the glass, wondering absently whether it was time to have it "touched up" again. It was not a very satisfactory process, imparting a lustreless greenish tinge. Often she wished that Jo had not inherited her colouring, for the red-gold lights in Jo's hair contrasted cruelly with the results of Anthea's "touching up." Perhaps she would try that new hairdresser who was advertising in all the women's papers. He might be able to do something about it. Then her mind returned to her grievances. They *deliberately* shut her out of their lives . . . There was Jo, going out with her undergraduate friends or entertaining them in her austerely furnished bed-sitting-room, and never once suggesting that Anthea should join the party. Piers' friends were so impossible that nothing would have induced Anthea to entertain them or be entertained by them. Even the two younger children still at school seemed to have joined the conspiracy. Anthea had arranged a special "treat" for Prue's fifteenth birthday last month, only to discover that Prue herself had arranged to celebrate the day by a "hike" and picnic with some of her schoolfellows. Her face had registered undisguised consternation when Anthea suggested driving out by car and joining the picnic tea . . . Roger, now thirteen, came home from school for the holidays — a polite stranger, courteously but firmly resisting all her attempts to mother him and order his life.

It would have been easier to bear if Jim had understood and sympathised, but, when she complained, he patted her on the back and said, "Nothing to worry about, old lady. They're growing up, that's all." Yet it seemed to her only yesterday that they had looked to her for everything, that the whole house had revolved about her . . . Even the efficiency at which everyone had once marvelled was not needed any longer. Her maids had been with her since the children were babies. They were well-trained automatons. The house seemed to run itself . . .

Her feelings of resentment deepened as she brooded on her wrongs, fastening round her neck the string of pearls that Jim had given her when Piers was born. She had worn out her youth drudging for them, and she got no gratitude, no appreciation . . . Forty-two . . . Well, she certainly wasn't going to spend the rest of her life sitting by the fireside with Jim. Jim himself seemed to face the prospect with equanimity. Occasionally she could persuade him to take her out in the evenings, but he did it reluctantly, and the entertainment had to be on strictly conventional lines — dinner at the Savoy or Berkeley (he disliked "amusing" places) and a play that had been seen and recommended by someone they knew. Afterwards, he would refuse all her efforts to induce him to go on to a dance or a night club and they came straight home to bed. In any case, she found these evenings with Jim indescribably boring. He had sunk so deep into his rut of routine that she could foretell his every word, almost his every movement. And his spreading girth and thinning hair terrified her, making her feel that he was dragging her down with him against her will into the abyss of old age.

So she had begun to "live her own life", as she put it to herself. Jim was making money, in spite of the depression, and she found many ways of spending it. At all costs she must be assured that she was young, beautiful, charming. And she found plenty of people to assure her, plenty of places where she could forget her fears. There were night clubs, dances and the new indoor skating rinks that were being opened all over London. She had taken lessons in Contract Bridge as soon as she heard of it. She had been among the first to see Al Jolson in the new talking picture "The Singing Fool" at the Regal. She had worn beach pyjamas on her last summer holiday . . . And, as she needed to be perpetually assured that she was young and beautiful, she had begun to take a young man about with her — to night clubs, cinemas, dances and skating rinks. He was always handsome, charming and immaculately turned-out, but he was not always the same young man. He changed, in fact, very frequently. Either he began to make love to her, which offended her, or he failed to make love to her, which equally offended her. Generally, after a few meetings, he began to bore or irritate her, or, even if that did not happen, he gradually became elusive and hard to pin down to times and places, and she would find that he was going about with a girl of his own age, which infuriated her afresh on each occasion. However, he was easy enough to replace. There seemed to be an endless supply of young men — handsome, charming, immaculately turned-out — all willing to go about with Anthea and prove to her that she was still attractive.

Even this her family refused to take seriously. They talked about "Ma's young men" with indulgent amusement. "Ma's gone gay," said Piers. "She's turned into a cradle-snatcher." . . . "Don't be impertinent, Piers," Anthea had said coldly, and Piers had apologised, but with a twinkle in his eye. Jim might at least have been jealous, she thought resentfully, when she brought the young men home and flirted with them under his nose, but he only said, "That's all right, old girl. You go out and have your fling. Does you good. As long as you don't try to drag me out, too . . ." And he would burrow more comfortably into his deep armchair, thrusting his slippered feet to the blaze.

"You know, your technique's a bit old-fashioned, Ma," said the irrepressible Piers. "Girls don't flirt like that nowadays. They're more subtle . . ."

She drew her lipstick carefully over her lips, then stood back, throwing another anxiously appraising glance over her reflection. The dress, of dull black satin, fitted like a glove. Thank goodness she'd kept her figure . . . Her skin was hardly lined at all . . . Very few crow's-feet round her eyes . . . Her neck, of course . . . Beside her reflection seemed to come a sudden vision of Jo's face — the eyes soft and dewy, the skin satin-smooth as a baby's. A stab of horror shot through her heart. Surely she wasn't jealous of her own child, her little Jo . . . Then she hardened herself and gathered her armour of grievances around her . . . Jim neglected her . . . The children shut her out of their lives . . . Jo went her way with her own friends, refusing the help and guidance that Anthea would so gladly have given. And again Anthea imagined the daughter she would have liked to have — docile and sweet, willing to be her companion, to let her choose her clothes and arrange her pleasures . . . After all, that was what a mother was for . . . Her thoughts turned to Cherry, as they had frequently done lately. Though she had clung obstinately to her decision, she had often felt ashamed of her refusal to take Cherry into her home . . . Perhaps this was her punishment for refusing. Perhaps Cherry would have been the "little daughter" she longed for . . .

She glanced at her watch. Time she started . . . She had arranged to meet the new young man at three-thirty. She had been introduced to him at the Millers' yesterday, just when Jimmie Pelham had fallen from favour and the post was vacant. While having dinner with Jimmie the night before, she had caught him in an exchange of half-smiles with a pretty girl at the next table, and when he rang up the next morning, she had replied coldly that she was too busy at present to arrange another meeting. So that Karl Zimmern was a godsend. He was tall, fair and very good-looking, with a manner of shy formal courtesy that was a welcome contrast to Jimmie's off-handedness. Moreover he was a German, and Germans were fashionable just now. One looked with kindly patronage on the Weimar Republic, struggling nobly towards the ideals of universal peace and brotherhood, on the young student in Tyrolese costume, rucksack on shoulder, striding through the Black Forest or the Rhine valley, hand in hand with his equally suitably-garbed Gretchen, sleeping in the clean austerity of the Youth Hostel, raising their fresh young voices to the strains of the mandolin. It was picturesque, innocent, a return to the golden age. One called it the "New Germany" or the "Real Germany" . . . And Anthea, flicked on the raw by that exchange of smiles between Jimmie and the unknown — smiles in which she read an amused contempt for his middle-aged companion — found Karl's diffidence and politeness very consoling. Moreover, as the evening wore on, she became aware of a strange new sensation that none of her other young men had aroused in her — a sensation that was heady, rejuvenating. Her heart quickened when her eyes met his, and she felt exuberantly, unreasonably happy. Her thoughts went back to Gerald Oxley. This was what she had felt for him and for no one else in the years between. She was bewildered, but beneath the bewilderment surged a wild sense of triumph. She wasn't too old to fall in love . . . Deliberately she surrendered to the sensation, deliberately encouraged it . . . He seemed a little surprised when she asked him to accompany her to the *thé dansant* this afternoon, but he thanked her with his formal, rather stilted politeness and accepted the invitation. The sense of happiness had sustained her all the way home. She kept summoning the memory of his handsome, clean-cut face, regular-featured, with crisp curling fair hair, and the expected thrill of delight never failed to shoot through her nerves. I wonder if he — feels the same, she thought. And the future, instead of being drab and dull and empty, as it had been for so long, was bathed in a rosy mist through which one could discern sunlit paths leading — who knew whither? She felt as eager and excited, as breathlessly, tremulously happy as a girl on the threshold of her first love affair.

But this morning she had awakened to a headache and a heavy sense of depression. I was mad, she said to herself . . . I must have had too much to drink. She had snapped at Jim and Jo at breakfast, grumbled at the perfect maids, and armed her spirit with its familiar panoply of grievances to hold at bay the new forces that threatened it.

But, as soon as she saw him waiting for her in the foyer, all her depression vanished. Her heart leapt, and her breath came and went unevenly. He bowed over her hand and presented her with a sheaf of lilies of the valley, which she pinned with trembling fingers in her coat. They secured a table for two, then joined the dancers on the dancing floor round which the tables were arranged. He danced stiffly and without much sense of rhythm, but the touch of his arm sent the blood racing through her body.

As they sat having tea together, a confused welter of thoughts raced through her mind. Why should she fight against it? She saw her life as a long grey stretch of monotonous duties, faithfully and self-sacrificingly performed without recompense or gratitude. I've got a chance of happiness at last . . . and I shall never have another. I've a right to it. Everyone has a right to just a little happiness in their lives . . . They wouldn't miss me if I went, and, if they did, it would serve them right. They don't appreciate me. I've never even travelled — except for a few stuffy cruises — because I've always been so busy with the children, and Jim would never go anywhere but Belton Sands after that first holiday there. She saw herself and Karl drifting down the canals of Venice in a gondola, watching the sunset over the desert . . . the Alps . . . the Italian lakes . . . Jim would divorce her, of course. Their home would be in Germany, she supposed. Perhaps he was poor, but that wouldn't matter. She had enough for both . . . She wondered how old he was. Probably very young . . . He had told her that he had just finished his course at Heidelberg University and was hoping for a professorship. She stifled the thought that she must be old enough to be his mother. In any case, such marriages often turned out very well. A woman at that age had learnt how to make a man comfortable, and what most men really wanted was mothering.

They stood in the foyer while the commissionaire summoned a taxi for her, and suddenly she felt that she could not bear to let him go, could not bear to lose the golden radiance that his presence shed over her, the glorious certainty of hope and youth and love.

"Won't you come back with me and have a drink?" she said, adding casually, "I'd like you to meet my husband."

He hesitated a moment, then accepted.

Jim was already back from the office when they reached home, and she glanced at her new cavalier as she introduced them, expecting to read surprise and horror on his face as he realised that she was married to this stout elderly man; but one could read little on his face. It was grave, intent and — heart-stirringly beautiful.

Jim questioned him about his impressions of England and the conditions in Germany, and she sat apart, sipping her sherry and watching him dreamily, numbed by happiness, seeing only those sunlit paths that led — who knew whither?

Then Jo came in from college. She wore a dark coat and skirt and carried her hat in her hand. Her red-gold hair was ruffled by the wind. She stood in the doorway, and she and Karl looked at each other. Jo caught her breath, and the boy turned pale. Anthea introduced them in a slow sulky voice.

"Be quick and change, Jo," she said. "It's almost dinner-time."

She meant that as a hint to Karl that it was time for him to go. She had been hoping that she could persuade him to stay to dinner, but now she decided suddenly that she did not want him to. But Jim, ever obtuse, had already issued the invitation, adding jocularly, "I expect we can manage to feed one more mouth, can't we, Mother?"

Anthea stiffened and set her teeth. She hated his calling her Mother. It relegated her to the dull and settled and middle-aged . . .

Jo came down to dinner, looking slender and lovely in a dress of dark-green velvet, made in mediaeval style, with long tight sleeves, tight pointed bodice and full gathered skirt. Her cheeks were flushed, and her bright hair was like an aureole. The boy watched her bemusedly, making no attempt to hide his admiration, and Anthea realised with a pang of despair how great a boredom his former manner of stilted courtesy had concealed.

After dinner he and Jo discussed England and Germany.

Jo's faith in the "New Germany" was almost fanatical.

"You've won your freedom," she said earnestly. "You must never let it go again."

"But we are so young in freedom," he said. "You are so old in it that you take it for granted. It is as natural to you as the air you breathe. We are a new nation. We do not know rightly how to use freedom, how to guard it. The Hohenzollerns are not the only enemies to our freedom."

"No, but you must have confidence in yourselves," said Jo. "The real Germany has awakened at last."

"Which is the real Germany?" he said with a puzzled frown. "Who knows? My father, when he was a little boy, lived in a barracks town where the recruits were drilled every day in the square. The sergeant was a big strong man and he would strike the recruits in the face or sometimes knock them senseless for trivial mistakes. Many of my father's schoolfellows enjoyed watching this and would go every day to watch the drilling on their way to school, but my father and one or two of his friends always went a longer way round in order to avoid seeing it. Which represents the real Germany — my father and his friends or the boys who liked to watch cruelty and the man who would strike his defenceless inferiors?"

"Your father and his friends," said Jo firmly. "The old Germany — the Germany of violence — is dead."

"Violence? Yes," he said musingly. "My country has always mistaken violence for strength. That has caused its downfall and may do so again . . . Even now, beneath the surface — so bright with hope and endeavour and our new ideals — are forces of darkness that sometimes make me afraid. They sleep, but they can so easily be awakened from their sleep . . ."

"You mustn't be afraid," flashed Jo. "You must believe in what you are creating. You must be willing to sacrifice everything to it."

A light seemed to spring into his face. It was the face of a Daniel, a St. George, a Sir Galahad.

"I and my friends are willing to do that," he said simply. "For Germany — *our* Germany, not the Germany of the Hohenzollerns and the Prussians — we would undergo the last torment, shed our last drop of blood."

Anthea and Jim listened in silence, sitting on either side of the fireplace. Anthea took out her knitting (she was knitting a pair of socks for Roger) and found that she could knit quite steadily, though her whole body felt numb with cold, and she avoided looking at Jo's face, radiant and lovely, with the bloom of youth on it.

They were discussing education now.

"Distortions of truth for whatever purpose are evil," Karl was saying. "They bring their own punishment."

Jim stifled a yawn, and the young man rose quickly.

"I am afraid I have stayed late," he said. "I am sorry . . ."

He took his leave of them, asking Jo with sudden stammering shyness if she would go with him to a concert at Queen's Hall the following Saturday. Jo agreed, her blue eyes fixed on him so steadfastly that she seemed to be promising much more than that.

When he had gone, Jo stood for a moment or two, gazing in front of her, then gave her head a little shake as if to bring herself back to earth.

"Well, I must go and do some work," she said.

"Yes," said Anthea, "it isn't often that you give us so much of your company in the evening."

She had surrendered to Fate, but she couldn't resist just that . . .

"Not a bad fellow for a German," said Jim when Jo had gone upstairs.

"Did you think so?" said Anthea indifferently.

"Didn't you?"

"I found him rather boring."

"Oh well," said Jim indulgently, "as one gets older, young people do seem a bit boring — except one's own." He smiled. "Jo fairly bowled him over, didn't she, the little monkey!"

A maid entered with the evening post on a tray.

"Only one — for you," said Jim, handing her a letter. She read it in silence.

"It's from Helena," she said at last. "Father wants us all to go over for his sixtieth birthday on the 20th. I suppose we could manage it . . ."

"Rather!" said Jim, going to the decanter to pour himself out his usual "nightcap". "Spot of whisky, my dear?"

"No, thanks."

"How is the old boy?"

"A little better. He and Helena are both hoping that this Pisany treatment will do him good." She read through the letter again. "Helena's worried about Cherry. She's leaving school and they both want to fix something up about her before they go abroad."

"I thought your Aunt Lilian . . ."

"Aunt Lilian seems to have washed her hands of her, and anyway she's been going off the rails a bit more than usual lately. She's taken to drinking again. I don't mean she ever gave it up, of course . . . Who was it told us she took drugs as well?"

"Dunno . . . One of your scandal-mongering friends, I expect."

"Anyway, Helena's going to see Clive about it. After all, she's Clive's job, isn't she?" She became thoughtful. "Jim . . ."

"Um?"

"If Clive doesn't want her, would you have any objection to my telling Helena that we'll have her here?"

"Not a bit," said Jim heartily. "I've often felt that we ought to have done something for the kid."

Chapter Seventeen

Helena leant back in a corner of the railway carriage, gazing unseeingly out of the window. At her heart dragged the familiar weight of anxiety that always accompanied her when she left Arthur, for however short a time, and she would be away on this occasion for the whole day. Still — he had been better lately, full of hope that the Pisany treatment would effect at least a partial cure, and he was as anxious as she was to get Cherry's future settled before they went.

She had left him sitting in the sun on the terrace, a rug over his knees, his papers and books on a table by his side. His parchment-like skin was stretched tightly over his cheek-bones, his face was furrowed by pain, his body thin and wasted, but he had smiled at her cheerfully as he said goodbye.

"Now don't worry," he had said affectionately. "Try to forget your old man of the sea while you're away. I promise I'll be good."

As the train sped on, part of her was still there with him, protecting, soothing . . . but, so accustomed was she to this division of herself, that her mind was at the same time busy with the problem of Cherry.

She had approached both Clive and Lindsay without success, and Anthea's offer to take Cherry into her home had come as a great relief. It was, in the circumstances, the best solution of the problem.

Her thoughts went back to the time when Lilian had first taken charge of Cherry, and the child had been like a new toy. She had rented a cottage in the New Forest, bought a pony, a dog, a kitten, fitted her up with a wardrobe of ridiculously expensive clothes and filled a nursery with ridiculously expensive toys. So devoted was she to the child that she was jealous of every other influence. She would not engage a nurse or a governess or even send her to school. She played with her, rode with her, read to her, put her to bed herself — often at unduly late hours — and fed her on unduly rich and exciting food. Cherry was a little bewildered, more than a little homesick, grave, silent, remote. Because Lilian could be gay and charming and kind and was the only person she had to love, she loved her, but she soon became obscurely aware of the lack of balance that underlay Lilian's charm, learnt to dread the precarious sharp-edged high spirits that were so quickly followed by black depression. There was a guarded, wary, unchildlike look in Cherry's eyes when Lilian was at her gayest. Lilian was never unkind to her, but on her bad days the blackness of her depression hung like a fog over everything. Tiring of country life, she took Cherry on a cruise. Friends of Helena's were on the same cruise, and they told Helena about it — Cherry treated like a doll, kept always at Lilian's side, appearing in a bewildering number of miniature "cruise outfits", brought down to dinner at night, dressed in elaborate ankle-length picture frocks of white satin or lace, her cheeks delicately rouged, her curls carefully "set". And there was always about her that withdrawn, unchildlike, guarded look . . .

Lilian made a large number of friends on the cruise, and, when they returned to England, engaged a nurse, and sent her to the Hampshire cottage with Cherry, while she amused herself in London with her new friends. After several months she went down to the cottage, nerve-racked and exhausted, had a violent scene with the nurse, sent Cherry to a boarding school and put the cottage in the house-agent's hands. After that she would sometimes take Cherry to London for the holidays, and, as she put it, "devote herself to the child", arranging a breathless succession of treats and parties, at the end of which Cherry would return to school paler than ever, with dark smudges of weariness beneath her eyes. Sometimes she would take her to a hotel in the country, where Cherry would be left, for the most part, to her own devices, while Lilian spent her time in the cocktail bar or playing bridge. Quite frequently she would forget all about her and leave her at school for several holidays running. There were times when, had it not been for Helena, Cherry would have gone about in rags. Then, after a long period of neglect, she would suddenly and for no apparent reason become Lilian's toy again, and would be taken about with her wherever she went, dressed in the height of juvenile fashion. As she grew from little-girlhood into the awkward stage of adolescence, Lilian's interest — fitful at the best of times — seemed to die away, and for the last few years she had ignored her altogether.

Helena had ascertained that the school to which Lilian had sent her was well-conducted, and on the rare occasions when Arthur seemed better had had her to stay at Hallowes for the holidays; but Arthur's health was so uncertain, and she could leave him so seldom, that on the whole she thought it better for the child to remain at school, where a holiday programme of games and expeditions was always arranged, than to hang about at Hallowes, where the entire regime of the house was necessarily ordered for the convenience of the invalid.

Still — something must be done about it now. Helena had written twice to Lilian without receiving any reply. That, of course, was characteristic of Lilian. She was so unreliable in every way that she was utterly unfitted to have charge of Cherry — apart from the fact that what was euphemistically called her "weakness" was growing on her with the years.

Helena had at first pinned her hopes on Clive, seeing him in a little house presided over by Cherry, becoming more human, less rigid under her influence. She thought of Jim's devotion to Jo, his pride in her, his deep protective love . . . and felt jealous of it on Cherry's behalf.

Clive had given up teaching soon after he had obtained the decree absolute. There had been no question, of course, of his staying at St. Michael's, and he had given his notice soon after her flight. But with the defection of Ronnie and Lindsay — the only two human beings whom he had admitted to his affection — the whole foundations of his life had shifted. He had obtained a post in a provincial grammar school whose pupils were chiefly the sons of small tradesmen. At St. Michael's he had been an unpopular master, but, partly because he had never fully realised his unpopularity, partly because he could keep his temper even under provocation, his discipline had been fairly good. It was a different man who went to Eshton Grammar School. Some cohesive force that had upheld him, giving him self-respect, self-confidence, even, as it seemed to some, conceit, had gone, and the whole structure had slipped and lay in ruins. He took for granted that everyone he met knew about Ronnie and Lindsay and discussed the affair behind his back with either amusement or contempt. There was something furtive and suspicious in his glance, which had once been frank and open. He recoiled in terror from any overtures of friendship. He lost his self-control and with it his power of discipline. His classes were pandemonium. The boys ragged him openly, and he screamed and raged at them. The head master gave him notice at the end of his first term.

He decided not to apply for another teaching post and obtained a post as curator of a museum in a small town on a part of the East Coast that was rich in fossils. His old hobby of geology now became his profession, and he had of late written several pamphlets on his discoveries, though he still avoided all personal contacts, even with his fellow enthusiasts. People had betrayed him, so he had withdrawn into the safer world of things. He was stiff and aloof in his manner and generally regarded as "queer", but he was successful in his new work, even occasionally giving rather dull lectures to clubs and societies interested in the subject.

He lived in rooms belonging to a retired housekeeper, who catered meticulously for his comfort, and her routine was as undeviating as clockwork. Nothing was a second out of its time or a fraction of an inch out of its place. Though he lived the life of an automaton, he was not unhappy . . .

Helena had set out hopefully on her visit to him, but her heart sank as his landlady showed her into his sitting-room. There was something dried-up and inhuman about the place.

Clive rose from his desk and came forward to greet her. He looked much older than his years. His mouth was harshly set, yet something cringing and beaten in his eyes denied the harshness, begged you to have pity on him, to leave him alone . . .

"It was good of you to come, Mater," he said. "I got your letter this morning." (Knowing him, she had given him no chance to shirk the meeting.) "Sit down, won't you? Mrs. Hart's just bringing up tea. How's Father?"

"A little better." She sat down and began to draw off her gloves. "I can't stay long, Clive. I want to catch the 5.40 back. I told you in my letter what I was coming for, didn't I? I want to talk to you about Cherry."

His thin hands, setting out a low tea-table before the fire, trembled and fumbled with the catch. His face was downbent, but she noticed how the veins stood out on the hollow temples. Before he could speak, the door opened and Mrs. Hart came in with a tray. She was typical of the class to which she had once belonged — an upper servant in a large household — elderly, impeccably neat, in black dress and long white apron, with an aloof rather chilling air. A lifetime of "service" had made her as much an automaton as Clive himself. Her face was a mask. She moved soundlessly as if on wheels. She had served Clive conscientiously and efficiently for ten years, but he had never asked her a single question about her personal life, and she would have been slightly affronted had he done so. He was her "gentleman", and there the matter began and ended. She greeted Helena respectfully, then dropped her eyes to arrange the tea-table — the tea exactly as Clive liked it, bread and butter exactly as Clive liked it, Clive's favourite jam and cakes, made by Mrs. Hart herself from old family recipes. She put the cosy over the tea-pot and slid from the room. Helena's heart sank still lower. Had she been foolish to come? One could not imagine Cherry in this *menage*. But if Cherry came, of course, Clive must move into a flat or a little house. Surely he was not yet too old to be moulded into some semblance of humanity . . . Again she saw Jo sitting on the arm of Jim's chair, tracing the line of his receding hair with one finger, laying her cheek on the bald patch . . . saw Jim tenderly framing Jo's face between his thumb and forefinger . . .

189

Clive, sitting down to pour out tea, was obviously nervous. His hands clattered jerkily among the tea things.

"I thought that Lilian . . ." he began.

"Lilian isn't fit to have charge of her," said Helena firmly. "She's drinking heavily again. At the best of times, you know, she's not reliable."

Clive had readily agreed to Lilian's taking responsibility for Cherry. He would have let her adopt her legally had it not been that Arthur had objected, insisting that the child was ultimately Clive's responsibility.

"Well, then——" said Clive, handing her a cup with an unsteady hand and shifting his eyes from hers.

"Your father and I are going abroad, you know," said Helena, "and, in any case, now that your father's health is so uncertain, Hallowes is no place for a young girl."

Clive seized on the excuse.

"Is this any better?" he said, waving his hand round the small book-lined room.

"No," admitted Helena, "but why need it be — this? You could take a house or a flat and let Cherry run it for you, with a maid to help her. She's a capable girl, and she's taken domestic economy at school. It would be better for you than this."

He shook his head, running his tongue over his dry lips.

"No, no," he protested. "I couldn't——"

"Clive, she's your responsibility. You can't get away from it. You were given the custody of her."

"Lilian——" he pleaded again.

"Lilian's impossible," said Helena shortly. "Your father would never agree to Lilian's having charge of her."

"She needn't leave school yet."

"You can't keep her at school for ever. When did you last see her, Clive?" He was silent, and she went on, "You haven't seen her since the night Lindsay took her away from you, have you? You've no idea what a darling she is. Clive, you'll be cutting something lovely out of your life if you turn her away."

She took a snapshot out of her bag and handed it to him. He

did not take it, but he had seen it before he could avert his eyes, and she realised that he only saw Lindsay in the pale oval face, dark eyes and soft dark hair. He pushed back his chair and rose abruptly, turning away to his desk. As he turned, she caught the look of shrinking terror on his face.

"It's no use, Mater," he said in a muffled voice. "I couldn't . . ."

"You mean you won't," she persisted.

"I couldn't." He took out his handkerchief and wiped the sweat furtively from his brow. "You can make what arrangements you like."

"You mean, you don't care what happens to her? You'd let her go to Lilian?"

"Lilian took on the responsibility for her. It's not my business now. I couldn't . . . You don't understand . . . I couldn't . . ."

She looked at him, half in pity, half in contempt.

"Would you let her go to Lindsay and Ronnie if they'd have her?"

His mouth twitched nervously and he nodded without speaking.

"It's your father who feels so strongly that one of her parents ought to have her," said Helena. "She must come to us, of course, if Lindsay won't have her. It's — hard on the child, Clive."

He spoke almost inaudibly.

"It was none of my doing."

She realised that in some obscure way he identified Cherry with Lindsay, included her in the same soul-sick bitterness.

"I suppose this is final?" she said. "Your father won't be pleased."

He plucked at his lips with his thin fingers and muttered something else about "Lilian . . ." His face was ash grey, and he was trembling. She had pulled down the walls he had built up so carefully, invaded his warm world of unreality, letting in the cold wind of human responsibility, the icy blast of memory . . .

"Very well," she said. "I won't worry you any more . . . By the way, your father wants all of you to come down to Hallowes for his sixtieth birthday on the 20th. Will you be able to manage it?"

"It's a week-day, isn't it?" said Clive with obvious relief. "I'm afraid I can't get away during the week."

"I'll explain to him. And Cherry's being confirmed next Saturday. I suppose it's too much to ask you to come down to St. Monica's for it, but perhaps you'll at least think of the child . . ." She rose and drew on her gloves. "Well, I must go now . . . Don't bother to come down with me."

But he escorted her to the front door, padding down the stairs behind her in his morocco slippers.

"Goodbye," he said. "I hope the treatment will do Father good. Yes, Mrs. Hart," as Mrs. Hart slid noiselessly, deferentially into the hall, "you can clear away. We've finished tea . . ."

Her interview with Lindsay had been no more satisfactory. Lindsay lived in a bright warm circle of happiness with Ronnie and their three children. She had taught herself to ignore everything outside it . . . and Cherry was outside it. She had matured into full rich beauty; her happiness had given her poise and assurance, but, at the mention of Cherry, the old look of unhappiness and uncertainty came back into her face. Like Clive, she clung to the fiction of Lilian's responsibility. Driven from that, she pleaded Clive's. Then, "But don't you understand?" she said. "People here don't — realise about the divorce. They take for granted that Ronnie's my first husband. Oh, I know that they might find out any time, but it wouldn't be the same as having Cherry — living here. That would — rub it in all the time. How should I explain her to people? I'm sorry, Helena. I know it's hard on her, so hard that I can't bear to think of it, but my first duty is to Ronnie and the children. People are narrow-minded in a little place like this. Ronnie's doing so well. He drew up the plans for the new Town Hall, you know, and if people knew about Clive it would — make a difference. And, you see, Helena, the children don't know. Ronnie and I decided not to tell them till they were older. I *couldn't* have Cherry here . . ."

"Things might have been simpler if you'd left her with Clive in the first instance," said Helena.

Lindsay's thoughts went back to that night when she had taken Cherry to Hallowes. She saw a girl driven desperate by love and fear and suspense, but it didn't seem to be herself. She even saw Cherry in her embroidered muslin frock, playing with the chessmen on the drawing-room floor, but the child seemed to have no connection with herself.

"It was crazy of me," she agreed, and added, "I shan't tell Ronnie about it, Helena. He's so terribly — kind. It would worry him, and he's just got the job of designing the new wing of the hospital."

Helena looked at her a moment or two in silence, then said,

"You're happy, aren't you, Lindsay?"

Lindsay drew a deep sigh.

"I'm happier than I dreamed anyone could be, happier than I could tell you. Ronnie and I were made for each other . . . I was so young when I met Clive. Why didn't someone warn me that it was just a schoolgirl infatuation? Marrying Clive is the one regret of my life. I've never regretted leaving him."

She showed Helena snapshots of the children and of Ronnie, talked of the children's cleverness, of the progress Ronnie was making . . . It caught at Helena's heart to think of Cherry left out in the cold beyond this warm bright circle of love . . . but she realised that it would be useless to persist.

"Well, I'm glad you're happy, my dear," she said at last. "And don't worry about Cherry. Her grandfather and I will see to her."

"Surely she can take up a career of some sort. Girls do, you know."

"Even so, she'll need a home," said Helena rather drily. "Girls do, you know."

Lindsay gave a twisted smile.

"I know how it seems to you," she said. "I know I'm selfish. I think happiness does make one selfish. I'd give myself to be chopped in pieces for Ronnie or the children, but no one else is — real, not even Cherry . . . You've always been so sweet to me. Try not to hate me . . ."

Helena kissed her.

"I don't, my dear."

On the way home her thoughts went over the other possibilities that had at various times suggested themselves to her. She had

more than once considered approaching Lindsay's parents, but Mr. Malvern had, at the time of the divorce, adopted the attitude of the Victorian parent, forbidding anyone to hold any communication with his erring daughter or even to mention her name in his presence. Since then he had, gradually and chiefly through the children, been induced to resume relationships and was now a devoted grandparent. But, like Lindsay, he had brought himself to ignore her first marriage and everything connected with it. Oddly, it was Cherry, not the other three children, whom he regarded, half unconsciously, as representing the family disgrace. She was the Weatherleys' responsibility — Arthur's or Clive's, he didn't care which. He disliked even to hear her mentioned. In any case the twins were both married now and the family had left Cokers End
. . .

So Helena was now on her way to St. Monica's for Cherry's confirmation and to talk things over with her. She hoped that Cherry would be sensible about Anthea's offer. It was not ideal, of course. Anthea, a "perfect mother" when her children were babies, was proving that possessiveness and vanity had formed a large part of her much-vaunted maternal instinct. Still — there was Jim, a solid rock of kindness and justice. And there were the young people, filling the house whose routine was ordered for their convenience. It was, at any rate, the best that offered . . .

She arrived at the school in time to arrange the veil over Cherry's shining head and fasten round her neck the gold cross and chain that she had brought as a confirmation present. After the service, most of the parents had tea with their children in the head mistress's drawing-room, but Cherry had asked permission for Helena to have tea alone with her in the little waiting-room, known as the "ante-room". "We have things to discuss," she had explained.

Helena made her way from the chapel down the long corridor to the room reserved for them. Everything was scrupulously clean, but the place had a bare institution-like atmosphere that always chilled her. It pained her to think that this was the only real home Cherry had known . . . A maid brought in tea and Cherry joined her a few minutes later. She had changed from her confirmation dress and looked fragile and overgrown in her school uniform of navy-blue serge with white collar and cuffs. Helena was struck again by her likeness to Lindsay. Her face wore that unconscious look of pathos that youth imparts to some faces and that Lindsay's had worn . . .

"It was sweet of you to come, darling," she said, "and I know you must be tired . . . Here's a footstool. Let me put your feet on it."

"No, I'm not a bit tired," smiled Helena, "and I've never acquired the footstool habit, you know."

"You've never had time to, have you?" said Cherry. "I'll use it, then." She sat down on the footstool at Helena's feet. "I used to sit like this, didn't I, when I was a little girl and came to stay with you at Hallowes, and you read *Alice in Wonderland* and the *Just So Stories* to me.

"I wish you could have come oftener . . . Oh, I mustn't forget to give you Grandpa's present." She took a book out of her bag. "He sent you this with his love. It's his first edition of George Herbert. His father gave it to him for his confirmation present and he's so fond of it that he wanted you to have it. I think he knows 'The Church Porch' by heart. It's full of deliciously unworldly worldly wisdom. He's marked most of his favourite lines."

She turned over the pages and read:

"For he that needs five thousand pounds to live
Is full as poor as he that needs but five.

Here's another:

"Laugh not too much; The witty man laughs least,
For wit is news only to ignorance."

She bent down so that Cherry, too, could see the pages.

"Who fears to do ill, sets himself a task;
Who fears to do well, sure should wear a mask."

Cherry read out the next marked lines:

"Envy not greatness; for thou mak'st thereby
Thyself the worse and so the distance greater.

Oh, and he's marked a whole verse here:

"Be useful where thou livest; that they may
Both want and wish thy pleasing presence still.
Kindness, good parts, great places are the way
To compass this. Find out men's wants and will;
And meet them there. All worldly joys go less,
To the one joy of doing kindnesses."

"How sweet of him to give it me!" said Cherry, still turning over the pages. "I shall love it . . . Give him my love and thanks and tell him I'll write."

"I will, dear . . . And he wants you to come down to Hallowes on the 20th, for his sixtieth birthday. I've asked Miss Crane and she says you may come."

Cherry looked up with a smile of pleasure. So grave was she ordinarily that when she smiled it was as if a light shone through every feature.

"How lovely!"

"He wants all the family to come, as it will be his last opportunity of seeing them before we go abroad."

The smile died from Cherry's face, leaving it pinched and drawn, and, for a moment, stripped of its youth.

"Is——?" she began, and stopped.

"No, dear, your father can't come," said Helena levelly, "but we're hoping that Aunt Anthea and Uncle Bill and their families will be there . . . Now, Cherry, let's discuss our business, shall we? You want to leave school next year?"

Cherry nodded.

"I've got a suggestion to make that I hope you'll agree to. I've heard from your Aunt Anthea, and she and Uncle Jim want you to go to live with them when you leave school. There are young people there—Jo and Piers — and it would be much more suitable for you than any other arrangement . . . You do agree, don't you, dear?"

Cherry shook her head.

"I'm going to live with Aunt Lilian."

"But, my dear——"

Cherry put her hand into her pocket and drew out a letter.

"I heard from her yesterday. She wants me to leave school at once and go to her."

She handed the letter to Helena, and Helena read it with a sinking heart. It was Lilian at her worst — full of maudlin self-pity and hysterical protestations of affection. It was unlikely that she had been quite sober when she wrote it. She gave it back to Cherry in silence.

"So, you see," said Cherry simply, "it's all settled."

"Now, listen to me, Cherry," said Helena. "Neither Grandpa nor I want you to go to Aunt Lilian. She isn't fit to have charge of you. I don't know how much you know about——"

"I know that she drinks too much," put in Cherry calmly. "I knew that, of course, when I was a little girl. That's why she needs me, and that's why I must go to her."

"It's quite impossible, Cherry. You've no idea what it means to have to cope with that sort of thing."

Cherry gave her a little one-sided smile.

"I've more idea than you think," she said. "I coped with it when I was with her before. When you — love a person, you don't mind."

"Cherry, darling, we want you to be happy . . ."

"Then let me go to her," burst out Cherry. "She's always been good to me. Don't you remember how she took me when I was a little girl and no one else wanted me? And she gave me such wonderful times! I shall never forget those holidays I used to spend with her — the pony, and the Zoo and the pantomimes. And now she needs me. Gran, can't you understand? She's the only person in all my life who's ever needed me." Helena's throat contracted.

"When did you last see her, Cherry?"

"Oh, I know what you mean," flashed Cherry. "She wouldn't need me if she weren't — like that and getting worse. She says she'll — try if I go to her."

"She won't, Cherry."

197

"I don't care. I won't let her down after all she's done for me. I don't care how hard it is if I can repay her a little for all she's done for me."

"She hasn't done much lately."

"You've read her letter. She's been too ill and unhappy to care about anything."

"Cherry, I know that things have been hard on you——"

But Cherry repudiated pity with a quick tremulous sensitiveness.

"No, Gran, they haven't. I've been very happy here. I shall be sorry to leave for lots of reasons. And you've always been angelic to me. I've been very very lucky."

Helena understood the pride that throughout her unfriended childhood had made Cherry avoid all mention of her parents and shrink from making any overtures to them. She had kept the hurt of their desertion of her and her desperate longing for their love hidden deep in her heart, and this had not made her bitter, but had given her, instead, an unchildlike quality of compassion and a flaming desire to repay any small kindness shown her.

"Let me tell Aunt Anthea and Uncle Jim that you'll go to them."

Cherry shook her head.

"I'm not particularly fond of Aunt Anthea, you know."

"Then come to us at Hallowes. We'd love to have you."

"And you'd kill yourself trying to do your duty to both me and Grandpa . . . No, I'm going to Aunt Lilian."

"My dear, you're only sixteen. You can't take the law into your own hands like this. Grandpa won't allow you to go to her."

Cherry raised her eyes, violet-blue and steadfast.

"He has no legal authority over me," she said. "Only Father has any legal authority over me, and he doesn't care what happens to me."

"My dear . . ." said Helena, laying her hand tenderly on Cherry's head.

This time Cherry did not repel her, but leant her head back against her knee, allowing the caress.

"We've never — talked much about it, have we, Gran?" she said in a low steady voice, "but I — understand. It isn't anyone's fault.

I suppose that I remind both of them of each other, and they want to forget each other."

"I think that's it," said Helena.

"So you mustn't try to stop me going to someone who *needs* me."

Pity for this unwanted child of Clive's tore at Helena's heart, but she said firmly,

"We shall both forbid it, Cherry, and Grandpa will insist on your father's forbidding it."

Cherry, who had been turning over the pages of her book, looked up with a faint smile.

"You can tell Grandpa that I'm taking a leaf out of his book. There's a verse here that begins 'Thy friend put in thy bosom' and goes on,

> If cause require thou art his sacrifice;
> Thy drops of blood must pay down all his fear.

And Aunt Lilian *is* my friend. I know that things won't be easy when I go to her, but I'm going." Her smile had died away, and her face was grave and earnest. "I'd go to her if I had to be killed for it."

Helena sighed.

"Well, let's not talk of it any more now, darling. You'll be coming to Hallowes on the 20th, and you can have a talk with Grandpa about it . . . The taxi will be here in a few minutes. Let's walk round the grounds before it comes. I'd like to see them again."

They walked round the grounds, Helena's arm through Cherry's, and Cherry chattered like a schoolgirl, telling her of her various friends and of the term's doings. They did not mention Lilian again, but, beneath the fragility and childishness, Helena was aware of something as inflexible as steel . . . She's trying to reassure me and make me happy, she thought — she hates to hurt anyone — but she was speaking the literal truth. She'd go to Lilian if she had to be killed for it . . .

"Take care of yourself and Grandpa, darling," said Cherry, hugging her when she said goodbye, "and I'll see you on the 20th."

But on the morning of the 20th Cherry received a wire: "Party postponed. Grandpa not so well. Letter following." Even as Cherry read it, she knew that he was dead.

PART VI

1937

Chapter Eighteen

Anthea's Silver Wedding

Billy entered the studio carrying a small parcel wrapped up in brown paper.

"Hello," said Leslie, looking up from the sketch on which she was working. "Did you manage to find something?"

"More or less," said Billy, beginning to unwrap the parcel. "I say, that's jolly good," he went on, leaning over her shoulder to examine the sketch, which portrayed a glamorous female in Victorian costume engaged in opening a small frilled parasol.

"It's foul," said Leslie calmly.

"What is it advertising? Parasols?"

"No. Face powder. The idea being that, whereas Grandmamma needed a parasol to protect her delicate complexion, the users of Knightsbridge Face Powder are in need of no such protection. Subtle, isn't it?"

"It's jolly good," repeated Billy stoutly.

"Ordinary, darling."

"Nothing you do could be ordinary."

Leslie glanced at the walls, on which hung a selection of her most uncompromisingly impressionist landscape paintings.

"Well, as long as it doesn't affect my real work, I don't mind. Sometimes I'm even optimistic enough to imagine that it improves my draughtsmanship."

Leslie now had a contract with a large firm of advertisement agents and was making a good income. She needed the money, as the children were both at public schools, and their fees, together with incidental expenses, mounted to a considerable sum.

The mine had been sprung by the children themselves. They had come into her studio one morning, when she was working on a cubist representation of a still-life group arranged on a table near her, and taken their stand, one on either side of her easel.

"May we speak to you, Mother?" Gavin had said.

"Certainly," said Leslie, her paint-brush poised in mid-air.

"Would you mind frightfully," Gavin had continued, "if we left Gorselands?"

Leslie stared from one to the other in amazement.

"But — I thought you were so happy there!"

"Oh yes, we are," he said, "but we've been talking it over and we don't want to grow up cranks."

Leslie laid down her paint-brush, and her astonishment changed to bewilderment.

"Cranks?" she repeated.

"Yes," said Gavin gently. "Like the people who come to your discussion groups, you know."

"We'd rather be ordinary people like Daddy," put in Elaine.

Gavin took up the strain.

"There's no discipline at Gorselands, and discipline is frightfully important. I mean, we're *happy* there, but it isn't any preparation for life."

"Who on earth has been talking to you like that?" said Leslie.

"Oh, we've *heard* people talking like that, of course," said Gavin, "but that wouldn't have made any difference if we hadn't agreed with them. It's not — sudden. We've been feeling like that for some time, and we've talked it over very thoroughly, haven't we, Elaine?"

Elaine nodded and repeated what was her sole contribution to the discussion, "We want to be ordinary people like Daddy."

Leslie argued and reasoned, pointing out the drawbacks of the public school system and the benefits of an education that encouraged initiative and individuality.

"You're interested in art, you know, Gavin. You love painting and modelling. That sort of thing is ridiculed and repressed in a public school."

"I don't think it is," said Gavin judicially. "It's rather encouraged nowadays. I've met several public school boys who are interested in art and are quite happy at school. And individuality, of course, is all very well, but one has to live in a community, and that's why discipline is important. And a man ought to be able to fight for his country."

"*Gavin!*"

"Daddy did," said Elaine.

"—so I'd like to be somewhere where there's an O.T.C.," continued Gavin. "Internationalism and pacifism are fine ideals, I know, Mother, but, with the Nazis in power in Germany, we can't afford them any longer."

There was something stricken in Leslie's eyes as she looked again from one to the other.

"I'd hoped that you two would be citizens of the new world," she said, "a world where all the barriers that divide humanity into petty little cliques had been broken down, and war was only an evil memory."

"We'd like to be," said Gavin. "Perhaps we shall be one day . . . but what we feel is that we ought to be preparing ourselves for the world as it is now."

"You've no idea what life at a public school is, Gavin. You've never been beaten. You wouldn't like it."

"Oh, I daresay there's a good deal I shouldn't *like*, but I've thought it all out, and, if you and Daddy don't mind, and if it isn't too expensive, that's the sort of education I'd rather have."

Leslie took up her paint-brush with her old brisk business-like air.

"Well, it's no good deciding anything in a hurry," she said. "Let's give ourselves a week to consider it and talk it over, and, if you feel the same at the end of a week, we'll see what we can do about it."

At the end of a week of discussion and argument the children were still of the same mind, and Leslie yielded with characteristic good sportsmanship.

"I think they're completely and utterly wrong," she said to Billy, "but, after all, they have their own lives to live, and I haven't any right to interfere."

So Gavin was now at Billy's old school and Elaine at a famous girls' boarding school in the West country. Leslie had decided that, if they were to be victims of the "old education", they should at least have the best it had to offer.

In order to meet the increased expenses, Leslie had turned to commercial work, still carrying on her "real work" as best she could. She was a successful commercial artist, for her talent gave even to the drawings she strove to make conventional an individuality that took the public taste. She shouldered this fresh burden gallantly, never betraying the deep disappointment it had caused her and striving to adapt herself to the new order of things.

The children asked their school friends to the house and must not be ashamed of it. She learnt to cook. The house was run on more conventional lines, though she clung determinedly to her old circle, and the "discussion group" still took place weekly in the lounge.

Billy accepted the change with relief. He had conscientiously upheld Leslie's earlier regime, but he felt more at home in a regime where a parent can give an order to his children and expect to be obeyed. Oddly, too, it seemed to establish more friendly relations. Billy was secretly proud of his son — artistic and sensitive but doggedly determined to acquire manliness at all costs and to avoid the reproach of being a "cissie." He got on well at school, for he was good at games, mediocre at lessons, keen and friendly and devoid of "side". His schoolfellows forgave him for his artistic proclivities when it was realised that he himself set little store by them.

Billy had opened his parcel and brought out a silver cigarette box, which he was regarding with a critical frown.

"Will it do?" he said. "It's terribly ordinary, of course, but silver does seem to tend to ordinariness."

"Jim and Anthea will love it," said Leslie.

"Good! I'll pack it up and post it."

"It's a frightful bore," said Leslie, "but don't you think we ought to take it round? . . . I mean, just to see if she's had any news of Jo."

"I suppose so," said Billy. "As a matter of fact it has been rather on my conscience lately. Anthea and I never had much in common, but, when Mother was alive, she used to send all of us each other's news and we kept more or less in touch. But now——" He ended the sentence with a shrug.

Helena had died only a few months after her husband. While her whole life centred in Arthur's sick-room and her every minute was occupied in waiting on him, watching by him, attending to his needs, she had seemed well and happy and younger than her years. When what her friends called her "release" came and she was free at last to "live her own life", she seemed suddenly to become an old woman and had died peacefully in her sleep during an attack of bronchitis that the doctor had right to the end persisted in calling "slight".

Piers, now a medical student at Guy's, still attended Leslie's discussion group regularly, despite Anthea's opposition, identifying himself more wholeheartedly than ever with the Left Wing that was gaining so many supporters and that was considered by an ever-increasing number of people to offer the; only cure for the world's confusion and suffering.

"I did ring up Anthea this morning," said Leslie, "to ask if she'd had any news, and she hadn't."

"Poor old Anthea!" said Billy. "She's going through a bad patch, and she's not made for bad patches."

Elaine entered the room. She had come home from school that morning and still wore her school uniform. She sat astride a chair, sturdy legs wide apart, arms resting on the chair back, and looked at the cigarette box.

"What's that for?" she asked.

"It's for Aunt Anthea's silver wedding present."

"Are you going to the party?"

"There's not going to be a party. It's been put off because Uncle Jim's gone out to Germany to try to bring Jo home."

"But Jo's home's *in* Germany."

"She's not happy there. Uncle Karl's in a concentration camp and — people are not being kind to Jo."

"Why not?"

"Because she doesn't like the Nazis."

"I don't like them, either, but, if she feels like that, why doesn't she come home?"

"The Nazis don't let people come home, and — I don't suppose she wants to, as long as Uncle Karl's there." She looked at Billy. "I think Jim's only wasting his time and probably making things worse for her."

"Perhaps, but the suspense was breaking him down. He's always been so devoted to Jo."

"I know, but, after all, it was Jo herself who asked him to leave her alone."

After the Nazi seizure of power, letters from Karl and Jo had become more and more infrequent till finally a Dutchman had brought a letter from her to Jim, which he had smuggled out of Germany, telling him that Karl had been put into a concentration camp because of his anti-Nazi activities, that Jo herself was constantly watched and had been questioned several times by the Gestapo, that all her letters were opened and that it was no longer safe for her to write to him or receive letters from him. She was expecting a baby in five months' time . . .

"She is right," the Dutchman had said, "and you would be foolish to try to communicate with her. You can have no conception of the terror that fills that country. Left alone, they may grow tired of spying on her and — questioning her. Should you — force matters, it may only precipitate trouble. She knows too much, has seen too much. They would not let her come to England, 'to spread', as they say, 'atrocity stories'. They would not let you see her, to hear 'atrocity stories' from her. People — vanish in that country. There are 'accidents', fabricated charges of treason . . ."

Tormented by anxiety and suspense, losing all his former geniality and placidity, growing manifestly older from day to day, Jim had for some time abided by Jo's decision. Then, suddenly, one evening he had announced to Anthea that he could endure the suspense no longer and that he had arranged to go to Germany alone the next day to find Jo and if possible bring her home.

"She won't come," wailed Anthea miserably, "and you'll never get home alive and—"

"I can't help it, Anthea," said Jim. "I must see her. I can't go on like this any longer."

That had been more than a week ago, and Anthea had had no news from him since.

"I suppose we ought to go," said Leslie. "She sounded in a pretty bad way on the telephone . . . I'm rather funking her . . . I hope Piers is there. It is his vacation, isn't it?"

"Yes, but I think he said something about going on a walking tour. He wasn't at your discussion group last night, was he?"

"No. Neither were you."

"You know it was my Terriers night."

"I know. You're all crazy. Simply *working* to bring war about. Still — it's no use talking to you."

Elaine drew a stick of liquorice out of her blazer pocket, put one end into her mouth, took an experimental suck, then withdrew it and said,

"Mary Dakers said they used to have a German boy to stay with them every summer, but, when he came over for the Coronation this year, he spat at their Union Jack, so they're not going to have him again . . . He'd always seemed nice till then," she added, replacing the stick of liquorice in her mouth.

A pale frightened-looking maid opened the door to them and showed them into the morning-room, saying, "I'll tell Madam you're here. I don't know if she'll see you. She's — in trouble."

When she had gone, Billy and Leslie looked at each other.

"I hope she's not had bad news," said Billy.

Then Anthea entered. She had evidently been crying, and her hair fell untidily about her flushed swollen face.

"Anthea!" said Billy. "Jo——"

"It's not Jo," said Anthea. "It's Piers, and it's all your fault. I'll never forgive you, either of you, as long as I live . . ."

Her face crinkled up and she sank down into an armchair.

"But, Anthea——"

She threw a crumpled sodden ball of paper towards them. It fell at Billy's feet, and he picked it up, opening it carefully.

Dear Dad and Mother,

I didn't go on a walking tour with Peter, and I shall be in Spain by the time you get this. Peter's going to post it to you. I'm sorry to spring it on you, but I knew it was no good asking your permission. I'm sorry, too, that I've had to go before finishing my medical training, but the bit I've done will be useful over there, anyway.

Don't worry. I'll come back all right.

Love to you all,
Piers

"And it's all your fault," sobbed Anthea. "It's that wicked nonsense he learnt at your house. He brought back the most frightful books on Communism and if he's killed it'll be all your fault . . . Oh, why had he to go there? It hadn't anything to do with him. If it hadn't been for you, he'd never have thought of it . . ."

"Anthea, I'm so *sorry*" said Leslie, "but—"

The door opened, and Prue came in, wearing her outdoor things. She was a tall girl of twenty-one, dark in colouring and rather like Jim, but without his clumsiness of build. She had followed Jo's example and insisted on going to college, where she was working for a degree in History.

She looked from one to another of the group, and caught her underlip in her teeth with a quick intake of breath.

"Jo—?"

"No, it's not Jo," said Billy, handing her the note.

She read it in silence.

Anthea raised her swollen face.

"It's all their fault," she said. "It was they who taught him this wicked nonsense. They've driven him to his death. They're murderers, and if there's any justice in the world they'll be made to pay for it . . . They sit smug at home and drive children like Piers into that hell . . ."

Prue sat on the arm of her chair and laid a hand gently on Anthea's disordered hair, her eyes still fixed on the note.

"It wasn't because of Aunt Leslie he did it, Mother," she said. "It was because of Jo and Karl. He told me he was going to, but I didn't know it would be so soon." Anthea raised her blotched distorted face.

"He *told* you?"

Prue nodded.

"Yes. It was because of what they'd done to Jo and Karl. He said he'd got to *do* something. It was no good just sitting back and feeling indignant . . . It wasn't only Jo, of course. He'd met refugees who'd told him things that — one wouldn't have believed possible. But, because he loved Jo and Karl, it all seemed to have been done to *them,* somehow . . . Anyway, he *had* to go."

"You *wicked* girl, not to tell me! We could have stopped him. We could have——"

"You couldn't have stopped him," said Prue.

There came the sound of wheels on the drive outside, and Billy looked out of the window.

"It's Jim," he said, "and — he's got Jo with him." Just at first when Jo entered the room — hatless and wearing a soiled, patched coat of camel's hair — Leslie felt a cold shiver run up her spine, as if she were seeing a ghost. The blue eyes, set in darkened hollows, held a curious blank look, such as one sees in the eyes of blind men. The cheeks were grey and sunken, the mouth set tightly in lines of strain. She moved jerkily, like an automaton. Even her once bright hair looked dull and lifeless. But when she smiled it was the old Jo — vital, undefeated.

She left the protective circle of Jim's arm to go to Anthea, kneeling by her chair and putting her arms about her, while Anthea sobbed helplessly on her shoulder.

Jim stood, watching them . . . then took a cigarette-case from his pocket with trembling fingers. The lines on his face had deepened; its muscles were taut. He looked as if he had not slept for nights.

"You got my letter, didn't you?" he said to Anthea.

"No. . ."

"I wrote . . . I ought to have telephoned when I got to England, but"— he gave a short tremulous laugh — "I was scared of leaving her even to telephone, and I think she was scared of being left, though she wouldn't show it. There's a sort of— scared feeling over there that gets into your blood. Half of them are so scared they hardly dare breathe, and the other half— Gosh! The whole thing beats me. It's like a nightmare." Usually inarticulate, relief and emotion had made him almost garrulous, and he continued, "The kid doesn't look too good, does she? But we'll soon have her looking her old self. She's been ill . . . Hello, Billy, 'lo, Leslie. Glad to see you. Gosh! It's grand to be back again!" He sat down suddenly on a small chair by the window as if he could stand no longer, but his eyes remained fixed on Jo with a kind of hungry tenderness. He lit his cigarette and smiled shakily. "Can't believe I've really got her . . ."

"How did you manage it?" said Billy.

He felt it almost a desecration to witness Jo's reunion with her mother and sister, and had crossed over to the window, where Jim was sitting.

"Palm-greasing, chiefly," said Jim. "They're far from incorruptible, you know. I had to pay three thousand altogether."

"Good Lord!"

"I'd have given every penny I have in the world to get her out," said Jim simply, "and I suppose they knew it."

Jo had kissed Anthea and Prue affectionately but in a curious dream-like way, as if, thought Leslie, watching, her real self were not there at all. She seemed to be consoling Anthea rather than being consoled by her. She was dry-eyed and spoke in a low, steady deliberate voice, as if she had learned in a hard school not to let it tremble.

"Where's Karl?" said Prue suddenly.

Jim frowned at her, but Jo answered in that new steady monotone that was so unlike the voice they remembered.

"He's dead. They sent me his ashes from the concentration camp."

"Oh, Jo!" wailed Anthea. "What—? Did they tell you?"

"For God's sake, Anthea!" said Jim, but Jo answered quietly,

"He was tortured to death . . . Someone who was there at the same time told me."

"How cruel to tell you!" flashed Prue.

Jo looked at her with widened eyes.

"No, Prue, it wasn't. We must know what we have to fight against. It's — better to know."

"I think the kid ought to go to bed," put in Jim. "She's tired out."

Jo smiled at him. As in all her slightest movements, there was something schooled and steady in the smile, something suggestive of self-control acquired and maintained at tremendous cost.

"I don't want to," she said. "It's so — comfortable here."

She had sunk back into an armchair, opening her travelling coat and letting her eyes close for a moment, as if yielding involuntarily to her weariness. The shadows of her thick lashes darkened the hollows round her eyes.

Anthea's gaze had flashed up and down the thin body in the threadbare, badly-fitting dress.

"*Jo!*" she cried. "You——"

Jo opened her eyes.

"I had a miscarriage," she said.

"Tell them the whole bloody story," burst out Jim in a white heat of rage that made them all turn to look at him in amazement. "They'll have to know sooner or later . . . The devils were kicking an old woman in one of their filthy Jew-baiting orgies, and, when Jo tried to interfere, they knocked her down and kicked her, too . . . And I had to soft-soap the bastards and cringe to them. God! I wish I'd had the guts to stick a knife into one of them!"

Anthea broke out again into wailing.

"Oh, why did you ever marry him, Jo? We warned you not to. Everyone warned you. I wish you'd never met him . . ."

Don't, Mother," said Jo softly. "You don't understand. None of you understands . . ."

She sat motionless, gazing in front of her, while Anthea wailed and Jim tried unavailingly to console her . . . She was still living in those years she had spent with Karl, before the horror had closed around them. Nothing that had happened afterwards had been able to cloud their radiance. They alone were real. The rest was as unreal as an evil dream. Her thoughts did not have to go *back* to those years of hope and life and happiness. They were there with her in the present — every minute of every day — and nothing could take them from her. She drew strength and courage and — compassion from them. A new self had been born in those days, a self armoured and equipped to endure without flinching the blows that were to come . . . At first when she heard of his death she had thought that he was trying to console her by drawing her thoughts back to re-live those days again in memory. Only gradually did she realise that those years were still with her, that Karl was still with her. There were, of course, dark hours of horror when her imagination saw his broken bleeding body, but they passed, and she saw him again as he was — beautiful as a young sun-god, full of hope and courage and faith.

"Now we've got her home, old lady," Jim was saying, as he patted Anthea's shoulder and stroked her hair, "there's nothing else to worry about."

But Anthea's sobs increased. He caught the word "Piers . . ."

"What about Piers?" he said.

"He's gone to Spain," said Prue, handing him the note.

He read it through in silence, then,

"What on earth's happened to the world?" he said helplessly.

"We bring them up so carefully," sobbed Anthea, "and look after them and nurse them through their illnesses and worry if they even get a cold, and are so careful what they eat and — and all for this . . . for *this*!"

"Hush, Mother," said Jim. "Remember Jo."

Jo was reading the note, and a light had sprung into her tired eyes.

"I'm glad," she said softly.

"What's the *good* of it all!" moaned Anthea. "Nothing seems *safe* any more."

"We don't want safety . . ." said Prue.

"Oh, you *talk*," said Anthea. "Talk won't give me back my baby Piers . . . my baby Jo . . ."

"You've got your baby Jo back, old lady," said Jim.

Anthea shook her head and said nothing.

"You understand, don't you, Daddy?" said Jo.

He nodded, but the lines round his mouth had tightened and he looked an old man.

"We ought to go," said Leslie, rising. "We really only came to bring you —" She paused, then went on apologetically: "It seems so unimportant, as things are, but it's your silver wedding day and . . . She handed the parcel to Anthea.

"So it is, old lady," said Jim, putting his hand on Anthea's shoulder. "We've been through a lot, but we've still got each other."

Anthea was unwrapping the parcel.

"Oh, it's sweet," she said. "Thank you so much."

"By the way, this came this morning," said Prue, taking a small packet from the mantelpiece. "I forgot to tell you."

Anthea opened it and took out a set of silver salt-cellars. Jim picked up the letter that fell from it and read,

Dear Aunt Anthea and Uncle Jim,
    This is from Aunt Lilian and myself, with our best wishes and hoping you will have many happy returns of the day.
                                Much love from
                                Cherry
    P.S.— I do hope that you have had news of Jo.

Jo, who had closed her eyes again for a moment, opened them suddenly.

"Cherry?" she said. "Surely she isn't still with Aunt Lilian?"

Anthea shrugged. She seemed a little cheered by her presents.

"Yes . . . Your father and I did our best, but she refused to listen to reason."

"Have you seen her lately?"

"No. Lilian's *quite* impossible, you know. The last time they came here, Lilian got drunk and was so rude to me that I swore I'd never have her in the house again."

"It's — hard on Cherry," said Jo slowly.

"She's no one to blame but herself," said Anthea. "We offered her a home and she refused."

Leslie and Billy were very silent on the way home.

"Gosh, that poor kid!" said Billy as they entered the gate of the little house in the garden city. "One can hardly bear to think what she's been through."

"When first I saw her," said Leslie, "I thought, she's the ghost of her old self. Then later I thought, No, not the ghost, the *spirit* . . ."

Chapter Nineteen

Cherry stood at the foot of the stairs, listening . . .

She and Lilian had had tea together over the sitting-room fire, then Lilian had said,

"I feel rather tired, dear, so I think I'll go to bed. I've got a nice book, and I'll light my bedroom fire and have a real rest. I shan't want any supper, darling, and I shall probably be fast asleep, so don't disturb me."

But Cherry had not lived with her all these years for nothing. She knew that cunning light in the pouched eyes, that artless, casual affectionate tone. She had, in fact, recognised the well-known signs for some days past the restlessness, the fidgeting, the swift alternations of irritability and affectionateness, as Aunt Lilian fought the familiar losing battle with her demon. It was not even much of a battle these days. It was merely a planning of the campaign, an arrangement for supplies. And Cherry, on her side, organised her forces, watching her unceasingly, searching the little cottage for secret stores, accompanying her wherever she went, despite rebuffs and insults. It was difficult to see how Aunt Lilian could have managed to smuggle as much as a bottle into the cottage this time. But then it always was difficult to see how she managed it . . . Some loopholes could not be closed. There was, for instance, the daily woman who came to clean the cottage in the mornings. Cherry had long ago abandoned the attempt to keep a maid. No maid would put up with Aunt Lilian . . . But Mrs. Andrews had seemed so respectable, so kind. She had promised Cherry so faithfully not to yield to Aunt Lilian's entreaties to buy drink for her, But, of course, Aunt Lilian did not stop at entreaties. She was willing to pay any money when the craving came upon her.

Cherry had gone up to her room about an hour later and tapped gently at the door. There had been a slight pause before Aunt Lilian said "Come in", but, when Cherry entered, she was sitting up in bed, wearing a dressing jacket, absorbed apparently in her novel. A bright coal fire burned on the hearth.

"Are you sure you don't want anything else?" Cherry had said, throwing a quick glance round the room.

"No, thank you, dear," Aunt Lilian had said, giving a good imitation of a smothered yawn. "I'm just dropping off . . ."

Cherry went downstairs again. There was no doubt now. Aunt Lilian's flushed cheeks and the little secret smile that played round the corners of her mouth told their own story. She had started drinking again. Sometimes she drank herself into a stupor and slept, but that did not often happen. Oh well . . . Cherry braced herself for whatever might be coming. The long hours of the night seemed to stand before her like an enemy massed for battle . . .

She went to the window of the little sitting-room and moved the curtain slightly to look out at the desolate countryside. The cottage stood by itself at the end of a lane, several miles out of the village, and they had lived in it now for about three years. Aunt Lilian was better without neighbours. At any time she was touchy and uncertain-tempered, ready to make scenes in public on the slightest provocation, while, in her bouts of drinking, she was outrageous. Things had been more peaceful generally since they came to the cottage. At first Aunt Lilian had been so delighted with it that Cherry had hoped it might effect a cure, but she had been quickly disillusioned.

She put some coal on the fire, then went to the foot of the stairs to listen again . . . The whistling of the wind was the only sound. She returned to the sitting-room and took from the writing-table the letter she had received from Anthea that morning.

Dear Cherry,
    Thank you both so much from Uncle Jim and myself for

your beautiful present. You will be pleased to hear that
Uncle Jim brought Jo back yesterday, but we heard the
same day that Piers had gone out to this horrible war in
Spain, which made us very sad.

Our love and thanks to you both,
Aunt Anthea

P.S.—You will be sorry to hear that Karl has died in Germany.

Jo . . . Piers . . . Cherry had not seen Jo since her wedding. She
had looked so lovely, and Karl, standing there by her side, golden
as a young Viking, clean and straight and vivid as a sword-blade,
had been a fitting mate for her . . . Then, of course, the day had
been spoilt because Aunt Lilian had drunk too much champagne
and become quarrelsome.

There had been brighter patches in her life with Lilian, of course
— times in which she had been pleasant and tractable, holidays
taken in the little car that Lilian had bought and Cherry had learnt
to drive, but even these had never been quite free from anxiety,
had terminated frequently in scenes of which Cherry, hardened as
she was to them, could not remember without burning shame. And
the dark patches had been very dark . . . There had been an occasion
earlier in the year when, as the culmination of a night of horror,
Lilian had driven Cherry out of doors, and she had taken refuge
with the doctor, firmly determined, not for the first time, never to
return.

Both the doctor and his wife had frequently tried to persuade
her to leave Lilian.

"The thought of you alone with that old devil worries me to
death," the doctor had said. "She'll do you a real mischief one of
these days. I know the sort. She's dangerous when she's in drink.
Haven't you anyone you could go to? Are both your parents dead?"

"No, they're alive," said Cherry, "but they're divorced."

"And neither of them wants you."

"Yes."

"It's damnable."

"I used to think so," said Cherry with her faint smile, "but I've got used to it now."

"Well, you must leave that drunken old termagant. Haven't you any other relatives?"

Cherry straightened her thin shoulders.

"Yes, lots, and they're very kind and they'd — have me, but I'd rather be on my own . . ."

"Well, you're not going back to her, remember."

But Lilian had come round the next day, full of maudlin penitence.

"Don't leave me, Cherry," she had pleaded. "You're all I've got in the world. I couldn't face life without you. I'll kill myself if you go. I swear I will. Cherry, I'll never be like that again. I didn't know what I was doing till today and then I could have killed myself. Cherry, you don't know how I've suffered. It wasn't me, darling . . . You know how I love you. You're all I've got in the whole world. You were my baby. Don't you remember those days, darling? You can't leave me now after all we've meant to each other. I've had my lesson. I'll be different. I swear I will . . ."

And she broke into the usual fit of hysterical sobbing.

"I can't help it," said Cherry to the doctor, as she prepared to return to the cottage with Aunt Lilian. "I shouldn't know a moment's peace, thinking of her, wondering what she was doing. She — needs me so terribly. I believe she *would* kill herself if I left her."

"Maybe she would," said the doctor, "and I don't see that anyone would be the worse . . . Anyway, she'll probably kill you if you don't."

"I can manage her," said Cherry.

"No one can manage a woman like that when she's in drink," said the doctor . . . "Now promise me one thing, Cherry. When she gets drunk you must lock her into her bedroom or whatever room she happens to be in and leave her to it. And you must ring me up and let me know. Will you promise?"

"Yes."

He had told Lilian of this, and humbly, penitently, Lilian had agreed.

"Yes, darling, do lock me in. It will make me happier to think that you're going to do that."

"And," went on the doctor sternly, "if ever you lay a finger on this child, I'll have you summoned for assault. I give you fair warning."

"I'd rather die than hurt Cherry," Lilian had protested brokenly.

The doctor snorted and said nothing.

The thought of the doctor and his kind little wife was a comfort to her now, as she stood listening at the foot of the stairs.

She returned again to the sitting-room and, taking up a book, tried to read, but her mind was so intent on listening that the words she read conveyed no meaning to her. As the wind howled round the cottage, she seemed suddenly to see it as it would look from outside — small and undefended, set in a desolate expanse of fields and woods, miles away from any other habitation . . . and she was conscious of an immense loneliness, such as even she had never known before.

She made a determined effort to fix her mind on her book . . . She didn't know how long she had been reading when she became aware of small furtive sounds upstairs. Aunt Lilian was moving about in her bedroom. Cherry put down her book and went to the foot of the stairs again, her heart pounding against her ribs. The small furtive sounds continued. Then, through them, came a laugh, low-pitched but distinct . . . Suddenly Cherry felt afraid . . . In all her dealings with Aunt Lilian she had never felt afraid before. It must be the effect of the weird howling of the wind and the odd momentary glimpse she had caught of the desolation of the little cottage in the empty countryside. She stood there, trying to conquer her fear, digging her teeth into her underlip . . . and again that low laugh came from Aunt Lilian's bedroom. An icy chill crept through Cherry's veins at the sound, and a curious prickly sensation over her scalp.

She went to the writing-table, took a key from one of the drawers, and, going quietly upstairs, slipped it into the lock and turned it. Aunt Lilian heard the sound, and her voice rose, ugly and thickened, in a snarl of anger. Cherry ran downstairs, drawing a breath of relief when she reached the sitting-room. But fear was still with her. Her pulses pounded in her ears so loudly as almost to drown the snarling voice from upstairs. Gradually the voice died away, and Cherry sank down upon the hearth-rug, kneeling in front of the fire, trying to control the chattering of her teeth . . . Aunt Lilian was quiet for so long that Cherry began to think she must have gone to sleep, but suddenly there came the sounds of pounding upon the door upstairs and above it Aunt Lilian's voice.

"Open the door, d'you hear, you dam' little bitch! Open the door . . . D'you hear me?"

Louder bangs showed that she was attacking the door with a chair. Cherry leapt to her feet, and, going to the telephone, rang the doctor's number. A maid answered.

"I'm sorry, miss. He's over at Wenham's farm. Mrs. Wenham's having her first an' she's having a bad time. He said he probably wouldn't be back till morning . . . The mistress? She went over to see her sister this morning and she's staying the night there. Can I take any message?"

"No, thank you," said Cherry, putting back the receiver.

The bangs upstairs increased in violence, alternated by the sounds of the smashing of crockery. Aunt Lilian had evidently begun the familiar process of wrecking her room. There had been times when, after one of her drunken fits, she had left every article of furniture in her room damaged beyond repair. Then her voice rose again, thicker and more inarticulate.

"I'll teach you . . . set fire to the bloody place . . . serve you right . . . you white-faced little slug, you! . . . Listen . . . I'll count ten, an' if you've not opened the door by then I'll set fire to it . . . Burn it down. One . . . two . . . three . . ."

Cherry crouched, tense and motionless, listening. Aunt Lilian might forget her intention while she was counting . . . but, if she didn't, she was quite capable of carrying it out. Cherry remembered the open coal fire in her bedroom.

". . . nine . . ."

Cherry slipped upstairs and turned the key in the lock, then stood back, flattening herself against the wall. The door was flung

222

wide, and Aunt Lilian staggered out onto the landing. She wore a loose dressing-gown that emphasised the lines of her coarsened, sagging body, and her grey hair fell untidily about her face. She passed Cherry without seeing her and went slowly, unsteadily downstairs. Cherry stayed where she was for a few moments then followed her and stood in the doorway of the sitting-room. Aunt Lilian was opening the top of the piano, in which several months ago she had hidden a bottle of whisky. It had been discovered by Cherry, and Aunt Lilian, confronted by it, had expressed surprise and artlessly supposed that it must have been put there by Mrs. Andrews. Her fuddled mind had gone back to it, and evidently she expected still to find it there. She turned her flushed bloated face to Cherry.

"Where is it?" she said, enunciating her words with difficulty. "I put it here . . . Where is it?"

"There isn't anything there, Aunt Lilian," said Cherry gently. "Come back to bed."

Aunt Lilian was still fumbling among the piano wires.

"Put it here," she said. "Where's it gone?"

"Don't you remember?" said Cherry steadily. "We took it out a long time ago. There isn't anything there."

Aunt Lilian's voice arose in a thick bellow of rage, her words almost indistinguishable.

"Drunk it youself, have you? I'll teach you, you dam' little hypocrite . . . Give me that bottle of whisky, d'you hear, or I'll—"

She advanced threateningly upon Cherry, and again fear gripped Cherry's heart. Her lips were white, but she stood her ground and answered quietly,

"There's no whisky anywhere here, Aunt Lilian. You'd better go back to bed. I'll bring you some coffee."

Suddenly Aunt Lilian changed her tactics and began to whine.

"Cherry, darling, give it me . . . Think of all I've done for you . . . Don't be cruel to me now I'm a poor old woman . . . Darling . . . My baby . . ." She put her arms round Cherry, and her drink-laden breath sent a wave of nausea through her. "Don't love poor old woman any more," whimpered Aunt Lilian. "Don't want to

223

kiss her . . . Where is it, Cherry darling? Where's poor old woman's bottle of whisky?"

Cherry pushed her gently back into a chair.

"I'll make you some coffee," she said. "I won't be a minute."

"Don't want coffee," whined Aunt Lilian. "Want bottle whisky."

Cherry went into the kitchen and put the kettle on the gas ring. Aunt Lilian's whining voice went on in the sitting-room, changing again gradually to anger. Cherry stood in the doorway again, watching her as she went about the room, searching for her whisky . . . smashing whatever came in her way. She opened the little china cabinet and flung cups, plates and saucers into the hearth. She took up a cushion and ripped it open, flinging the stuffing about her in handfuls. She lifted up a small table and threw it against the wall, splintering the glass of a picture that hung there . . .

Cherry watched in silence, hoping that, as sometimes happened, she would exhaust herself and sink into a stupefied sleep. She stopped suddenly, surveyed the scene of destruction around her and laughed — a high-pitched foolish cackle of exaltation. "Burn the place down," she said excitedly. "Burn it down and bloody little bastard with it . . . Good riddance . . ."

She seized a newspaper that lay on a table near her, thrust it into the heart of the fire and drew it out, flaming like a torch. Cherry darted forward, snatched it out of her hand and put it onto the fire, pressing it down with the poker. She turned too late to see Aunt Lilian bending over her, her face a bestial mask of rage. Before she could rise to her feet the clutching hands were at her throat and she was forced down onto her back. She struggled vainly . . . The hands closed more tightly. She could see the blotched twisted face a few inches from hers . . . the glaring eyes . . . the open dripping mouth . . .

Then the door was flung wide, and a girl, wearing a soiled patched camel-hair coat, entered. In a flash she was across the room, pulling back Aunt Lilian's bulk, bending over Cherry . . . It was some moments before Cherry realised what had happened. She sat up, gasping for breath, her hands at her throat.

"Jo!" her lips said soundlessly.

"Don't try to speak yet," said Jo, "and don't try to get up." She took a cushion that had escaped Aunt Lilian's investigations and put it under Cherry's head. "God! She'd nearly killed you. Your face was black when I came in . . ."

Cherry's eyes were roving anxiously round the room.

"She went upstairs," said Jo drily. "It may have sobered her for a bit. Anyway, I'll deal with her if she comes down again." She smiled and answered the question in Cherry's eyes. "You're wondering what brought me . . . Well, I've not been able to get you out of my head ever since I came back to England and heard you were still with Aunt Lilian. I kept thinking of you down here alone with that drunken beast, and I couldn't understand how it, was that they all took it as a matter of course and behaved as if it weren't their business . . . And then this afternoon I suddenly felt so anxious about you that I couldn't bear it a moment longer. Mother was out, so I just left a note for her and got into the car and ran down . . . I suppose your guardian angel came to fetch me — and only just in time! Now don't move yet, Cherry. I'm going to make a cup of tea. I'll hear if she comes down again . . ." Her eyes roved round the wrecked room. "You poor kid! What a time you must have had!"

About a quarter of an hour later Cherry rose unsteadily to her feet. There were blue marks on her throat, but she could breathe freely and speak in a whisper.

"Jo," she said, "I can never thank you . . ." She stopped and listened. There was no sound from upstairs. "I must go up to her, Jo. She'll have gone to sleep just anyhow. I won't try to get her to bed, but I must just put the eiderdown over her, so that she won't catch cold."

"I'll see to it," said Jo. "You stay where you are." She went upstairs and opened Aunt Lilian's door. A piercing gust of air met her. The curtains were drawn back, the window wide open. The moonlight showed her an empty room, with smashed toilet-ware and a broken mirror scattered on the carpet.

She crossed the room and leant out of the window. Aunt Lilian's body lay huddled on the stone-flagged path beneath.

PART VII

1940

Chapter Twenty

Prue's Wedding

Jo and Cherry ran down the platform and scrambled into a carriage just as the train began to move out.

They had been up all night, driving an ambulance through the London *blitz,* and had barely had time to change out of their uniforms before starting.

"We're clean, at any rate," panted Cherry, as she sank down into a corner seat. "I thought I'd never come unblacked."

"Sure you got the glass out?" said Jo, looking down anxiously at Cherry's bandaged hand.

"Yes . . . It wasn't much."

Through the sound of the train they suddenly heard the wailing notes of the siren.

"Another one!" said Jo. "Hope the flat will still be standing when we get home."

Jo had taken the flat soon after her return from Germany and had thrown herself wholeheartedly into work for the refugees. It had, she knew, been a bitter disappointment to her parents — especially to her father — who had hoped that she would now take her place at home as daughter of the house.

"I feel hateful about it," she had said to Cherry, "and, of course, I can't make them understand, though Daddy does try. I'm sorriest about Daddy because he's always been so good to me. But — I can't just go home and be 'Daddy's darling'. They want to pet me and look after me, and I don't want to be petted and looked after. I haven't time for it, and I can't risk being — weakened. I need all my strength for my work . . . They want to make me —forget, and I don't want to forget. I'm terribly sorry they're hurt, but —

they think I'm the same person I was when I went away, and I'm not. I'm so different that I couldn't go back to it, however hard I tried. I don't — belong to them any more."

After Aunt Lilian's funeral, Cherry had joined Jo, seeing to the domestic side of the regime, but throwing herself into the work as energetically as Jo. The two girls got on together excellently. They had much in common, and both had been through a hard school of suffering. Beneath their appearance of youth and fragility lay a courage and strength and capacity for endurance beyond what would seem to be its limits. Cherry was the weaker of the two, but she drew strength from Jo.

Many of the people who worked with her and knew her history were puzzled by Jo.

"You ought to hate them even more than we do," said a woman who had been roused to fury by the tales of the refugees' suffering, "and you don't seem to hate them as much."

"Perhaps I don't," said Jo slowly. "Just as when you're out there you pass to something beyond fear, so you can pass to something beyond hatred. It's — so important to keep our vision clear, and hatred and bitterness cloud it. We're fighting something so monstrously evil that no one who hasn't lived with it can know how evil it is. If we're to conquer it, we can't afford to fritter our strength away on emotions . . . can't afford to hate. You hate something that you can — partially, at any rate — understand. This is beyond understanding, beyond hatred. We can only fight it blindly . . ."

After Munich she and Cherry had taken courses in First Aid and were now attached to a stretcher-party unit, taking their ambulance night after night through fires and falling bombs.

Clive had been killed in the early days of the Battle of Britain — killed, appropriately enough, in his museum, surrounded by his fossils and geological specimens. Cherry, unwilling to revive the old feelings of bitterness, had not wanted to go to the funeral, but Jo had persuaded her. He had been killed by blast, and there were no wounds on his body, and, when Cherry stood by the coffin and looked down at the thin worn face, marked by weariness and premature old age, all her bitterness was swept away on a wave of compassion, and she had stooped down to touch the furrowed brow with her lips.

Clive's lawyer had written to tell Lindsay of his death, and Lindsay, breaking the silence of years, had written to Cherry, saying that she had been unable to go to the funeral but was coming up to London next Tuesday and hoped that Cherry would meet her for lunch . . . So deep had been the emotion connected all her life with Lindsay that Cherry could not sleep at all the night before the meeting and set off for it pale and trembling. She returned still pale, but with an air of what Jo called to herself "release". She looked, thought Jo, like a prisoner set free after lifelong imprisonment, still too much bewildered to realise her freedom.

She said nothing to Jo about the meeting till just before they went to bed. Jo had made some cocoa and noticed that Cherry had not touched hers, but was sitting gazing unseeingly in front of her.

"Hurry up, old girl," she said. "We've got to be at the post tomorrow morning."

Cherry looked up at her as if suddenly realising her presence.

"Don't go yet, Jo. I want to — tell you about it."

Jo sat down again.

"Well, what was it like?"

Cherry was silent for a few moments, then said,

"Jo, I've dreamed of her and longed for her and — I used to cry myself to sleep for her night after night when I was a child. I suppose that I'd built up a picture of impossible perfection round the idea of her. And now at last I've met her, and (I wouldn't say it to anyone but you, Jo, but I've got to say it just once to get if off my chest) she's — ordinary. Pretty, of course, and well dressed, but — provincial, somehow, and smug. She showed me photographs of her children and told me how wonderful they were, and reeled off a lot of platitudes about the war . . . Did you ever see Ronnie?" Jo shook her head. "He sounds rather nice . . . but she's been too happy with him. I've often noticed that happiness makes people a little — stupid . . . Oh, Jo, to think how I've broken my heart over her! I used to offer the most outrageous sacrifices to God, in return for which I was to have a letter from her the next morning — a letter that never came . . . I used to pray myself dizzy . . . I used to have a pretended existence in which she and I lived together and were everything to each other. I couldn't have faced life without it . . . And now I've met her after all these years, and we haven't a single thing in common."

"I wonder what she thought of you," said Jo with a faint smile.

"I think she thought I was just dumb . . . She asked me to go and spend Christmas with them. That was Ronnie's idea, I gathered, but she wanted me to pretend to be her cousin, as her friends don't know anything about me. I think she was very much relieved when I said I couldn't go."

Jo looked at her. She was pale and still a little bewildered, but the old air of remoteness, of faint unhappiness, had gone. There was even a suggestion of vitality about her that had not been there before.

"It clears away a lot of old lumber, doesn't it?" she said.

Cherry rose and stretched.

"Yes . . . Lets air and light into a very unhealthy atmosphere. I can put it all behind me now and start fresh."

The two girls were now on their way to Prue's wedding. By a curious coincidence, she was marrying a young pilot attached to Cokers End Aerodrome. The aerodrome had been built on the fields behind Hallowes, and Hallowes itself, which had stood empty for some years, had been commandeered for billeting and messing accommodation. The lodge at the end of the long winding drive, where old Quimp used to live, was let to married officers, and Prue's fiancé had managed to secure it. The engagement had been a short one and the preparations for the wedding somewhat sketchy. Simon had been so busy with the Battle of Britain that he had barely had time even to get engaged.

"I love you terribly, darling," he had said to Prue, "but flying's got to come first. You understand, don't you?"

232

And Prue not only said that she understood, but really did understand.

Immediately on the outbreak of war, Jim had rejoined his old regiment, and Piers, safely back from the Spanish War, had been among the first to be sent out to France. He had recently returned from Dunkirk, still unscathed, but without any of his possessions. Roger, now at Oxford, wrote frequent eloquent letters to Jim, demanding permission to leave college and "join up," and threatening to do so without permission, if permission were withheld.

Anthea had remained in London till the beginning of the *blitz*, when she had closed the house and gone to live at a hotel in Torquay. There she found a community after her own heart, who spent their time playing bridge, dancing and going to the cinema, who still changed into elaborate toilettes every evening and demanded the best of everything to eat and drink as their exclusive right.

"It's lovely," she wrote, "to be able to forget the war."

Prue, who had obtained a post as welfare worker in a North London factory, refused all Anthea's invitations to join her in Torquay and took a room at a hostel near her factory, doing duty as a part-time warden at a neighbouring post.

Anthea was distracted by the news of her engagement to a young man whom she had never seen. She wrote:

Darling,
    Do take Mother's advice and wait. These hasty wartime marriages are most unwise. I daresay that he's everything you say he is, but it's going to be very difficult for these young men to get jobs after the war, and I don't suppose that there's much future in flying. Do wait till after the war, darling, then, if you both still feel the same, we can have a real wedding. I've got such lovely plans for a real wedding. One can't have one in war-time with all these stupid restrictions and red tape. You're my last little girl, you know, and I shan't have another chance, so you must let me have the sort of wedding I've been planning for you ever since you were tiny . . .

"Thank God for the war!" said Prue succinctly as she handed the letter to Simon.

Realising that Prue was not to be moved, Anthea wrote to Simon, asking him to come down to Torquay and have a talk with her. Simon replied shortly that he had so many dates with the Hun at present that he was afraid he could not make one with her as well. She wrote to Jim that the affair must be stopped at once, but Jim, who had met Simon and liked him, had no intention of stopping it, even if he could have done.

Surrendering to the inevitable, Anthea began to make plans to hold the wedding from her Torquay hotel and at Torquay's most fashionable church. She interviewed the manager of the hotel, arranged for a reception after the wedding that would surpass in smartness every other social function held at Torquay since the war began, issued informal invitations to everyone she knew, then told Prue of her plans. Prue's reply had sent Anthea in tears to her friends for sympathy.

"They're so *ungrateful*," she said. "One slaves and slaves for them and gets no gratitude . . . First there was Jo marrying that horrible German, and then, when we'd risked our lives rescuing her, going off with hardly a word of thanks to live in a slummy little flat that hadn't even a decent address and to hobnob with those disgusting refugees, who were probably nobodies at all in their own countries. Then there was Piers . . . going off to that horrible war in Spain that hadn't anything to do with him and, when he got back safely — no thanks to him at all, for he took *no* care of himself — going straight off to that wretched Dunkirk, where he lost every stitch of clothing he had, not to speak of a pair of field-glasses that his father and I had paid *pounds* for . . . And Roger writing the most ungrateful letters and threatening to throw up his whole career, when, if he'd only have the sense to *wait,* the war might be over before he was called up . . . And now Prue, turning up her nose at the sort of wedding any other girl would give her eyes for . . . It's so heartbreaking, after all one's *done* for them . . ."

She soon rallied her forces, however, and decided to open the

234

Hampstead house for the wedding. Having learnt wisdom, she said little to Prue about the preparations she intended to make . . . but, by what seemed to Anthea a piece of personal spite on Hitler's part, a land mine fell near the house a few days after she had come to this decision, and it was completely wrecked.

"Simon talks of 'dates with the Hun'," said Anthea caustically, "but he doesn't seem to have been exactly on the spot on this occasion."

Her next suggestion was a London hotel, but there Prue showed herself firm.

"I'd hate to be married from a London hotel," she said. "If I've got to be married from a hotel, I don't see why it shouldn't be the Red Lion at Cokers End. I remember it so well from the time when we used to go to stay with Gran, and I've stayed there so often since Simon and I got engaged that it's almost like home. Anyway, I love country pubs and I hate London hotels. I suppose it's unconventional, but that doesn't matter these days, and, as the family would have to travel to it in any case, it might as well travel to Cokers End as anywhere else . . . Would you mind terribly being married under the shadow of the aerodrome, Simon?"

"I'd love it," said Simon promptly.

Prue smiled at him.

"Actually you hate leaving it even to be married, don't you?"

He grinned.

"Well, it's rather my job at present. Other places don't seem quite real."

"And I'd adore it . . . It's a dear little church. Ronnie's father used to be vicar there. You don't know about that, of course. It's our family skeleton, and all very ancient history now. He ran away with Uncle Clive's wife . . . No, not the vicar. He was bats, I believe. It was Ronnie who did the running away . . . Simon, it *would* be fun, wouldn't it? I'll come down the day before, put up at the Red Lion, and we'll be married the next day, and then take the car and wander about till the petrol gives out."

"O.K. by me," said Simon. "What about your people? Thank Heaven mine are in India."

"Well, after all, it's *our* wedding. I'll tell them where we're going to be married, and they can come if they want to and stay away if they don't. The only person I really want is Jo — and Daddy, of course, if he can manage it."

Anthea travelled up from Torquay in a spirit of determined martyrdom. At one time she had decided to mark her disapproval of the whole affair by refraining even from buying a new hat, but the temptation of her favourite hat shop proved too great, and she bought finally not only a new hat but a new and very becoming two-piece of black with touches of ice blue, which considerably allayed her rancour. "Of course, I wouldn't have been seen dead in it before the war," she said, "but we've all got to make some sacrifices . . ."

Jim arrived in uniform just as the wedding was beginning and a wire came from Piers, who was undergoing a mysterious course of training in Scotland. Simon's best man was Freddie Dalton, whose face resembled that of a mischievous schoolboy, but who was, Simon had told her, the coolest devil on the station . . .

After the wedding they went over to the Red Lion to drink the newly married couple's health and then to Hallowes Lodge. It was a snug little place, comfortably furnished in plain cottage style.

"Surely, darling, you'll be able to get some help from the village," said Anthea plaintively, "if only for the rough."

"No, I shall see to it myself," said Prue. "Even the rough. I shall need something to fill in my time. I'm quite prepared to be the most neglected wife in history. I don't suppose that Simon will even remember I'm here most days."

"I warned you right from the beginning," said Simon, smiling at her, "that flying comes first."

"Oh, I know," she said. "I accept the condition. It's rather fun to *start* by being neglected. I shall carefully treasure my 'lines,' as you'll probably not recognise me after the war and deny ever having married me."

"Simon's the best pilot we've got," said Freddie, "and you'll have me to reckon with if you start putting him off his stride."

"Oh, I shan't," said Prue meekly. "As a matter of fact, I don't *want* to come first till after the war, and then — well" — she gave Simon a glance that was meant to be threatening — "'possessiveness' will hardly be the word."

Anthea was disposed to be tearful over the lodge.

"If I'd known," she said, "in the days when we lived at Hallowes and old Quimp and his wife *pigged* it in here, that it would ever be my daughter's home, it would have broken my heart."

"It's a jolly little place," said Jim. "I wouldn't mind living here myself, would you, Jo?" He took out his pipe and lit it. "By Jove! It's good to see you all again. You look marvellous, old lady. One would think you were the bride."

"Oh, well," said Anthea, bridling with pleasure, "one has a duty to oneself even in war-time." She looked disapprovingly at Prue's plain grey flannel coat and skirt. "How Prue can wear that old thing at her own wedding——"

"It's not old," said Prue indignantly. "I've only had it a few months."

"Yes, but people have *seen* it."

"Simon never knows what I have on, so why worry?"

"You *ought* to know what she has on, Simon," said Anthea severely. "It's not fair on a woman not to. I know, because Jim was just as bad." Her mind suddenly seized on another grievance. "And I do think that Roger might have sent a wire, even if he couldn't come."

"Oh," said Jim, diving into the pockets of his tunic and still chewing placidly on his pipe, "I meant to break it to you more gently, but I've had a letter from the authorities. Roger has vanished from the haunts of learning."

"*What!*" screamed Anthea.

"He said, you know, that, if I didn't give him permission to leave college and enlist, he'd do it without. I didn't give him permission, so I suppose he's done it without. I gather from the letter that quite a number of his friends have vanished with him. I suppose we shall hear from him sooner or later."

"But what are you going to *do* about it?" said Anthea wildly.

"Do? Nothing. Good luck to the lad, I say. I'm glad he had the guts to do it. I didn't want to take the responsibility of saying he could leave college, but, if he's willing to take it himself, well and good!"

"I simply don't know what to make of you all," said Anthea helplessly. "The whole world seems to have gone mad. There we were, a happy united family, only a year ago — or almost a year ago — and now what are we? *Scattered*! Nobody knows where Roger is. Nobody knows where Piers is — except that he's sure to be doing something wildly dangerous and unnecessary somewhere. There's Jo driving an ambulance and doing a whole lot of other things that are *not* a woman's work, and here's Prue marrying—" she caught herself up and ended lamely, "well, marrying."

"Have another glass of champagne, Mrs. Harborough," said Simon, grinning.

"You can call me Mother if you like," said Anthea graciously. "I've nothing against you *personally*, you know."

"Thank you, Mother," said Simon.

"Family life's gone by the board for the present, old lady," said Jim. "We've had to give it up in order to get it back, if you understand what I mean."

"Well, I don't," snapped Anthea.

"It's happening all the world over . . ."

"Oh, I know that . . . There's Leslie, who always said she wouldn't *have* a war, working at a First Aid post, and that child Gavin joining the L.D.V.s, and Billy in some out-of-the-way place or other——"

"Hello, Billy!" said Jim as Billy walked into the little room. "How are you, old chap?"

"Grand, thanks," said Billy. "Hello, everyone . . . I managed to get leave, so I thought I'd try to make it on the way home."

He was introduced to the bridegroom, kissed Prue and presented her with a cigarette-case and lighter.

"All I could find in the one-eyed hole I'm stationed in at present," he said.

"They're lovely, Uncle Billy," said Prue, kissing him again.

"Have some champagne, Billy," said Anthea. "We brought a bottle over from the Red Lion and Prue has some glasses here. It's certainly not the sort of wedding I'd have chosen, but——"

"Let's go out into the garden," said Jim, when Billy had drunk the health of the bride and bridegroom.

"Yes," agreed Anthea. "One can hardly breathe in this poky little hole. I don't know how Prue's going to endure it."

They walked up the drive and round the house. Through an open window they saw long lines of bare trestle tables.

"That was the drawing-room, wasn't it?" said Prue. "Gran used to make tea at a little table by the fireplace. She had one of those funny old-fashioned spirit kettles."

Another window showed a billiard table and card tables set along the wall.

"That was the library. Grandpa practically lived there, and no one had to disturb him."

They stood on the terrace looking at the overgrown neglected garden. From a window upstairs the strains of a gramophone rang out suddenly with "There'll always be an England."

"There used to be a little summer-house over there," said Prue. "It was on the edge of the wall, and you could watch the people passing in the lane beneath without their seeing you. We used to get a tremendous kick out of it."

"Let's see if it's still there," said Freddie. "We've never explored the place . . ."

"Yes, come on . . ." said Prue.

She and Simon and Freddie went down the terrace steps, crossed the lawn and disappeared among the trees. The others watched them go.

"He seems quite a gentleman," said Anthea, "but the whole thing's so — slap-dash."

Billy leant his arms on the stone parapet, half wishing he had not come. The place was full of ghosts . . . Helena stooping over her rose-beds on the lawn, now bare trodden earth . . . Arthur sitting in his chair in the corner of the terrace, where now a heap of sawn logs was stacked . . . Clive and Ronnie making their way down to their "place" under the beech tree . . . The house itself had been leisured and gracious. Something of Helena's spirit of serenity had seemed always to brood over it. Now it was shabby and restless — bare windows, peeling paint, grimy stone-work. What it housed now was urgent, vital, indomitable, but it was only the shell. It had lost the independent life of its own that it had once had. Though full to overflowing, it wore an empty beaten look.

The other three came slowly back across the lawn.

"It was still there," said Prue. "Very tumble-down, of course. We saw two old women passing in the lane below and they didn't see us. One still gets a kick out of it . . ." She turned and looked at the house. "It was a lovely place in the old days, wasn't it? Though I don't know how much was the place itself and how much was Gran . . . What's the first thing you remember here, Uncle Billy?"

Billy considered.

"Wasn't there some sort of beano when Father came back from the Boer War, Anthea? I seem to remember lugging his sword about."

"I think they took that from you before you came out," said Anthea. "There was a garden party and I remember you strutting about in his sun helmet and tunic."

"And I remember Jo's christening . . . You were very smug at your christening, Jo. I remember Clive making me hand round the christening cake before I'd had any myself."

He glanced quickly at Cherry, remembering how a mask used to close down over her face when either of her parents was mentioned. But her smile now was devoid of embarrassment or constraint.

"He would," said Anthea, and added hastily, "though, of course, one shouldn't say so, now the poor boy's dead."

"I feel we've barged in on your family life with a vengeance, nabbing this place," said Simon. "We're going to nab Four Elms next. You didn't live there, too, by any chance, did you?"

"That's where Mother used to live, isn't it?" said Cherry, and again Billy noticed that she spoke without the old constraint and shrinking. "Where have they gone to now?"

"We lost touch with them," said Anthea . . . "Do you know anything about them, Billy? They were Leslie's friends, weren't they?"

"Yes . . . I believe she hears from them occasionally . . . They went to the Slade with her, but never did much beyond painting frescoes all over the walls one summer when the old man was away. You could hear him bellowing for miles when he came back . . ."

The church clock struck five.

"Not a bad little church," said Simon. "I'm glad we got married in it. Decent padre, too."

"He's tidied up the Vicarage garden since our day," said Billy.

"Oh dear!" sighed Anthea. "How long are we going to have this dreadful war?"

"'If necessary, for years,'" quoted Freddie.

"'If necessary, alone,'" continued Billy.

They were silent, savouring that mood of exalted resolution that had seized the spirit of England when she was left, as it seemed, defenceless and alone.

"We're not alone really, you know," said Jo softly.

"We jolly well seem to be," said Freddie, "now that the French have ratted . . ."

"Do you mean the Angels of Mons stunt?" said Simon with a laugh. "I'd rather trust in tanks and guns."

"Why not both?" said Jo. "Do you remember how Christ said to Peter, 'Thinkest thou that I cannot pray to my Father, and he shall presently give me more than twelve legions of angels'? It was literally true. There *are* literally legions of angels, and they *are* literally sent to fight for us . . . Dunkirk was a miracle, and there will be other miracles."

"Savours of wishful thinking to me," said Freddie.

"Why not?" said Jo. "What's wrong with wishful thinking? It's only another name for faith. Don't you remember how St. Paul said that Jephthah and Saul and the other old warriors, 'By faith subdued kingdoms . . . waxed valiant in fight, put to flight the armies of the aliens'. They didn't neglect the weapons of war, but they knew that they were only half the battle . . ."

"Angels plus guns and tanks?" said Simon.

"Yes . . . We must go all-out for guns and tanks, but we mustn't get so busy over them that we lose touch with our allies."

"Our allies?"

"Our legions of angels. . ."

For a moment she saw Karl's face as she had known it, but lit by a radiance she had never seen before — a radiance so blinding that she felt dazzled . . .

"'We wrestle not against flesh and blood,'" quoted Prue dreamily.

"By Jove!" said Freddie, impressed. "You people do know your Shakespeare."

"It's all very well to talk like that," said Anthea, "but think of all these young lives wasted."

"Nothing's — wasted, you know," said Jo. "These boys — finish their work more quickly than people who live thirty or forty years longer, and, after all, in comparison with Eternity, what's thirty or forty years? And how can we say that they're *missing* anything? The Greeks used to say 'Whom the gods love, die young'. Are old men so much happier and better than young ones that we need regret those thirty or forty odd years? They probably go to something far more thrilling and real than anything those years would have had to offer . . . I expect that Christ's death at thirty seemed to many of His contemporaries the tragic cutting short of a life full of promise."

"I don't know where you pick up these ideas, Jo," said Anthea querulously. "You ought to get out more." Jo smiled at her.

"I get out quite a lot."

"I mean, to parties and things."

"There aren't any now, you know."

"But you wouldn't go to them when you could. It always makes people queer, not getting out."

"Come on, Freddie," said Simon. "Time we fetched the car from the garage." He turned to Prue. "Got all you want from the pub, dear?"

"I'll come with you and make sure," said Prue, slipping her arm through his.

"Poor old Jo!" said Simon as they walked down the drive. "She's had a rotten time, hasn't she, Prue? Did I tell you about her, Freddie? Her husband died in a concentration camp and she was going to have a kid but got mixed up in some Jew-baiting shindy and lost it. It's made her a bit — unlike other people."

"Y-yes," said Freddie, frowning thoughtfully, "but you can see she's—*got* something."

"Oh, yes," agreed Simon. "We need a few people who can see beyond their noses. Not many of us can." Prue squeezed his hand gratefully.

On the terrace, Anthea was recalling memories of her youth.

"We had a marvellous time on Clive's twenty-first birthday," she said. "Mine wasn't half so exciting, because Father was having one of his bad attacks, but we turned the whole place upside-down on Clive's, I remember . . . What was the name of the boy who made such a nuisance of himself to me, Jim?"

"Gerald Oxley?" said Jim.

"Yes, that was it. I remember he proposed to me at that dance of Clive's. He used to propose regularly. He was crazy about me. A stupid conceited boy. I couldn't bear him . . . But then," she sighed, "there was never any man in my life but you, Jim."

"And no other woman in mine, old lady," said Jim, taking her hand. "Regular Darby and Joan, aren't we?"

"Yes," said Anthea. "If Prue's half as happy as we've been . . . Mind you, it's not been easy. It's a whole-time job, you know, being wife and mother."

"You've been marvellous at it," said Jim.

"I wonder . . ." began Anthea, and stopped.

"Yes?"

She had been wondering whether to stop having her hair tinted and let it go grey. She'd have to do it sooner or later . . . but perhaps she needn't start yet. It would have such an odd piebald effect at first. No, she wouldn't start yet.

"Nothing, dear." She looked at Jo, who was gazing dreamily over the garden. "What are you thinking about, Jo?"

Jo turned to her.

"I was seeing old Father Time as a sort of watchman with a bell going round this house and calling out, 'Arthur's home-coming and all's well' . . . 'Jo's christening and all's well' . . . 'Clive's twenty-first birthday and all's well' . . ."

"But what about 1940?" said Anthea with a sigh.

Jo smiled.

"1940?" she said, "1940 and all's well."

THE END